Puffball

Fay Weldon

A KING PENGUIN
PUBLISHED BY PENGUIN BOOKS

PENGUIN BOOKS
Published by the Penguin Group
Viking Penguin, a division of Penguin Books USA Inc.,
40 West 23rd Street, New York, New York 10010, U.S.A.
Penguin Books Ltd, 27 Wrights Lane,
London W8 5TZ, England
Penguin Books Australia Ltd, Ringwood,
Victoria, Australia
Penguin Books Canada Ltd, 2801 John Street,
Markham, Ontario, Canada L3R 1B4
Penguin Books (N.Z.) Ltd, 182–190 Wairau Road,
Auckland 10, New Zealand

Penguin Books Ltd, Registered Offices:
Harmondsworth, Middlesex, England

First published in Great Britain by Hodder and Stoughton Ltd. 1980
First published in the United States of America by
Summit Books, an imprint of Simon & Schuster, Inc. 1980
Published in Penguin Books 1990

1   3   5   7   9   10   8   6   4   2

LIBRARY OF CONGRESS CATALOGING IN PUBLICATION DATA
Weldon, Fay.
Puffball/Fay Weldon.
p.   cm.
ISBN 0 14 01.3118 3
I. Title.
PR6073.E374P8   1990
823'.914—dc20   89–23231

Printed in the United States of America

KING PENGUIN

PUFFBALL

Born in England and raised in New Zealand, Fay Weldon received an M.A. in Economics and Psychology from St. Andrews University in Scotland, then turned to writing film scripts, plays, short stories, and novels. Her books include *The Cloning of Joanna May, The Hearts and Lives of Men, The Leader of the Band, The Shrapnel Academy, The Heart of the Country,* and *The Life and Loves of a She-Devil* (now the film *She-Devil*). She lives in London and in Somerset with her husband and two of her four sons.

Puffball

In the Beginning

Many people dream of country cottages. Liffey dreamed for many years, and saw the dream come true one hot Sunday afternoon, in Somerset, in September. Bees droned, sky glazed, flowers glowed, and the name carved above the lintel, half-hidden by rich red roses, was Honeycomb Cottage and Liffey knew that she must have it. A trap closed round her.

The getting of the country cottage, not the wanting – that was the trap. It was a snare baited by Liffey's submerged desires and unrealised passions, triggered by nostalgia for lost happiness, and set off by fear of a changing future. But how was Liffey, who believed that she was perfectly happy and perfectly ordinary, to know a thing like that? Liffey saw smooth green lawns where others saw long tangled grass, and was not looking out for snares.

Besides, as Liffey's mother Madge once observed, 'Liffey wants what she wants and gets cross with those who stand in her way.'

Richard stood in Liffey's way that hot September afternoon, and Liffey was cross with him. Richard had been married to Liffey for seven years, and responded, as spouses will, to the message behind the words, and not the words themselves.
'I want to live in the country,' said Liffey, remarkably enough, for she did not often put her wants and wishes so straightforwardly into words.
'We can't,' said Richard, 'because I have to earn a living,' and it was unlike him to disappoint her so directly, and so brutally.

Liffey and Richard seldom had rows, and were nearly always

polite to each other, which made them believe they were ideally suited and happily married. She was small and bright and pretty; and he was large, handsome and responsible. She was twenty-eight, and he thirty-two. Madge was relieved that Liffey was, so far, childless; but Richard's mother, although an Anglican, had already lit a candle to the Virgin Mary and prayed for the grandchild she could reasonably have expected five years ago. They had been married for seven years, after all.

'But we could be so happy here,' said Liffey. The cottage stood on rising ground, at a point where smooth fields met wooded hillside. It looked across the plains to Glastonbury Tor, that hummocky hill which rises out of the flat Somerset levels, and is a nexus of spiritual power, attracting UFOs, and tourists, and pop festivals, and hippies, and the drug squad. The cottage was empty. Spiderwebs clouded the latticed windows.

'We are happy where we are,' said Richard. Adding, 'Aren't we?' in a half threatening, half pleading tone of voice, so she was obliged to forget his crossness and kiss him, and say yes. And indeed, their city apartment was small, but convenient and comfortable, and Liffey had never before complained about it, nor had any real reason to. If she gave voice to worries they were not so much personal as ecological, and were about the way the earth's natural resources were being eaten up, and what was happening to the blue whale, and baby seals, and butterflies, and what deforestation did to the ozone layer above Brazil. Richard, who knew that new developments in nuclear, chemical and silicon chip technology would soon solve all such problems, laughed gently and comfortingly at her worries and loved her for worrying. He liked to look after her, or thought he did.

After they kissed, he took Liffey round to the back of the cottage, through hollyhocks and wallflowers, and there, in the long grasses down by the stream, made love to her. It was a decorous event, characteristic of their particular mating behaviour. Liffey lay still and quiet, and Richard was quick and dutiful.

'Isn't she skinny,' said Mabs, watching through field glasses from the bedroom of Cadbury Farm. Her husband Tucker took the glasses.

'They grow them like that in the city,' he said.
They both spoke in the gentle, caressing drawl of the West Country, mocking the universe, defying its harshness.
'You don't know they're from the city,' Mabs objected.
'They're not from round here,' said Tucker. 'No one round here does it in public.'

Cadbury Farm was made of stone, and so long and low and old it all but vanished into the fold of the hill above the cottage. Liffey and Richard, certainly, had not noticed it was there. Tucker's family had lived at Cadbury Farm, or on its site, for a thousand years or so. When Tucker moved about his fields, he seemed so much part of them he could hardly be seen. Mabs was more noticeable. She was reckoned a foreigner: she came from Crossley, five miles away. She was a large, slow, powerful woman and Tucker was a small, lithe man. So had her Norman ancestors been, ousting the small dark Celts, from which Tucker took his colouring and nature.

'Richard,' said Liffey, 'you don't think we can be seen?'
'Of course not,' said Richard. 'Why are you always so guilty? There's nothing wrong with sex. Everyone does it.'
'My mother didn't,' said Liffey, contradicting because the feeling of crossness had returned. Sexual activity can sweep away many resentments and anxieties, but not those which are bred of obsession and compulsion. 'Or only when she had me,' she amended.
'More fool her,' said Richard, who didn't want to talk about Liffey's mother. Richard's parents had described Liffey's mother, after the wedding, as wonderfully clever and eccentric, and Richard had watched Liffey carefully since, in case she seemed to be going the same way.

'If we lived in the country,' persisted Liffey, 'and had a bit of peace and quiet, I could really get down to writing my novel.' Liffey had secretarial training and did temporary work in offices from time to time, when it didn't interfere with her looking after Richard, but felt that such work could hardly, as she put it, fulfil her. So she wrote, in her spare time, poems and paragraphs, and ideas, and even short stories. She showed what she wrote to nobody, not even to Richard, but felt a certain sense of progress and achievement for having done it.

'You'd be bored to death,' said Richard, meaning that he feared that he would.

'You have your career and your fulfilment,' persisted Liffey, 'and what do I have? Why should your wishes be more important than mine?'

Why indeed? Richard could not even cite his money earning capacity in his defence, since Liffey had a small fortune of her own, left to her by a grandfather. And he had of late become very conscious of the communal guilt which the male sex appears to bear in relation to women. All the same, Liffey's words rang fashionable and hollow in the silence he allowed to follow them.

He made love to her again. Moral confusion excited him sexually – or at any rate presented itself as a way out of difficulty, giving him time to think, and a generally agreeable time at that.

'She's just a farmyard animal like any other,' said Tucker handing over the glasses to Mabs.

'Women aren't animals,' said Mabs.

'Yes, they are,' said Tucker, 'tamed for the convenience of men.'

Mabs put down her glasses and looked malevolently at her husband, frightening him into silence. Then she turned back to Liffey and Richard and watched some more.

'They're very quick about it,' she complained to Tucker. 'I

thought city folks got up to all kinds of tricks. Do you fancy her?'

'She's too skinny for my taste,' said Tucker.

'And you can do a lot better than him,' said Mabs, returning the compliment.

'I should hope so,' said Tucker, and did, pushing Mabs' old grey skirt up and reaching the oyster-coloured silk underwear beneath. She was fussy about what she wore next to her skin. She had surprisingly long and slender legs. Her bulk was contained in her middle parts. Tucker loved the way her sharp brown eyes, in the act of love, turned soft and docile, large irised, like those of his cows. The image of Liffey stayed in his mind, as Mabs had intended it should, and helped. Mabs made good use of everything that came her way, and Tucker did, too.

'If you would have a baby,' said Richard to Liffey, as they lay in the long grass, the late sun striking low across the land, 'there'd be some point in living in the country.' Liffey did not want a baby, or at any rate not now. She might be chronologically twenty-eight, but felt eighteen, and eighteen was too young to have a baby.

Liffey looked at Honeycomb Cottage. Generations of happy, healthy children, she thought, had skipped in and out of the door, along the path, under roses and between hollyhocks. There, loving couples had grown old in peace and tranquillity, at one with the rhythms of nature. Here she and Richard would be safe, out of the city which already had turned a few of his dark hairs grey, and was turning his interest away from her, and which threatened her daily with its pollutants and violence; the city: where there was a rapist round every corner, and rudeness at every turn, and an artificiality of life and manners which sickened her.

'All right,' said Liffey, 'let's have a baby.'

Panic rose in her throat, even as she spoke.

'All right,' said Richard, 'let's live in the country.'

He regretted it at once.

Mabs was in the yard of Cadbury Farm as Richard and Liffey drove back towards the main road along the bumpy track that passed both cottage and farm. Richard had to stop the car while Tucker drove his cows in. Mangy dogs strained and barked at the end of chains, and were yelled into silence by Mabs. She bent to give them bones and her rump was broad.

'So long as you don't ever let yourself go,' added Richard, and then Mabs stood straight and smiled full at Richard and Liffey. She was formless and shapeless in her old grey skirt and her husband's shirt. Her hair was ratty, she had unplucked whiskers on her double chin, and she weighed all of thirteen stone. But she was tall and strong and powerful, and her skin was creamy white.

'She looks like a horse,' said Liffey. 'Do you ever see me looking like a horse?'

'You'd better not,' said Richard, 'or we'll move straight back to town.'

Richard did not believe that Liffey, if offered the country, would actually want to live there. He believed he had called her bluff – which had begun to irritate him – and brought her a little nearer to having a baby, and that was all. He was realistic where Liffey was romantic, and trained, as business executives ought to be, in the arts of manipulation.

'Mind you,' said Liffey, 'horses are very friendly. There are worse things to be.'

Liffey, as horse, came from the Viennese stables. She tossed her head and neighed and pranced, precisely and correctly. She was trained in the arts of child-wifedom. Mabs, as horse, was a working dray – Tucker mounted her easily. She galloped and galloped and sweated and brayed, and what price breeding then? Who needed it? But how was Liffey to know a thing like that? Liffey never sweated, never brayed. Liffey made a sweet little mewling sound, as soon as she possibly could yet still carried conviction; a dear and familiar sound to Richard, for what their love-making might lack in quality was certainly made up for in frequency. Liffey felt that the act of copulation was a strange way to demonstrate the act of love, but did her best with it.

Tucker's cows moved on. Richard and Liffey left.

'They'll be back,' said Mabs to Tucker. He believed her. She seemed to have a hot line to the future, and he wished she did not. She had a reputation of being a witch, and Tucker feared it might be justified.
'We don't want city folk down Honeycomb,' protested Tucker.
'They might be useful,' said Mabs, vaguely. Glastonbury Tor was dark and rose sharply out of a reddish, fading sky. She smiled at the hill as if it were a friend, and made Tucker still more uneasy.

Inside Liffey (1)

There was an outer Liffey, arrived at twenty-eight with boyish body and tiny breasts, with a love of bright, striped football sweaters and tight jeans, and a determination to be positive and happy. Outer Liffey, with her fluttery smiley eyes, sweet curvy face, dark curly hair, and white smooth skin. And there was inner Liffey, cosmic Liffey, hormones buzzing; heart beating, blood surging, pawn in nature's game.

She put on scent, thrust out her chest, silhouetted her buttocks and drew male eyes to her. That way satisfaction lay: the easing of a blind and restless procreative spirit. How could she help herself? Why should she? It was her rôle in the mating dance, and Liffey danced on, as others do, long after the music stopped.

Liffey had lately been cross with Richard. Bad-tempered, so

he'd ask if her period was due, thus making her more irritable still. Who wants to believe that their vision of the world is conditioned by their hormonal state: that no one else is truly at fault, except that believing it makes them so?

'I've just had my period,' she'd say, 'as you surely ought to know,' and make him feel the unfairness of it all, that he should be spared the pain and inconvenience of a monthly menstrual flow, and she should not.
'Perhaps it's the pill,' he'd say.
'I expect it's just me,' she'd say, bitterly.

But how was one to be distinguished from the other? For Liffey's body was not functioning, as her doctor remarked, as nature intended. Not that 'nature' can reasonably be personified in this way – for what is nature, after all, for living creatures, but the sum of the chance genetic events which have led us down one evolutionary path or another. And although what seem to be its intentions may, in a bungled and muddled way, work well enough to keep this species or that propagating, they cannot be said always to be desirable for the individual.

But for good or bad – i.e. convenient for her, inconvenient for the race – Liffey had interfered with her genetic destiny and was on the pill. She took one tablet a day, of factory-made oestrogen and progesterone powders mixed. As a result, Liffey's ovarian follicles failed to ripen and develop their egg. She could not, for this reason, become pregnant. But her baffled body responded by retaining fluid in its cells, and this made her from time to time more lethargic, irritable and depressed than otherwise would have been the case. Her toes and fingers were puffy. Her wedding ring would not come off, and her shoes hurt. And although the extra secretions from her cervix, responding to the oestrogen, helped preserve her uterus and cervix from cancer, they also predisposed her to thrush infections and inconveniently damped her pants. Her liver functioned differently to cope with the extraneous hormones, but not inefficiently. Her carbohydrate metabolism was altered and her heart was slightly affected, but was strong and young enough to beat steadily and sturdily on.

The veins in her white, smooth legs swelled slightly, but they too were young and strong and did not become varicose. The clotting mechanism of her blood altered, predisposing her to thrombo-embolic disease. But Liffey, which was the main thing, would not become pregnant. Liffey valued her freedom and her figure, and when older friends warned her that marriage must grow out of its early love affair and into bricks and mortar and children, she dismissed their vision of the world as gloomy.

Was Liffey's resentment of Richard a matter of pressure in her brain caused by undue retention of fluid, or in fact the result of his behaviour? Liffey naturally assumed it was the latter. It is not pleasant for a young woman to believe that her behaviour is dictated by her chemistry, and that her wrongs lie in herself, and not in others' bad behaviour.

Holding Back

The next weekend Liffey and Richard took their friends Bella and Ray down to visit Honeycomb Cottage.

The trap closed tighter.

'When I say country,' said Richard, to everyone, 'I mean twenty miles outside London at the most. Somerset is impossible. But as a country cottage, it's a humdinger.' He had a slightly old-fashioned vocabulary.

Richard was, Bella always felt, a slightly old-fashioned young man. She wanted to loosen him up. She felt there was a wickedness beneath the veneer of well-bred niceness and that it was Liffey's fault it remained so firmly battened down.

'When I say have a baby,' said Liffey, 'I mean soon, very soon. Not quite now.'

Ray had a theory that wives always made themselves a degree less interesting than their husbands, and that Liffey, if married to, say, himself, would improve remarkably.

Bella and Ray were in their early forties and their friendship with Richard and Liffey was a matter of some speculation to Bella and Ray's other friends. Perhaps Bella was after Richard, or Ray after Liffey? Perhaps they aimed for foursomes? Or perhaps, the most common consensus, Bella and Ray were just so dreadful they had to find their friends where best they could, and choice did not enter into it.

Bella and Ray – who wrote cookery columns and cookery books – were a couple other couples loved to hate. Liffey and Richard, however, such was their youth and simplicity, accepted Ray and Bella as they were: liked, admired and trusted them, and were flattered by their attention.

Ray and Bella had two children. Bella had waited until her mid-thirties to have them, by which time her fame and fortune were secure.

When Bella and Ray saw the cottage they knew at once it was not for them to admire or linger by. Its sweetness embarrassed them. Their taste ran to starker places: they would feel ridiculous under a thatch, with roses round their door. They rather unceremoniously left Richard and Liffey at the gate and borrowed the car and went off to the ruins of Glastonbury to inspect the monks' kitchen with a view to a Special on medieval cookery.

'Richard,' said Liffey. 'The main-line station's only ten minutes by car, and there's a fast early train at seven in the morning which gets you in to London by half-past eight and a fast one back at night so you'd be home by half-past seven, and that's only half an hour later than you get home now.'

The Tor was distant today, swathed in mists, so that it rose as if from a white sea. And indeed, the surrounding plains, the levels, had once been marsh and sea until drained by monks to provide pasture.

'I want to live here, Richard,' said Liffey. 'If we live here I'll come off the pill.'
Richard nodded.

He opened Liffey's handbag and took out her little packet of contraceptive pills.
'I don't understand why someone who likes things to be natural,' he said, 'could ever rely on anything so unnatural as these.'

Richard took Liffey round to the field at the back and threw her pills, with some ceremony, into the stream, which recent rain had made to flow fast and free.

'I wonder what he's throwing away,' said Mabs watching through the glasses.
'So long as it's nothing as will harm the cows,' said Tucker. 'They drink that water.'
'Told you they'd be back,' said Mabs.

And Mabs and Tucker had a discussion as to whether it was in their best interests to have Richard and Liffey renting the cottage, and decided that it was, so long as they rented, and didn't buy. An outright purchaser would soon discover that the two-acre field, on the far side of the stream, belonged to the cottage, and not, as Tucker pretended, to Cadbury Farm. Tucker found it convenient to graze his cows there; but would not find it convenient to pay for grazing rights. 'You tell your sister to tell Dick Hubbard to keep his mouth shut about the stream field,' said Tucker.

Dick Hubbard was the estate agent responsible for Honeycomb Cottage, with whom Mabs' sister Carol was having an affair. Dick Hubbard was not married, but Carol was. Mabs disapproved of the relationship, and did not like Tucker mentioning it. Many things, these days, Mabs did not like. She did not like being forty any more than the next woman did; she was beginning to fear, for one reason and another, that she was infertile. She was, in general, suffering from a feeling she could only describe as upset – a wavering of purpose from day to day. And she did not like it.

'He'll keep it shut of his own accord,' said Mabs.

Something about Liffey upset her even more: the arrogant turn of her head as she sat in the car waiting for Tucker's cows to pass; the slight condescension in the smile; the way she leaned against Richard as if she owned him; the way she coupled with him, as she was doing now, in the open air, like an animal. Mabs felt that Liffey had everything too easy. Mabs felt that, rightly, Liffey had nothing to do in the world but enjoy herself, and that Liffey should be taken down a peg or two.

'Nice to have a new neighbour,' said Mabs, comfortingly, and Tucker looked at her suspiciously.

'I wouldn't fancy it down in the grass,' said Mabs. 'That stream's downright unhealthy, and nasty things grow there at this time of year.'

'You won't mind when I swell up like a balloon?' Liffey was saying to Richard.

'I'll love you all the more,' said Richard. 'I think pregnant women are beautiful. Soft and rounded and female.'

She lay on his chest, her bare breasts cool to his skin. He felt her limbs stiffen and grow tense before she cried out, her voice sharp with horror.

'Look! What are they? Richard!'

Giant puffballs had pushed up out of the ground a yard or so from where they lay. How could she not have noticed them before? Three white globes, giant mushroom balls, each the size and shape of a human skull, thinned in yellowy white, stood blindly sentinel. Liffey was on her feet, shuddering and aghast.

'They're only puffballs,' said Richard. 'Nature's bounty. They come up overnight. What's the matter with you?'

The matter was that the smooth round swelling of the fungus made Liffey think of a belly swollen by pregnancy, and she said so. Richard found another one, but its growth had been stunted by tangled conch-grass, and its surface was convoluted, brownish and rubbery.

'This one looks like a brain in some laboratory jar,' said Richard.

Him and me, thought Liffey, trembling as if aware that the invisible bird of disaster, flying by, had glanced with its wings. Him and me.

Bella and Ray came round from the back of the house.

'We knew we'd find you round here,' said Ray. 'Bella took a bet on it. They'll be at it again, she said. I think she's jealous. What have you found?'

'Puffballs,' said Richard.

'Puffballs!'

'Puffballs!'

Ray and Bella, animated, ran forward to see.

Liffey saw them all of a sudden with cold eyes, in clear sunlight, and knew that they were grotesque. Bella's lank hair was tightly pulled back, and her nose was bulbous and her long neck was scrawny and her eyes popped as if the dollmaker had failed to press them properly into the mould. Her tired breasts pushed sadly into her white T-shirt: the skin on her arms was coarse and slack. Ray was white in the bright sunlight, pale and puffy and rheumy. He wore jeans and an open shirt as if he were a young man, but he wasn't. A pendant hung round his neck and nestled in grey, wiry, unhuman hairs. In the city, running across busy streets, jumping in and out of taxis, opening food from the Take Away, they seemed ordinary enough. Put them against a background of growing green, under a clear sky, and you could see how strange they were.

'You simply have to take the cottage,' said Bella, 'if only to bring us puffballs. Have you any idea how rare they are?'
'What do you *do* with them?' asked Liffey.
'Eat them,' said Ray. 'Slice them, grill them, stuff them: they have a wonderful creamy texture – like just ripe Camembert. We'll do some tonight under the roast beef.'
'I don't like Camembert,' was all Liffey could think of to say.

Ray bent and plucked one of the puffballs from its base, fingers gently cupping its globe from beneath, careful not to break the taut, stretched skin. He handed it to Bella and picked a second.

Tucker came along the other side of the stream. Cows followed him: black and white Friesians, full bumping bellies swaying from side to side. A dog brought up the rear. It was a quiet, orderly procession.
'Oh my God,' said Bella. 'Cows!'
'They won't hurt you,' said Liffey.
'Cows kill four people a year in this country,' said Bella, who always had a statistic to back up a fear.

'Afternoon,' said Tucker, amiably across the stream.
'We're not on your land?' enquired Ray.
'Not mine,' said Tucker. 'That's no one's you're on, that's waiting for an owner.'
He was splashing through the water towards them. 'You thinking of taking it? Good piece of land, your side of the stream, better than mine this side.'

He was across. He saw the remaining puffball. He drew back his leg and kicked it, and it burst, as if it had been under amazing tension, into myriad pieces which buzzed through the air like a maddened insect crowd, and then settled on the ground and were still.

'Him or me,' thought Liffey. But just at the moment Tucker kicked she felt a pain in her middle, so she knew it was her, and was glad, in her nice way, that Richard was saved. Her tummy: his brain. Well, better kicked to death by a farmer than sliced and cooked under roast beef by Bella and Ray.

'If you want to spread the spores,' said Ray to Tucker, 'that's the best way.'
'Disgusting things,' said Tucker. 'No use for anything except footballs.'

He told them the name of the estate agent who dealt with the property and left, well pleased with himself. His cows munched solemnly on, on the other side of the brook, bulky and soft-eyed.
'I hate cows,' said Bella.
'I rather like them,' said Ray. 'Plump and female.'
Bella, who was not so much slim as scrawny, took this as an attack, and rightly so.

They drove back to London with Bella's mouth set like a trap and Ray's arm muscles sinewy, so tight was his grasp on the steering wheel. Liffey admired the muscles. Richard, though broad and brave, was a soft man; not fat, but unmuscled. Richard's hands were white and smooth. Tucker's, she had noticed, were gnarled, rough and grimy, like the earth. A faint sweet smell of puffball filled the car.

Inside Liffey (2)

The pain Liffey felt was nothing to do with Tucker's kicking of the puffball. It was a mid-cycle pain – the kind of pain quite commonly, if inexplicably, felt by women who take the contraceptive pill. It is not an ovulation pain, for such women do not ovulate. But the pain is felt, neverless, and at that time.

Liffey, on this particular September day, was twelve days in to her one-hundred-and-seventy-first menstrual cycle. She had reached the menarche rather later than the average girl, at fifteen years and three months.

Liffey's mother Madge, worried, had taken her to the doctor when she was fourteen-and-a-half. 'She isn't menstruating,' said Madge, bleakly. Madge was often bleak. 'Why?'
'She's of slight build,' the doctor said. 'And by and large, the lighter the girl, the later the period.'

Liffey, at the time, had no desire whatsoever to start menstruating, and took her mother's desire that she should as punitive. Liffey, unlike her mother, but like most women, had never cared to think too much about what was going on inside her body. She regarded the inner, pounding, pulsating Liffey with distaste, seeing it as something formless and messy and uncontrollable, and being uncontrollable, better unacknowledged. She would rather think about, and identify wholly with, the outer Liffey. Pale and pretty and nice.

It was not even possible to accept, as it were, a bodily status quo, for her body kept changing. Processes quite unknown to her, and indeed for the most part unnoticeable, had gone on inside Liffey since the age of seven when her ovaries had begun to release the first secretions of oestrogen, and as the contours of her body had begun their change from child to woman, so had vulva, clitoris, vagina, uterus, fallopian tubes and ovaries, unseen and unconsidered, begun their own path to maturity. The onset of menstruation would occur when her body dictated, and not when the doctor, or Madge, or Liffey felt proper.

Her menstrual cycle, once established, was of a steady, almost relentless twenty-eight-day rhythm, which Liffey assumed to be only her right. Other girls were early, or late, or undecided: trickled and flooded and stopped and started. But as the sun went down every twenty-eight days, from the one-hundred-and-eighty-fourth calender month of her life,

Liffey started to bleed. Being able so certainly to predict this, gave her at least the illusion of being in control of her body.

Liffey never enquired of anyone as to why she bled, or what use the bleeding served. She knew vaguely it was to do with having babies, and thought of it, if she thought at all, as all her old internal rubbish being cleared away.

The mechanics of her menstrual cycle were indeed ingenious.

Lunar month by lunar month, since she reached the menarche, Liffey's pituitary gland had pursued its own cycle: secreting first, for a fourteen-day stretch, the hormones which would stimulate the growth of follicles in Liffey's ovaries. These follicles, some hundred or so cyst-like nodules, in their turn secreted oestrogen, and would all grow until, on the fourteenth day (at any rate in the years she was not taking the pill) the biggest and best would drop off into the outer-end of one of Liffey's fallopian tubes and there, unfertilised, would rupture, allowing its oestrogen to be absorbed. This was the signal for the remaindered follicles to atrophy: and for Liffey's pituitary to start secreting, for a further twelve days, a hormone which would promote the formation of a corpus luteum which would secrete progesterone and flourish until the twenty-sixth day, when the pituitary withdrew its supplies. Then the corpus luteum would start to degenerate and on the twenty-eighth day be disposed of in the form of menstrual flow – along, of course, with the lining of Liffey's uterus, hopefully and richly thickened over the previous twenty-eight days to receive a fertilised ovum, but so far, on one-hundred-and-seventy occasions, disappointed.

The disintegration and shedding of the uterus lining, signalled by the withdrawal of oestrogen, would take three days and thereafter the amount of blood lost would gradually diminish as the uterus healed.

On this, the twelfth day into Liffey's cycle, the seventy-seventh follicle in the left fallopian tube was outstripping its fellows, distending the surface of the ovary as a cystic swelling almost half an inch in diameter – but owing to the fact that Liffey had been taking the pill, her body had been hoodwinked so that the ovum would have no time to actually fall, but would merely atrophy along with its fellows.

Did a tremor of disappointment shake Liffey's body? Did the thwarting of so much organic organisation register on her consciousness? Certainly she had a pain, and certainly Mabs' eyes flickered as Liffey winced, but that too could be coincidence.

Mothers

Mabs and Tucker walked up to Honeycomb Cottage. They liked to go walking over their land, and that of their neighbours, just to see what was happening. As people in cities turn to plays or films for event, so did Mabs and Tucker turn to the tracks of badgers, or observe the feathers where the fox had been, or the owl; or fret at just how much the summer had dried the stream, or the rain swelled it. A field, which to a stranger is just a field, to those who know it is a battleground for combatant plant and animal life, and the traces of victory and defeat are everywhere.

Tucker came across another puffball and kicked it, taking a run, letting a booted foot fly, entering energetically into the conflict. 'Nasty unnatural things,' said Mabs. She remembered her mother before her sister Carol had been born, and the swollen white of her belly as she lifted her skirt and squatted to urinate, as was her custom, in the back garden. Mabs' mother Mrs Tree thought it was wasteful to let good powerful bodily products vanish down the water closet. This belief was a source of much bitterness and shame to her two daughters, and one of the reasons they married so early.

Mrs. Tree was a herbalist, in the old tradition. Her enemies, and she had many, said she was a witch, and even her friends recognised her as a wise woman. On moonlit nights, even now, she would switch off the television and go gathering herbs – mugwort and comfrey, cowslip and henbane, or any of the hundred or more plants she knew by sight and name. She would scrape roots and strip bark, would simmer concoctions of this or that on her gas-stove, at home with distillations and precipitations. The drugs she prepared – as her mother's before her – were the same as the local doctor had to offer; psychoactive agents, prophylactics, antiseptics, narcotics, hypnotics, anaesthetics and antibiotics. But Mrs. Tree's medicines served, in overdose, not just to restore a normal body chemistry, but to incite to love and hate, violence and passivity, to bring about increased sexual activity or impotence, pain, irritability, skin disease, wasting away, and even death. She made an uneasy mother.

'Does your mother use puffballs?' Tucker asked Mabs. Mabs didn't reply and he knew he should not have asked. She liked to pretend that her mother was just like anyone else. But Tucker, as was only natural in the circumstances, would roll food around in his mouth before he swallowed, searching for strange tastes. Such knowledge passed from mother to daughter.

'Puffballs are too nasty even for my mum,' said Mabs, presently. 'They're the devil's eyeballs.'

'Isn't it dark and poky!' said Mabs, pushing open the front door of Honeycomb Cottage. 'I'd rather have a nice new bungalow any day. But the view's good, I'll say that.'

Mabs waved at Glastonbury Tor, in a familiar kind of way, as she went inside. The sun was setting behind the hill, in a blood red sky.

'I wonder if they'll live like pigs,' said Mabs, 'the way they act like pigs,' and she looked at Tucker slyly out of the corner of her eye so that he started grunting and waddling like a pig and pushed her with his belly into the corner and bore down upon her, laughing: and they made love in the red light that shone in diamonds through the latticed windows.

'So she's too skinny for you, is she,' said Mabs, presently.

'Yes,' said Tucker.

'You might have to learn to like it,' said Mabs. 'Just once or twice.'

'Why's that?' asked Tucker, surprised.

'It's important to have a hold,' said Mabs. 'You can't be too careful with neighbours.'

'You wouldn't like it,' said Tucker. 'Not one bit.'

'I'm not the jealous type,' said Mabs. 'You know that. Not if there's something to be got out of it. I don't mind things done on purpose. It's things done by accident I don't like.'

They walked back hand in hand to Cadbury Farm. She was so large and slow, and he was so small and lively, they had to keep their hands locked to stay in pace with one another.

The dogs in the courtyard barked and Tucker kicked them. 'They're hungry,' Mabs protested.

'A good watchdog is always hungry,' said Tucker. 'That's what makes it good.'

The children were hungry as well, but Mabs reserved her sympathy for the dogs. Mabs had five children. The eldest, Audrey, was fourteen. The youngest, Kevin, was four. Mabs slapped small hands as they crept over the tabletop to steal crusts from the paste sandwiches she prepared for their tea. All her children were thin. Presently Mabs picked up a wooden spoon and used that as a cane, to save her own hand smarting as she slapped. One of the children gave a cry of pain.

'You shouldn't have done that,' said Tucker, taking notice.

'My children. I do as I please.' She did, too, according to mood.

'You're too hard on them.'

26

She said nothing.

Her breasts were full and round beneath the old sweater. Tucker's eyelids drooped in memory of them.

'Get the bleeding sauce,' Mabs shouted at Eddie. Eddie was her third child, and irritated her most, and she slapped and shouted at him more than she did the others. He took after her, being large and slow. She preferred her children to take after Tucker. That cruel audacity which in Mabs was almost attractive, was in Eddie something nasty and sly: she had slapped and startled him too often: he lived in the expectation of sudden disaster, and now cringed in corners. Nobody liked him. He was eight now and it would be the same when he was eighty. Audrey, Mabs' eldest, looked after him. She was kind where her mother was cruel, and clever at her books. Mabs took her books away because she put on airs.

Mabs and Tucker ate fish fingers and tinned spaghetti. The children made do with the sandwiches.

That night Mabs sat at the window and watched a sudden storm blow up over the Tor. Black clouds streamed out from it, like steam from a kettle, and formed into solid masses at the corners of the sky. Lightning leapt between the clouds. Thunder rumbled and rolled, but the rain did not start.

'Come to bed,' said Tucker.

'There are people in Honeycomb Cottage,' said Mabs. But Tucker couldn't see them, although he came to stand beside her. Lightning lit up the interior of the rooms, and made strange shapes which could have been anything.

'What sort of people?' he asked, cautiously.

'Him and her,' said Mabs. 'It won't be long now.'

'At it again, are they?'

'No,' said Mabs. 'They were in opposite corners of the room. She was holding a baby.'

'I know what's the matter with you,' said Tucker. 'You want another baby.'

'No I don't,' she said, but he knew she did. Her youngest child was four years old. Mabs liked to be pregnant. Tucker wondered how long it would be before she began to think it was his fault, and what means she would find to punish him. 'Come to bed,' he said, 'and we'll see what we can do.'

It was a rare thing for him to ask. Usually she was there first, lying in wait, half inviting, half commanding, a channel for forces greater than herself. Come on, quick, again, again! Impregnate, fertilise; by your will, Tucker, which is only partly your will, set the forces of division and multiplication going. Now!

Inside Liffey (3)

Liffey was off the pill.
Liffey's pituitary gland was once more its own master and stimulated the production of oestrogen and progesterone as it saw fit: no longer, by its inactivity, hoodwinking her body into believing it was pregnant. Liffey became a little thinner: her breasts a little smaller: her temperament a little more volatile. She was conscious of an increase in sexual desire although she was still obliged to pretend, for Richard's sake, and in the interest of her own self-esteem, to have orgasms. Not that this affected her fertility, for orgasm and ovulation in the human female are not connected, as in other species they sometimes are. And although sexual desire itself can on occasion prompt ovulation, overriding the pituitary's clock-work timing, the element of surprise which brings this rare phenomenon about (and much distress to rape victims and deflowered virgins) was not present in Richard's love-making with Liffey.

Liffey's menstrual cycle was thus quickly restored to its normal rhythm. Liffey, all the same, did not become pregnant.

Two more lunar months went by. Two more ova dropped, decayed and were disposed of.

Liffey's chance of becoming pregnant, which was ninety-five per cent when she was a teenager, was by now down by some six per cent and would continue to diminish, slightly, year by year, as would Richard's, until by the time he was sixty, his fertility rate would be down by ninety per cent, and hers, of course, would be nil.

In their favour, both were still young: intercourse occurred at least four times a week, and Richard's sperms were almost always present in the outer part of Liffey's fallopian tubes, waiting for ovulation to occur. Against them, was the fact that Richard had flu in November, and his sperm count was perhaps temporarily rather low: and Liffey had only just come off the pill. There were the many other statistical probabilities of conception to take into account. Had Liffey known all this, she would perhaps not have lain awake at night, fearing – for although she did not want a baby she certainly did not want to be infertile – that she was barren and that some cosmic punishment had been visited upon her.

It was a matter of time, nothing else, before she conceived.

In-Laws and Secretaries

Liffey's mother Madge was a lean, hard-drinking, prematurely white-haired teacher of chemistry in a girls' school in East Anglia. She had never married, nor wished to, and Liffey was not so much a love child as a gesture of defiance to a straitlaced world. Madge had thought to bear a warrior son, but had given birth to Liffey instead, and Liffey had compounded the error by attempting, throughout her childhood, to chirrup and charm her way into Madge's affections.

Madge, hearing that Liffey was trying to have a baby, commented then to a friend, 'Silence for six months and then this. Not that she's pregnant, not that she's miscarried – just that she's *trying* to have a baby. How's that for a piece of non-news?' 'I expect she thought it would please you,' said the friend, who was only there for the whisky.

'It doesn't,' said Madge. 'Liffey is an only child and an only grandchild. Nature is clearly trying to breed the line out. Trust Liffey to interfere with the proper course of things.'

Madge did not want Liffey to be pregnant. She did not want to think of herself diluting down through the generations. She craved mortality.

Richard's father, on the other hand, living in early retirement in a fisherman's cottage in Cornwall, was glad to think that his line might well continue, now that Liffey was off the pill. Richard's mother was made nervous by the news – as if some trouble, pacing for years behind at a steady distance, had suddenly broken into a jog and overtaken her. She started knitting at once, but there was a tenseness in her hands, and the nylon wool cut into her fingers.

The Lee-Foxes looked a placid enough couple – well-heeled, grey-haired, conventional and companionable – but the effort to appear so cost them a good deal in nervous energy. He had ulcers; she, migraines.

'It's too early to start knitting,' said Mr. Lee-Fox. 'She's not even pregnant: they're just trying.'

'Richard always does what he sets out to do,' said Mrs. Lee-Fox, loyally.

'Your fingers are bleeding,' said Mr. Lee-Fox. 'Whatever is the matter?'

She wept, for answer.

'Little garments,' said Mr. Lee-Fox, in wonder, 'stained by blood and tears!'

Mr. Lee-Fox could not understand why, having worked

hard to achieve a reasonable home and a happy life and done so at last, troubles should still keep occurring. It was his wife's fault, he concluded. She was discontented by nature. He hoped, for his son Richards's sake, that Liffey was not the same.

'You mustn't worry,' he said. 'Liffey will come through with flying colours. Wait and see.'

Liffey was at the time extremely discontented, which made her more loving and lively than ever. Chirruping and charming. Sometimes, when she woke up in the apartment, opening her eyes to the concrete wall of the house next door, and the sound of traffic instead of the sound of birds, she thought she was a child again, and in her mother's house.

The trouble was that Richard, telephoning Dick Hubbard the estate agent about Honeycomb Cottage, had been told that the cottage was for sale, and not to rent, and Richard had said they could not afford it.

'We could spend some of my money,' said Liffey.
'No, we couldn't,' said Richard firmly. 'I'm not going to live off you. What kind of man would that make me?'

By mutual consent, throughout their marriage, Liffey's money had been used to buy small things, not large things. Confectionery as it were, but not the matrimonial home.

'Then let's sell this place and buy that.'
'No. It isn't ours to sell.'

The apartment had been a wedding gift from Mr. and Mrs. Lee-Fox. Disapproving of Liffey as a bride for Richard, they had sacrificed their own comfort and security and spent an inordinate amount on the present. Thus they hoped both to disguise their feelings and remain securely sealed in the ranks of the happy and blessed.

When Richard came home from his boarding school bruised

and stunned, victim of bullying, they would seem not to notice.

'Such a wonderful school,' they'd say to friends. 'He's so happy there.'

Liffey searched the newspapers for cottages to rent but found nothing. Another month passed: another egg dropped, and failed. Liffey bled; Richard frowned, perplexed.

Liffey took a temporary job in a solicitor's office. The quality of her cooking deteriorated. She served Richard burnt food and tossed and turned all night, keeping him awake. She did not know she did it, but do it she did. She had come off the pill, after all, and still they lived in London.

'If Liffey can't have children,' asked Annie, Richard's secretary, 'would you stick by her?'

'Of course,' said Richard immediately and stoutly. But the question increased his anxiety.

Annie read cookery books in her lunch hour, propping them in her electric typewriter. She took an easy and familiar approach to her job, and felt no deference towards anyone. She had spent a year working in the States and had lost, or so it seemed to Richard, her sense of the nuances of respect owing between man and woman, powerful and humble, employer and employed.

Her fair hair hung over the typewriter like a veil. She had a boyfriend who was a diamond merchant and one-time bodyguard to General Dayan. She had wide blue eyes, and a rounded figure. Liffey had never seen her. Once she asked Richard what Annie looked like – tentatively, because she did not want to sound possessive or jealous.

'Fat,' said Richard.

And because Annie had a flat, nasal telephone voice Liffey had assumed she was one of the plain, efficient girls whom large organisations are obliged to employ to make up for the pretty ones they like to keep up front.

Besides.

When Richard and Liffey married they had agreed to tell one another at once if some new emotional or physical involvement seemed likely, and Liffey believed the agreement still held.

Christmas approached, and Liffey stopped work in order to concentrate upon it, and decorate the Christmas tree properly. She had her gifts bought by the second week in December, and then spent another week wrapping and adorning. She was asked to Richard's office party but didn't go. She did not like his office parties. Everyone looked so ugly, except Richard, and everyone got drunk.

Liffey arranged to meet Richard at a restaurant after the party. She expected him at nine. By ten he had not arrived, so she went round to the office, in case he had had too much to drink or there had been an accident. In no sense, as she explained and explained afterwards, was she spying on him.

The office was a massive new concrete block, with a marble-lined lobby and decorative lifts. Richard's employers were an international company, recently diversified from oil into films and food products – the latter being Richard's division, and he a Junior Assistant Brand Manager. If it were not for Liffey's private income, she would have had to work and earn, or else live very poorly indeed. As it was, lack of financial anxiety made Richard bold in his decisions and confident in his approach to his superiors, which was duly noted and appreciated, and boded well for his future.

Liffey went up in the lift to Richard's office, walking through empty corridors, still rich with the after-party haze of cigarette smoke and the aroma from a hundred half-empty glasses. From behind the occasional closed door came a cry, or a giggle or a moan. Liffey found Richard behind his desk, on the floor with Annie, who was not one of the plain ones after all, just plump and luscious, and all but naked, except for veils of hair. So was Richard.

Liffey went home by taxi. Richard followed after. He was maudlin drunk, sick on the step, and passed out in the hall. Liffey dragged him to bed, undressed his stubborn body and left him alone. She sat at the window staring out at the street.

She felt that she was destroyed. Everything was finished – love, trust, marriage, happiness. All over.

But of course it was not. Richard's contrition was wonderful to behold. He begged forgiveness: he held Liffey's hand. He pleaded, with some justification, total amnesia of the event. Someone had poured vodka into the fruit cup. It was Annie's fault, if anyone's. Richard loved Liffey, only Liffey. Love flowed between them again, lubricating Liffey's passages, promoting spermatogenesis in Richard's testes, encouraging the easy flow of seminal fluid from seminal vesicles and prostate to the entrance of the urethra, and thence, by a series of rhythmic muscular contractions, into Liffey.

Love, and none the worse for all that: but earthly love. Spiritual love, the love of God for man, and man for God, cannot be debased, as can earthly love, by such description.

Still Liffey did not get pregnant.

Annie was transferred to another office. After the annual Christmas party there was a general shifting round of secretarial staff. A stolid and respectful girl, Miss Martin, took Annie's place. Her plumpness was not soft and natural, as was Annie's, but solid and unwelcoming, and encased by elasticated garments. Her face was impassive, and her manner was prim; Richard was not attracted to her at all, and was relieved to find he was not. He had lately been having trouble with sudden upsurges of sexual interest in the most inappropriate people. He confided as much in Bella.

'For heaven's sake,' said Bella, 'you can't be expected to stay faithful to one person all your life, just because you married them.' Richard quite disliked Bella for a time, for giving

34

voice to what he saw as cheap and easy cynicism. He still believed in romantic love, and was ashamed of his lapse with Annie: his sudden succumbing to animal lust. He decided that Liffey and he would see less of Bella and Ray.

Christmas Pledges

Liffey's birthday was on Christmas Day, a fact which annoyed Madge, who was a proselytising atheist.

They were to spend Christmas with Richard's parents. They journeyed down to Cornwall on the night of Christmas Eve: there was a hard frost. The night landscape sparkled under the moon. Richard and Liffey were drunk with love and Richard's remorse. The back of the car was piled high with presents, beautifully wrapped and ribboned. They took with them a thermos of good real coffee, laced with brandy, and chicken sandwiches. They went by the A303, down past Windsor, on to the motorway, leaving at the Hungerford exit, and down through Berkshire and Wiltshire, crossing Salisbury Plain, where Stonehenge stood in the moonlight, ominous and amazing, dwarfing its wire palisade. Then on into Somerset, past Glastonbury Tor, into Devon and finally over the Tamar Bridge into Cornwall.

Liffey loved Richard too much to even mention Honeycomb Cottage, although they passed within five miles of it.

Christmas Day was bright, cold, and wild. Mr. and Mrs. Lee-Fox's cottage was set into the Cornish cliffs. A storm arose, and sea spray dashed against the double glazing but all was safe and warm and hospitable within. The roast turkey was magnificent, the Christmas tree charming, and Liffey's presents proved most acceptable – two hand-made patchwork quilts, one for each twin bed. Liffey loved giving. Her mother, Madge did not. They had once spent Christmas

35

with Madge, rather than with Richard's parents, and had a chilly bleak time of it. Madge liked to be working, not rejoicing.

Mr. and Mrs. Lee-Fox agreed, under their quilts on Christmas night, that at least Liffey kept Richard happy and lively, and at least this year had worn a T-shirt thick enough to hide her nipples.

On their way back to London they made a detour out of Glastonbury and into Crossley, and passed Dick Hubbard's estate agency. There was room to park outside, for the Christmas holiday, stretching further and further forward to grab in the New Year, kept most of the shops and offices closed. And Dick Hubbard's door was open. Richard stopped.

'Townspeople,' said Dick Hubbard, looking down from his private office on the first floor. 'Back from the Christmas holidays, and looking for a country cottage to rent, for twopence halfpenny a week. They're out of luck.'
He was a large, fleshy man in his late forties, at home in pubs, virile in bed; indolent. His wife had died in a riding accident shortly after his liaison with Carol had begun. Carol was smaller and slighter than her sister Mabs, but just as determined.
'There's Honeycomb Cottage,' said Carol.
'That's for sale, not for rent. I'm holding on until prices stop rising.'
'Then you'll hold on for ever,' said Carol. 'And in the meanwhile it will all fall down. Mabs says it's already an eyesore. She's quite put out about it.'
'Mabs had better not start interfering,' said Dick, 'or she'll lose her grazing.' But no one in Crossley, not even Dick Hubbard, liked to think of Mabs being put out, and when Richard and Liffey enquired about Honeycomb Cottage, they were told it was to rent on a full repairing lease for twenty pounds a week.
'Done,' said Richard.

36

'Done,' said Dick Hubbard.
They shook hands.

'In the country,' said Liffey, as they got back into the car, 'the word of a gentleman still means something. People trust one another. You're going to love it, Richard.'
'It's certainly easy to do business,' said Richard.

They decided to rent the London apartment to friends, and let the income from one pay for the outgoings on the other. 'We could get thirty a week for the flat,' said Liffey. And the extra can pay for your fares.'

It was a long time since she had been anywhere by train.

After Richard and Liffey had gone, Dick Hubbard returned to his interrupted love-making with Carol.
'Didn't they even ask for a lease?' asked Carol.
'No,' said Dick.
'You'll do all right there,' said Carol.
'I know,' said Dick.

Friends

On the morning of December 30th, Liffey rang up her friend, Helen, who was married to Mory, an architect. The friendship was not of long standing. Liffey had met Helen in the waiting room of an employment agency a year ago, and struck up an acquaintance.

After the manner of young married women, still under the obligation of total loyalty to a husband, Liffey had cut loose from her school and college friends, as if fearing that their very existence might merit a rash confidence, a betrayal of her love for Richard. She made do, now, with a kind of surface intimacy with this new acquaintance or that, and since she did not offer any indication of need or distress, or any real exchange of feeling, the friendships did not ripen.

Liffey did not like to display weakness: and weakness admitted is the very stuff of good friendship.

Mory and Richard had met over a dinner table or so, and discussed the black holes of space, and Richard, less acute in his social than his business relationships, thought he recognised a fellow spirit.

So now Liffey went to Helen and Mory for help.

'Helen? Sorry to ring so early but Helen we've rented a *most darling* cottage in the country and now all we have to do is find someone for this flat and we can move out of London in a fortnight, and I was wondering if you could help?'
There was a pause.
'How much?' enquired Helen.
'Richard says forty pounds a week but I think that's greedy. Twenty would be more like it.'
'I should think so,' said Helen. 'If you can't find anyone Mory and I could take it, I suppose, to help you out.'
'But that would be wonderful,' cried Liffey. 'I'd be so grateful! You'd look after everything and it would all be safe with you.'

Liffey sorted, washed, wrapped, packed and cleaned for two weeks. Friends rather mysteriously disappeared, instead of helping. She had no idea she and Richard had accumulated so many possessions. She gave away clothes and furniture to Oxfam. She found old photographs of herself and Richard and laughed and cried at the absurdity of life. She wrapped her hair in a spotted bandana to keep out clouds of dust. She wanted everything to be nice for Helen and Mory. Charming, talented, scatty Helen. Mory, the genius architect, temporarily unemployed. Lovely to be able to help!

'Friendship,' Liffey said, 'is all about helping.'
'Um,' said Richard. Five years ago the remark would have enchanted, not embarrassed him.
'Don't you think so, Bella,' persisted Liffey, not getting the expected response from Richard.

'I daresay,' said Bella, politely. Ray was out visiting friends who had a sixteen-year-old daughter he was helping through a Home Economics examination. Bella was in a bad, fidgety mood. Richard knew Ray was making her unhappy and from charity had lifted the embargo on the friendship. And Bella was being very kind; the kindest, in fact, of all their friends, offering packing cases, time, concern, and showing an interest in the details of the move. Now, on the eve of their departure for the country, she gave them spaghetti bolognese. The sauce came from a can. Richard followed Bella into the kitchen. Liffey had gone to the bathroom.

'Liffey's a lucky little girl,' said Bella, 'having a husband to indulge her so.'

Bella kissed Richard full on the lips, startling him.

'If you're not careful,' said Bella, 'Liffey will still be a little girl when she's got grey hairs and you're an old, old man.'

She dabbed his mouth with a tissue.

'You're going to hate the country,' said Bella. 'You're going to be so lonely.'

'We have each other,' said Richard.

Bella laughed.

Liffey came back from the bathroom with a long face.

'No baby?' asked Bella.

'No baby,' said Liffey. 'I'm sorry, Richard. Once we're in the country I'm sure it will happen.'

The removal van arrived on the morning of Wednesday, January 7th. Liffey's period was soon to finish. She was in a progesterone phase.

Richard took the day off from work. They followed the furniture van in the car, and left the key under the mat for Mory and Helen. There was no need of a lease, or a rent-book, between friends.

'Goodbye, you horrible town,' cried Liffey. 'Hello country! Nature, here we come!' Richard wished she wouldn't, Bella's words in his mind. And, he rather feared, Bella's lips. He had never thought of her as a sexual entity before.

Mory and Helen moved in a couple of hours after Richard and Liffey had left. With them came Helen's pregnant sister and her unemployed boyfriend, both of whom now had the required permanent address from which to claim Social Security benefits.

Honeycomb Cottage, in January, was perhaps colder and damper than Liffey had expected, and the rooms smaller: and the banisters had to come down before any furniture could get in, and Richard sawed the double bed in two to get it into the bedroom, but Liffey was happy, brave and positive, and by Wednesday evening had fires lit, decorative branches, however bare, in vases, and a cosy space cleared amongst chaos for a delicious celebration meal of bottled caviar, fillet steak (from Harrods), a whole pound of mushrooms between them, and champagne.

'All this,' marvelled Liffey, 'and five pounds a week profit!' She'd forgotten how much she'd asked Helen to pay, in the end. 'You're leaving out the fares,' murmured Richard, but not too loud, for it was always unkind to present Liffey with too much reality all at once. Fares would amount to some thirty pounds a week. Liffey had bought a whole crate of new books – from thrillers, new novels, to heavy works on sociology and philosophy, which she intended to dole out to Richard day by day, for the improvement of his mind on the morning journey, and his diversion on the evening train – and Richard was touched.

'It's very quiet,' said Richard, looking out into the blank, bleak wet night. 'I don't know what you're going to do with yourself all day.'
'I love the quietness,' said Liffey. 'And the solitude. Just you and me – oh, we are the most enviable of people! Everyone else just dreams, but we've actually done it.'

That night they slept on foam rubber in front of the fire, but did not make love, for they were exhausted. Richard wondered why someone so old and scraggy and cynical as

Bella should be so attractive. Perhaps true love and sexual excitement were mutually exclusive.

Realities

On Thursday morning Liffey's little alarm watch woke them at six. Liffey was up in a trice to make Richard's breakfast. The hot water system was not working and there was ice in the wash basin, but he laughed bravely. Liffey had the times of the trains written out and pinned up above the mantelpiece. She tried to light the kitchen stove but the chimney was cold, and filled the room with smoke. She could not get the kettle to boil: she plugged in the toaster and all the electricity in the house fused: she could not grind the coffee beans for coffee. The transistor radio produced only crackle – clearly here it would need an aerial. Richard stopped smiling. Liffey danced and kissed and pinched and hugged, and he managed a wan smile, as he found the old candles he'd noticed in the fuse box.

'I suppose, darling, they'd die if you took another day off work?'
'Yes, they would,' said Richard, longing for the warmth and shiny bright order of the office, and the solidarity of Miss Martin who never pranced or kissed, but offered him hot instant coffee in plastic mugs at orderly intervals.

Richard left the house at seven-thirty. Castle Tor station was twelve minutes' drive away, and the train left at seven fifty-two.
'Allow lots of time,' said Liffey, 'this first morning.'

Richard was delayed by the cow mire outside Cadbury Farm. The little Renault sank almost to its axles in the slime, for it had thawed overnight, and what the day before had been a hard surface now revealed its true nature. But revving and reversing freed the vehicle, though it woke the dogs, and he arrived, heart beating fast, at Castle Tor station at seven fifty. The station was closed. As he stood, open-mouthed, the fast train shot through.

Richard arrived back at Honeycomb Cottage at five minutes past eight. He stepped inside and slapped Liffey on the face, as she straightened up from lighting the fire, face blackened by soot.

Castle Tor station was closed all winter. Liffey had been reading the summer timetable. The nearest station was Taunton, on another line, twenty miles away. The journey from there to Paddington would take three hours. Six hours a day, thirty hours a week, spent sitting on a train, was clearly intolerable. And another eight hours a week spent driving to and from the station. To drive to London, on congested roads, would take even longer.

Richard hissed all this to Liffey, got back into his car, and drove off again.

Liffey cried.

'I wonder what all that was about,' said Tucker, putting down the field glasses.
'Go on up and find out,' said Mabs.
'No, you go,' he said.

So later in the morning Mabs put on her Wellington boots and her old brown coat with the missing buttons and paddled through the mire to Honeycomb Cottage and made herself known to Liffey as friend and neighbour.

'Do come in,' cried Liffey. 'How kind of you to call! Coffee?'

Mabs looked at Liffey and knew she was a bubble of city froth, floating on the scummy surface of the sea of humanity, breakable between finger and thumb. Liffey trusted the world and Mabs despised her for it.
'I'd rather have tea,' said Mabs.

Liffey bent to riddle the fire and her little buttocks were tight

and rounded, defined beneath stretched denim. The back-side of a naughty child, not of a grown woman, who knows the power and murk that lies beneath, and shrouds herself in folds of cloth.
So thought Mabs.

Liffey was a candy on the shelf of a high-class confectioner's shop. Mabs would have her down and take her in and chew her up and suck her through, and when she had extracted every possible kind of nourishment, would spit her out, carelessly.

Liffey looked at Mabs and saw a smiling, friendly country-woman with a motherly air and no notion at all how to make the best of herself.

Liffey was red-eyed but had forgiven Richard for hitting her. She could understand that he was upset. And it had been careless of her to have misread the train timetable. But she was confident that he would be back that evening with roses and apologies and sensible plans as to how to solve the commuting problem. And if it were in fact insoluble, then they would just have to move back into the London apartment, apologising to Mory and Helen for having inconvenienced them, and keep Honeycomb as a weekend cottage. Liffey could afford it, even if Richard couldn't. His pride, his vision of himself as husband and provider, would perhaps have to be dented, just a little. That was all.

Nothing terrible had happened. If you were an ordinary, reasonably intelligent, reasonably well-intentioned person, nothing terrible could happen. Surely.

Liffey shivered.
'Anything the matter?' asked Mabs.
'No,' said Liffey, lying. Lying was second nature to Liffey, for Madge her mother always spoke the truth. Families tend to share out qualities amongst them, this one balancing that, and in families of two, as in the case of Madge and Liffey, the result can be absurd.

At that very moment Mory, who had brutal, concrete architectural tastes, looked round Liffey's pretty apartment and said, 'Christ, Liffey has awful taste!' and then, 'Shall we burn *that*?' and Helen nodded, and Mory took a little bamboo wall shelf and snapped it between cruel, smooth, city hands and fed it into the fire so that they all felt warmer.

'I hope Dick Hubbard's given you a proper lease,' said Mabs.
'You can't trust that man an inch.'
'Richard sees to all that,' said Liffey and Mabs thought, good, she's the fool she seems.

Mabs was all kindness. She gave Liffey the names of doctors, dentist, thatcher, plumber and electrician.
'You don't want to let this place run down,' she said. 'It could be a real little love nest.'

Liffey was happy. She had found a friend in Mabs. Mabs was real and warm and direct and without affectation. In the clear light of Mabs, her former friends, the coffee-drinking, trinket-buying, theatre-going young women of her London acquaintance, seemed like mouthing wraiths.

A flurry of cloud had swept over from the direction of the Tor and left a sprinkling of thin snow, and then the wind had died as suddenly as it had sprung up, and now the day was bright and sparkling, and flung itself in through the window, so that she caught her breath at the beauty of it all. Somehow she and Richard would stay here. She knew it.

Mabs stood in the middle of her kitchen as if she were a tree grown roots, and she, Liffey, was some slender plant swaying beneath her shelter, and they were all part of the same earth, same purpose.

'Anything the matter?' asked Mabs again, wondering if Liffey were half-daft as well.

'Just thinking,' said Liffey, but there were tears in her eyes. Some benign spirit had touched her as it flew. Mabs was uneasy: her own malignity increased. The moment passed.

Mabs helped Liffey unpack and put straight, and half-envied and half-despised her for the unnecessary prodigality of everything she owned – from thick-bottomed saucepans to cashmere blankets. Money to burn, thought Mabs. Tucker would provide her with logs in winter and manure in summer: she's the kind who never checks the price. A commission would come Mabs' way from every tradesman she recommended. Liffey would be a useful source of income.

'Roof needs re-doing,' said Mabs. 'The thatch is dried out: it becomes a real fire-risk, not to mention the insects! I've a cousin who's a thatcher. He's booked up for years but I'll have a word with him. He owes me a favour.'
'I'm not certain we'll be able to stay,' said Liffey sadly, and Mabs was alerted to danger. She saw Liffey as an ideal neighbour, controllable and malleable.
'Why not?' she asked.

Public tears stood in Liffey's eyes at last, as they had not done for years. She could not help herself. The strain of moving house, imposing her will, acknowledging difficulty, and conceiving deceit, was too much for her. Mabs put a solid arm round Liffey's small shoulders, and asked what the matter was. It was more than she ever did for her children. Liffey explained the difficulty over the train timetable.
'He'll just have to stay up in London all week and come back home weekends. Lots of them round here do that,' said Mabs.

Liffey had not spent a single night apart from Richard since the day she married him, and was proud of her record. She said as much, and Mabs felt a stab of annoyance, but it did

45

not show on her face, and Liffey continued to feel trusting.
'Lots of wives would say that cramped their style,' said
Mabs.
'Not me,' said Liffey. 'I'm not that sort of person at all. I'm a
one-woman man. I mean to stay faithful to Richard all my
life. Marriage is for better or worse, isn't it.'
'Oh yes,' said Mabs, politely. 'Let's hope your Richard feels
the same.'
'Of course he does,' said Liffey stoutly. 'I know accidents
can happen. People get drunk and don't know what they're
doing. But he'd never be unfaithful; not properly unfaithful.
And nor would I, ever, ever, ever.'

Mabs spent a busy morning. She went up to her mother and
begged a small jar of oil of mistletoe and a few drops of the
special potion, the ingredients of which her mother would
never disclose, and went home and baked some scones, and
took them up to Liffey as a neighbourly gesture and when
Tucker came home to his mid-day meal told him to get up to
Liffey as soon as possible.
'What for?' asked Tucker.
'You know what for,' said Mabs. She was grim and excited
all at once. Liffey was to be proved a slut, like any other.
Tucker was to do it, and at Mabs' behest, rather than on his
own initiative, sometime later.
'You know you don't really want me to,' said Tucker,
alarmed, but excited too.
'I don't want her going back to London and leaving that
cottage empty for Dick Hubbard to sell,' said Mabs,
searching for reasons. 'And I want her side of the field for
grazing, and I want her taken down a peg or two, so you get
up there, Tucker.'
'Supposing she makes trouble,' said Tucker. 'Supposing
she's difficult.'
'She won't be,' said Mabs, 'but if she is bring her down for a
cup of coffee so we all get to know each other better.'
'You won't put anything in her coffee,' said Tucker,
suspiciously. 'I'm a good enough man without, aren't I?'
Mabs looked him up and down. He was small but he was

wiry; the muscles stood out on his wrists: his mouth was sensuous and his nostrils flared.

'You're good enough without,' she said. But in Mabs' world men were managed, not relied upon, and were seldom told more than partial truths. And women were to be controlled, especially young women who might cause trouble, living on the borders of the land, and a channel made through them, the better to do it. Tucker, her implement, would make the channel.

'I'll go this evening,' he said, delaying for no more reason than that he was busy hedging in the afternoon, and although he was annoyed, he stuck to it.

Liffey ate Mabs' scones for lunch. They were very heavy, and gave her indigestion.

A little black cat wandered into the kitchen, during the afternoon. Liffey knew she was female. She rubbed her back against Liffey's leg, and meowed, and looked subjugated, tender and grateful all at once. She rolled over on her back and yowled. She wanted a mate. Liffey had no doubt of it: she recognised something of herself in the cat, which was hardly more than a kitten and too young to safely have kittens of her own. Liffey gave her milk and tinned salmon. During the afternoon the cat sat in the garden and toms gathered in the bushes and set up their yearning yowls, and Liffey felt so involved and embarrassed that she went and lay down on her mattress on the floor, which was the only bed she had, and her own breath came in short, quick gasps, and she stretched her arms and knew she wanted something, someone, and assumed it was Richard, the only lover she had ever had, or ever – until that moment – hoped to have. Gradually the excitement, if that was what it was, died. The little cat came in; she seemed in pain. She complained, she rolled about, she seemed talkative and pleased with herself.

Farmyards, thought Liffey. Surely human beings are more than farmyard animals? Don't we have poetry, and paintings, and great civilisations and history? Or is it only men who have these things? Not women. She felt, for the first time in her life, at the mercy of her body.

Richard, four hours late at the office, had to fit his morning's work into the afternoon, re-make appointments, and re-arrange meetings. It became obvious that he would have to work late. His anger with Liffey was extreme: he felt no remorse for having hit her. Wherever he looked, whatever he remembered, he found justification for himself in her bad behaviour. Old injuries, old traumas, made themselves disturbingly felt. At fifteen, he had struck his father for upsetting his mother: he felt again the same sense of rage, churned up with love, and the undercurrent of sadistic power, and the terrible knowledge of victory won. And once his mother had sent off the wrong forms at the wrong time and Richard had failed as a result to get a university place. Or so he chose to think, blaming his mother for not making his path through life smooth, recognising the hostility behind the deed, as now he blamed Liffey, recognising her antagonism towards his work. It was as if during the angry drive to the office, a trapdoor had opened up, which hitherto had divided his conscious, kindly, careful self from the tumult, anger and confusion below, and the silt and sludge now surged up to overwhelm him. He asked Miss Martin to send a telegram to Liffey saying he would not be home that night.

Miss Martin raised her eyes to his for the first time. They were calm, shrewd, gentle eyes. Miss Martin would never have misread a train timetable.
'Oh Mr. Lee-Fox,' said Miss Martin. 'You have got yourself into a pickle!'

Farmyards

Mabs' children came home on the school bus. Other children wore orange arm bands, provided by the school in the interests of road safety. But not Mabs' children.

48

'I'm not sewing those things on. If they're daft enough to get run over they're better dead. Isn't that so, Tucker?'

Today the children carried a telegram for Liffey. Mrs. Harris, who ran the sub post-office in Crossley had asked them to take it up to Honeycomb Cottage. They gave it instead to Mabs, who steamed the enevelope open, and read the contents, more for confirmation than information, for Mrs. Harris had told the children, who told Mabs, that Richard would not be coming home that night. He was staying with Bella, instead.

Bella? Who was Bella? Sister, mistress, friend?

Tucker consented to take the telegram up to Liffey. No sooner had he gone than Mabs began to wish he had stayed. She became irritable, and gave the children a hard time along with their tea. She chivvied Audrey into burning the bacon, slapped Eddie for picking up the burnt bits with his fingers, made Kevin eat the half-cooked fatty bits so that he was sick, and then made Debbie and Tracy wipe Kevin's sick up. But it was done: they were fed. All were already having trouble with their digestions, and would for the rest of their lives.

When Mabs was pregnant she was kinder and slower, but Kevin, the youngest, was four, and had never known her at her best. He was the most depressed, but least confused.

Liffey, wearing rubber gloves and dark glasses as well as four woollies, opened the door to Tucker. She knew from his demeanour that he had not come to deliver telegrams, or to mend fuses (although he did this for her, later) but to bed her if he could. The possibility that he might, the intention that he should, hung in the air between them. He did not touch her, yet the glands on either side of her vaginal entrance responded to sexual stimulation – as such glands do, without so much as a touch or a caress being needed – by a dramatic increase in their secretions.

Like the little black cat on heat, thought Liffey. Horrible!

She made no connection between her response and Mabs' scones, with their dose of mistletoe and something else. How could she?

I am not a nice girl at all, thought Liffey. No. All that is required of me is the time, the place, and the opportunity: a willing stranger at the door unlikely to reproach me; and dreams of fidelity and notions of virtue and prospects of permanence fly out the window as he steps in the door.

Love is the packet, thought Liffey, that lust is sent in, and the ribbons are quickly untied.

If I step back, thought Liffey, this man will step in after me and that will be that.

Come in, come in, Liffey's whole body sang, but a voice from Madge answered back, 'Wanting is not doing, Liffey. Almost nothing you can't do without.'
Liffey did not step back. She did not smile at Tucker. But her breath came rapidly.

Tucker introduced himself. Farmer, Neighbour. Mabs' husband. Owner of the field where the black and white cows grazed. Kicker of puffballs. Liffey remembered him now, by his steel-capped boots. She remained formal, and friendly. But Tucker *knew*, and knew that she knew, what there could be, was to be, between them.
Tucker handed over the telegram.
'My husband can't get back this evening,' said Liffey, brightly and briskly, reading it. She knew better than to betray emotion at such a time. But she minded very much.

A fighter plane zoomed over the Tor, startling both, and was gone. Tucker Pierce smiled at Liffey. Liffey's eyelids drooped as other parts of her contracted, in automatic beat. Oh, little black cat, squirming over the cool ground, the better to put out the fire within! Tucker moved closer. Liffey stood her ground, chanting an inner incantation, of nonsense and aspiration mixed. Richard, I love you, Richard, I am spirit, not animal: Tucker, in the name of love, in the name of God, in the name of Richard, flawed and imperfect as he is; Tucker, stay where you are.

Tucker stayed; Tucker talked, still on the step.
'Come the spring,' said Tucker, 'you'll be wanting our cows in your field. Keep the grass and the thistles down.'
'Not to mention the docks,' said Tucker. 'Docks can be a terrible nuisance.'
'Don't thank me,' said Tucker. 'We're neighbours, after all.'
'Any little bits and pieces you need doing,' said Tucker. 'Just ask.'
'Looks cosy in there,' said Tucker, peering over Liffey's shoulder into the colourful warmth within. 'I see you've a way with rooms: making them look nice, Feminine like.'

And indeed Liffey had: tacking up a piece of fabric here, a bunch of dried flowers there. She adorned rooms as she hesitated to adorn herself. She loved silks and velvets and rich embroideries and plump cushions and old, faded colours.

Tucker looked longingly within. Liffey stood her ground.
'Come on down to the farm,' said Tucker, remembering Mabs' instructions, 'and have a cup of coffee with Mabs.'
'Mabs is always glad of company,' lied Tucker. 'One thing to be on your own when you expect it,' observed Tucker, with truth. 'Quite another when you don't. You'll be feeling lonely, I dare say.'
'Not really,' said Liffey, with as much conviction as she could muster. 'But I'd be glad to use your telephone, if I could.'

They walked down together, along the rutted track. Tucker Pierce, farmer, married, father of five, muddy-booted, dirty-handed, coarse-featured, but smiling, confident and easy, secure in his rights and expectations. And little Liffey, feeling vulnerable and flimsy, a pawn on someone else's chessboard, not the Queen. She saw herself through Tucker's eyes. She saw that her frayed jeans could represent poverty as well as universal brotherhood, and skinniness malnutrition, rather than the calculated reward of a high protein, low calorie diet.

Liffey had to run to keep up with Tucker. Her country shoes, so absurdly stout in London, appeared flimsy here, while his clumsy boots moved easily over the hollows and chasms of the rutted path.
'It's quiet up here,' said Tucker, turning to her.
Not here, she thought, not here in the open, like an animal: and then, not here, not anywhere, never!

Liffey rang Richard's office from the cold hall of Cadbury Farm. Miss Martin said Richard was not available, having gone to a meeting at an outside advertising agency, and she did not expect him back.
'Didn't he leave a message?'
'No.'

Liffey rang Bella and the au-pair girl Helga answered. Bella and Ray were dining out, with Mr. Lee-Fox. Perhaps if Liffey rang later? At midnight?
'No. It wouldn't be practical,' said Liffey.
'Any message?'
'No,' said Liffey.

'You do look cold,' said Mabs. 'Pull a chair to the fire.'
And she poured Liffey some coffee, in a cracked cup. The coffee was bitter.

Mabs chatted about the children, and schools, and cows and smoking chimneys. Tucker said nothing. The kitchen was large, stone flagged, handsome and cold. The same pieces of furniture – substantial rather than gracious – had stood here for generations – dresser, tables, sideboards, chairs – and were half-despised, half-admired by virtue of their very age.

Tucker and Mabs boasted of the price they would fetch in the auction room, while using the table, almost on purpose, to mend sharp or oily pieces of farm machinery, and the edge of the dresser for whittling knives, and covering every available surface with the bric-à-brac of everyday life – receipts, bills, brochures, lists, padlocks, beads, hair rollers, badges, lengths of string, plastic bags, scrawled addresses, children's socks and toys, plasters, schoolbooks, and tubes of this and pots of that. Neither Mabs nor Tucker, thought Liffey, marvelling, were the sort to throw anything away, and had the grace to feel ashamed of herself for being the sort of person who threw out a cup when it was chipped; or a dress when she was tired of it, or furniture when it bored her.

Cadbury Farm, she saw, served as the background to Tucker and Mabs' life, it was not, as she was already making out of Honeycomb Cottage, a part, almost the purpose, of life itself.

Liffey went home as soon as she politely could.
'It's getting dark,' said Mabs. 'Tucker had better go with you. I'm not saying there's a headless horseman out there, but you might meet a flying saucer. People do, round here. Mostly on their way home from the pub, of course. All the same, Tucker'll take you. Won't you, Tucker?'
'That's right,' said Tucker.

But Liffey insisted on going by herself, and then felt frightened and wished Tucker was indeed with her, whatever the cost, particularly at that bend of the road where the wet branches seemed unnaturally still, as if waiting for something sudden and dreadful to happen. But she hurried on, and pulled the pretty curtains closed when she got to the cottage, and switched on the radio, and soon was feeling better again, or at any rate not frightened; merely angry with Richard and upset by her own feelings towards Tucker, and fearful of some kind of change in herself, which she could hardly understand, but knew was happening, and had its roots in the realisation that she was not the nice, good, kind, pivotal person she had believed, around whom the rest of an imperfect creation revolved, but someone much like anyone else, as nice and as good as circumstance would allow, but not a whit more: and certainly no better than anyone else at judging the rightness or wrongness of her own actions.

Desire for Richard overwhelmed her when she lay down to sleep on the mattress on the floor. It was, for Liffey, an unusual and physical desire for the actual cut and thrust of sexual activity, rather than the emotional need for tenderness and recognition and the celebration of good things which Liffey was accustomed to interpreting as desire, for lack of a better word. Presently images of Tucker replaced images of Richard, and Liffey rose and took a sleeping pill, thinking this might help her. All it did was to seem to paralyse her limbs whilst agitating her mind still more; and a sense of the blackness and loneliness outside began to oppress her, and an image of a headless horseman to haunt her, and she wondered whether choosing to live in the country had been an act of madness, not sanity, and presently rose and took another sleeping pill, and then fell into a fitful sleep, in which Tucker loomed large and erect.

But she had locked the door. So much morality, prudence, and the habit of virtue enabled her to do.

In Residence

At the time that Liffey was taking her second sleeping pill Bella offered one to Richard. Bella sat on the end of his bed, which Helga the au-pair had made up out of a sofa in Bella's study. Bella wore her glasses and looked intelligent and academic, and as if she knew what she was talking about. Her legs were hairy beneath fine nylon. Richard declined the pill.
'Liffey doesn't believe in pills,' he said.
'You aren't Liffey,' said Bella, firmly.
Richard considered this.
'I decide what we *do*,' said Richard, 'but I let Liffey decide

what's good for us. And taking sleeping pills isn't, except in extreme circumstances, and by mutual decision.'

'Liffey isn't here,' Bella pointed out. 'And it was she who decided you'd live in the country, not you.'

It was true. Liffey had edged over, suddenly and swiftly, if unconsciously, into Richard's side of the marriage, breaking unwritten laws.

'You don't think Liffey misread the timetable on purpose?' He was on the downward slopes of the mountain of despondency, enjoying the easy run down: resentments and realisations and justifications rattled along at his heels, and he welcomed them. He wanted Bella to say yes, Liffey was not only in the wrong, but wilfully in the wrong.

'On purpose might be too strong,' said Bella. 'Try by accident on purpose.'

'It's unfair of her,' said Richard. 'I've always tried to make her happy, I really have, Bella. I've taken being a husband very seriously.'

'Bully for you,' said Bella, settling in cosily at the end of the bed, digging bony buttocks in.

'But one expects a return. Is that unreasonable?'

'Never say one,' said Bella. 'Say "I". "One" is a class-based concept, used to justify any amount of bad behaviour.'

'Very well,' said Richard. '*I* expect a return. And the truth is, Liffey has shown that she doesn't care for my comfort and convenience, only for her own. And when I look into my heart, where there used to be a kind of warm round centre, which was love for Liffey, there's now a cold hard patch. No love for Liffey. It's very upsetting, Bella.'

He felt that Bella had him on a pin, was a curious investigator of his painful flutterings. But it was not altogether unpleasant. A world which had been black and white was now transfused with colour: rich butterfly wings, torn but powerful, rose and fell, and rose again. To be free from love was to be free indeed.

Bella laughed.

55

'Happiness! Love!' she marvelled. 'Years since I heard anyone talking like that. What do you mean? Neurotic need? Romantic fantasy?'

'Something's lost,' he persisted. 'Call it what you like. I'm a very simple person, Bella.'

Simple, he said. Physical, of course, was what he meant. Able to give and take pleasure, and in particular sexual pleasure. Difficult, now, not to take a marked sexual interest in Bella; she, clothed and cosy on his bed, and he, naked in it, and only the thickness of a quilt between them. Or if not a sexual interest, certainly a feeling that the natural, ordinary thing to do was to take her in his arms so that their conversation could continue on its real level, which was without words. The very intimacy of their present situation deserved this resolution.

These feelings, more to do with a proper sense of what present circumstances required than anything more permanent, Richard interpreted both as evidence of his loss of love for Liffey, and desire for Bella, and the one reinforced the other. That, and the shock of the morning, and the evidence of Liffey's selfishness, and the sudden fear that she was not what she seemed, and the shame of his striking her, and the exhaustion of the drive, and the stirring up of childhood griefs, had all combined to trigger off in Richard's mind such a wave of fears and resentments and irrational beliefs as would stay with him for some time. And in the manner of spouses everywhere, he blamed his partner for his misfortunes, and held Liffey responsible for the cold patch in his heart, and the uncomfortably angry and anxious, lively and lustful thoughts in his mind: and if he did not love her any more, why then, it was Liffey's fault that he did not.

'All I can say,' said Bella, 'is that love or the lack of it is made responsible for a lot of bad behaviour everywhere; and it's hard luck on wives if misreading a train timetable can herald the end of a marriage: but I will say on your behalf, Richard, that Liffey is very manipulative, and has an emotional and sexual age of twelve, and a rather spoilt twelve at that. You'll just have to put your foot down and move back to London, and if Liffey wants to stay where she is, then you can visit her at weekends.'

'She wouldn't like that,' said Richard.

'You might,' said Bella. 'What about you?'

Spoilt. It was a word heard frequently in Richard's childhood.

You can't have this: you can't have that. You don't want to be spoilt. Or, from his mother, I'd like you to have this but your father doesn't want me to spoil you. So you can't have it. It seemed to Richard, hearing Bella say 'spoilt' that Liffey had been the recipient of all the good things he himself had ever been denied, and he resented it, and the word, as words will, added fuel to his paranoic fire, and it burned the more splendidly.

As for Bella – who had thrown in the word half on purpose, knowing what combustible material it was – Bella knew she herself was not spoilt, and never had been. Bella had been obliged to struggle and work for what she now had, as Liffey had not, and no one had ever helped her, so why should it be different for anyone else?

Richard sat up in bed. His chest was young, broad and strong. The hairs upon it were soft and sleek, and not at all like Ray's hairy tangle.

'I wish I could imagine Liffey and you in bed together,' said Bella. 'But I can't. Does she know what to do? Nymphet Liffey!'

Bella had gone too far: approached too quickly and too near, scratched Liffey's image which was Richard's alone to scratch. Whatever was in the air between herself and Richard evaporated. Bella went back to her desk, typing, and Richard lay back and closed his eyes.

The wind rose in the night: two sleeping pills could not wipe out the sound or ease the sense of danger. Liffey heard a tile fly off the roof: occasionally rain spattered against the window. She lay awake in a sleeping bag on a mattress on the floor. The double bed was still stacked in two pieces against the wall. Liffey ached, body and soul.

Liffey got up at three and went downstairs and doused the fire. Perhaps the chimneys had not been swept for years and so might catch light. Then she would surely burn to death. Smoke belched out into the room as the hot coals received the water. Liffey feared she might suffocate, but was too frightened to open the back door, for by letting out the smoke she would let the night in. When she went upstairs the night had become light and bright again; the moon was large: the Tor was framed against pale clouds, beautiful. Liffey slept, finally, and dreamt Tucker was making love to her on a beach, and waves crashed and roared and stormed and threatened her, so there was only desire, no fulfilment.

When she woke someone was hammering on the front door. It was morning. She crawled out of the sleeping bag, put on her coat, went downstairs and opened the door.
It was Tucker. Liffey stepped back.
Tucker stepped inside.
Tucker was wearing his boots, over-trousers tucked into them, a torn shirt, baggy army sweater, and army combat-jacket. His hands were muddy. She did not get as far as his face.
'Came up to see if you were all right,' said Tucker.
'I'm fine,' said Liffey. She felt faint: surely because she had got up so suddenly. She leaned against the wall, heavy-lidded. She remembered her dream.
'You don't look it,' said Tucker. He took her arm; she trembled.
'How about a cup of tea?' said Tucker. He sat squarely at the kitchen table, and waited. His house, his land, his servant. Liffey found the Earl Grey with some difficulty. Richard and she rarely drank tea.

'It's very weak,' said Tucker, staring into his cup. She had not been able to find a saucer and was embarrassed.

'It's that kind of tea,' said Liffey.

'Too bad Hubby didn't come home,' said Tucker. 'I wouldn't miss coming home to you. Do you like this tea?'

'Yes.'

'I don't,' said Tucker. He stood up and came over to stand behind her, pinioning her arms. 'You shouldn't make tea like that. No one should.'

His breath came warm and familiar against her face. She did not doubt but that the business of the dream would be finished. His arms, narrowing her shoulders, were so strong there was no point in resisting them. It was his decision, not hers. She was absolved from responsibility. There was a sense of bargain in the air: not of mutual pleasure, but of his taking, her consenting. In return for her consent he offered protection from darkness, storm and fire. This is country love, thought Liffey. Richard's is a city love: Richard's arms are soft and coaxing, not insistent: Richard strikes a different bargain: mind calls to mind, word evolves word, response evokes response, is nothing to do with the relationship between the strong and the weak, as she was weak now, and Tucker strong upon her, upon the stone floor, her coat fortunately between her bare skin and its cold rough surface, his clothing chafing and hurting her. Tucker was powerful, she was not: here was opposite calling to opposite, rough to smooth, hard to soft, cruel to kind – as if each quality craved the dilution of its opposite, and out of the struggle to achieve it crested something new. This is the way the human race multiplies, thought Liffey, satisfied. Tucker's way, not Richard's way.

But Liffey's mind, switched off as a pilot might switch off manual control in favour of automatic, cut back in again once the decision of abandonment had been made. Prudence returned, too late. This indeed, thought Liffey, is the way the human race multiplies, and beat upon Tucker with helpless, hopeless fists.

It was the last day of her period. Surely she could not become pregnant at such a time? But since she had stopped taking the pill her cycle was erratic and random: what happened hardly deserved the name of 'period': she bled for six days at uneven intervals, that was all. Who was to say what was happening in her insides? No, surely, surely, it would be all right, must be all right; even if it wasn't all right, she would have a termination. Richard would never know: no one would ever know.

She was worrying about nothing: worrying even as she cried out again in pleasure, or was it pain: Tucker now behind her, she on her side, held fast in his arms. They were like animals: she had not cared: now she began to: she wanted Richard. Where was Richard? If he hadn't missed his train none of this would have happened. Richard's fault. It could not happen again: it must not happen again: she would have to make clear to Tucker it would not happen again: so long as he understood what she was saying, peasant that he was. Even as she began to be horrified of him he finished, and whether she was satisfied or not she could not be sure. She thought so. It was certainly a matter of indifference to Tucker. He returned to the table and his cold tea. He wanted the pot filled up with boiling water. She obliged in silence, and poured more.
'I suppose you could develop a taste for it,' he said. 'But I'd better be getting back to Mabs.'

He left. Liffey went back to bed, and to sleep, and the sleeping pills caught up with her and it was two in the afternoon before she woke again, and when she did, the dream of Tucker and the actuality of Tucker were confused. Had it not been for the state of her nightshirt and the grazing on her legs and the patches of abraded roughness round her mouth, she would have dismissed the experience altogether as the kind of dream a woman dreams when she sleeps alone for the first time in years. But she could not quite do that.

Liffey balanced the incident in her mind against Richard's scuffling with his secretary at the office party, and decided that the balance of fidelity had been restored. There was no need to feel guilty. At the same time there was every reason not to let it happen again. She had the feeling Tucker would not return, at any rate not in the same way. He had marked her, that was all, and put her in her proper place. She felt sure she could rely upon his discretion. She was even relieved. Now that Richard had been paid out, she could settle down to loving him again. She felt she had perhaps been angrier with him than she had thought.

'Well?' enquired Mabs, when Tucker returned. The children were off on the school bus. Eddie had a bruise on his back. She had given him a note to take to his teacher saying he had a sore foot and could he be excused physical training, which was done in singlet and pants.
'Skinny,' complained Tucker. 'Nothing to it.'
She pulled him down on top of her, to take the taste of Liffey out of him as soon as possible.
'Not like you,' said Tucker. 'Nothing's like you.'
'But we'll get the cows in her field,' Mabs comforted herself.
'We'll get whatever we want,' said Tucker. He felt the distress in her and kissed her dangerous eyes closed, in case the distress should turn to anger, and sear them all.
'She's just a little slut,' said Mabs. 'I knew she was from the way she talked. Don't you go near her again, Tucker, or I'll kill you.'

He thought he wouldn't, because she might.
If he'd been a cockerel, all the same, he'd have crowed.
Taking and leaving Liffey. He liked Liffey.

Mabs asked Carol, later, if she knew what it was her mother mixed in with the mistletoe, and Carol said no, she didn't. But whatever it was, it had got her Dick Hubbard.

'It's not that I believe in any of mother's foolery,' said Carol, 'any more than you do. It's just that it works. At least to get things started. It would never get a river flowing uphill – but if there's even so much as a gentle slope down, it sure as hell can start the flood.'

In Richard's Life

Richard, taking Bella's words to heart, if not her body to his, went round to the apartment before going to work, to explain to Mory and Helen that a mistake had been made, and that he and Liffey would have to return to London. Liffey, Richard had decided, would have to put up with using Honeycomb Cottage as a weekend retreat, and he would have to put up with her paying for its rent – not an unpleasant compromise for either of them – until his verbal contract with Dick Hubbard, to take the cottage for a year, could be said to have expired. 'Never go back on a deal just because you can,' Richard's father had instructed him, 'even if it's convenient. A man's word is his bond. It is the basis on which all civilisation is based.' And Richard believed him, following the precept in his private life, if not noticeably on his employers' behalf.

'Never let a woman pay for herself,' his mother had said, slipping him money when he was nine, so he could pay for her coffee, and confusion had edged the words deeply into his mind. 'Never spend beyond your income,' she would say, 'I never do,' when he knew it was not true.
Now he earnestly required Liffey to live within his income whilst turning a blind eye to the fact that they clearly did not: that avocados and strawberries and pigskin wallets belonged to the world of the senior executive, not the junior. The important thing, both realised, was to save face. She seriously took his housekeeping, and he seriously did not notice when it was all used upon one theatre outing.

It was difficult, Richard realised on the way up the stairs, to fulfil the obligation both to Dick Hubbard and to Mory, who had been promised a pleasant apartment and who now must be disappointed. It could not, in fact, be done; and for this dereliction Richard blamed Liffey. He resolved, however, out of loyalty to a wife whom he had gladly married, to say nothing of all this to Mory.

The familiar stairs reassured him; the familiar early morning smells of other people's lives: laundry, bacon, coffee. The murmur of known voices. This was home. Three days away from it and already he was homesick. He could never feel the same for Honeycomb Cottage, although for Liffey's sake he would have tried. Wet leaves, dank grass and a sullen sky he could persuade himself were seasonal things: but the running, erratic narrative of the apartment block would never be matched, for Richard, by the plodding, repetitive story of the seasons.

I am a creature of habit, said Richard to himself.

'I am a creature of habit!' Richard's mother had been accustomed to saying, snuggling into her fur coat, or her feather cushion, eyes bright and winsome, when anyone had suggested she do something new – such as providing a dish on Tuesday other than shepherd's pie, or getting up early enough in the morning to prepare a packed lunch for Richard, or going somewhere on holiday other than Alassio, Italy. 'I am a creature of habit!' Perhaps, Richard thought now, one day I will understand my mother, and the sense of confusion will leave me.

Richard knocked on his own front door. Helen's sister Lally, pregnant body wrapped in her boyfriend's donkey-jacket, opened the door. She wore no shoes. Richard, startled, asked to see Mory or Helen.
'They're asleep,' said Lally. 'Go away and come back later whoever you are,' and she shut the door in his face. She was very pretty and generally fêted, and saw no need to be

pleasant to strange men. She believed, moreover, that women were far too likely for their own good to defer to men, and was trying to stamp out any such tendency in herself, thus allying, most powerfully, principle to personality.

Richard hammered on the door.
'This is my home!' he cried. 'I live here.'
Eventually Mory opened the door. Richard had not seen Mory for three months. Then he had worn a suit and tie and his hair cleared his collar. Now, pulling on jeans, hopping from foot to foot, hairy chested, long haired, he revealed himself as what Richard's mother would describe as a hippie.
'Don't lose your cool, man,' said Mory. 'What's the hassle?'
'Is that really you?' asked Richard, confused more by the hostility in look and tone, than by the change in Mory's appearance, marked though it was.
'So far as I know,' said Mory, cunningly.

He did not ask Richard in. On the contrary, he now quite definitely blocked the door, and Richard, who had just now seen himself as a knight errant, was conscious of a number of shadowy, barefoot creatures within, and knew that his castle had been besieged, and taken and was full of alien people, and that only force of arms would win it back.
Richard explained. He was cautious and formal.
'That's certainly shitsville, man,' said Mory, 'but it was on your say so we split, and our pad's gone now, and what are we supposed to do, sleep on the streets to save you a train journey? Didn't you see Lally was pregnant?'
Richard said he would go to law.
Mory said Richard was welcome to go to law, and in three years time Richard might manage an eviction.
'We've got the law tied up, man,' said Mory. 'It's on the side of the people, now. You rich bastards are just going to have to squeal.'

Mory's language had changed, along with his temperament. Richard remarked on it to Miss Martin, when he reached the office. He was already on the phone to his solicitor.

'He may have been popping acid,' remarked Miss Martin. 'Or he may have been like that all the time. People's true natures reveal themselves when it comes to accommodation. It's the territorial imperative.'

The solicitor sighed and sounded serious, and said Richard should come round at once.

Richard drove up to Honeycomb Cottage at eight that evening. He parked the car carefully on hard ground, in spite of his apparent exhaustion. He covered the bonnet with newspaper before he came in to the house. He did not mean to risk the car not starting in the morning. Liffey waved happily from the window. Last night's nightmares and suspicions, and the morning's bizarre event, were equally washed away in expectation, excitement and a sense of achievement. She had worked hard all day, unpacking, putting up curtains, lining shelves, chopping wood: reviving last night's uneaten sweet-and-sour-pork in the coal-fired Aga which, now it had stopped smoking, she knew she was going to love. She had the hot water system working and the bed assembled. She had bathed and put on fresh dungarees, and washed her nightshirt.

Richard was not smiling as he came in the room. He sank in a chair. She poured him whisky, into a warmed glass. That way the full flavour emerged.
He was silent!
'Haven't I worked hard? Do say I've done well. You've no idea how I missed you. There was such a wind, I was quite frightened in the night.'
Still he did not speak. Hearing her own voice in the silence she knew it was the voice of a child, playing bravely alone in its lighted bedroom, dark corridors between it and parents: making up stories, speaking aloud, filling up space, taking first one rôle, and then the other. Mournful, frightened prattle.
'Did you really stay with Bella?' She heard her own voice growing up, growing sour. No, she begged, don't let me. But she did.

'Why didn't you drive back last night? You must have known I'd be miserable on my own.'

Still silence.

'And you hit me.'

'Do shut up, Liffey,' said Richard, in a conversational and uncondemning voice, thus enabling her to do so. 'What's for supper?'

She fetched out the sweet-and-sour-pork. She lit the candles. They ate. It was almost what she had dreamed, except that Richard hardly said a word.

'We are in a mess,' said Richard over the devilled sardines she had prepared in place of dessert. She could see that getting to the shops would be difficult. She would have to get a telephone installed as soon as possible, if only in order to call taxis.

'We're not,' said Liffey, 'we're here, aren't we, and it's lovely, and if you say we have to move back to London I won't make any trouble. But I would like to stay.'

Did Liffey have Tucker in mind as she spoke? Opening up whole new universes of power, and passion; laying instinct bare.

'We can't move back to London,' said Richard, and even as Liffey's eyes lit up, said, 'I'm going to have to stay up in London during the week, and come back at weekends.'

Liffey wept. Richard explained.

'At least until we can get something sorted out with the lawyers,' said Richard. 'Three months or so, I imagine. I can stay with Ray and Bella, on their sofa. It won't be very comfortable but I can manage.'

Did Richard have Bella in mind as he spoke, filling his black-and-white world with rich colours of cynicism and new knowledge.

How long since Liffey had really wept? Not, surely, during

all the time she had been married to Richard. Tears had fallen from her eyes for the plight of the helpless, or for abused children, or forsaken wives, or for the tens of thousands swept away by floods in far-off places, but she had not wept for herself.

'I don't want to be away from you,' said Richard. 'Do you think I enjoy sleeping apart from you? But what else can I do?'

'Helen and Mory are supposed to be our *friends*,' wept Liffey.
'How can friends behave like that?'

Richard tried to console Liffey. He told her about army wives whose husbands were away for months at a time, and light-housemen, and submariners on nuclear submarines who sometimes didn't come home for years. And the wives of convicts and political prisoners.

'But those are other people,' cried Liffey. 'This is *me*.'

Richard told Liffey how nice she'd made everything in the cottage, and how he would look forward to coming home at the weekends, and how absence made the heart grow fonder and she believed him, and he believed himself, and they went to bed, tearful but entwined; and he fell asleep, so tired was he, before he could do more than embrace her, and in the morning both slept through the alarm, which was set for five-thirty, so that Richard had to leap out of bed and be gone before she could possibly speak to him.

Liffey without Richard

When Richard had gone Liffey snuggled back into the warm bed and half wondered and half wished that Tucker would come knocking at the door, but he did not. Liffey did not lust after Richard. She never had. They were too well suited, too polite for that. He could produce in her, by kissing and loving, a delicate desire: but not the personal, angry focusing of lust.

Liffey, waking properly a second time, with the winter sun shining across white frosted fields and the Tor raising its crystalline arm into a pale brilliant sky, felt happy enough. But realising that despondency might soon set in, Liffey made lists.

> Get telephone.
> Learn to drive.
> Organise shopping.
> Invite friends.
> Read gardening books.

Presently she added:
> Writing paper and stamps.

And then, later:
> Bicycle, to get to postbox. Powered bicycle, perhaps?

Later, she added:
> Write book.

That one frightened her. If there was time and opportunity she might actually have to, and be judged. She would rather have it as a dream, than a reality. She crossed it out.

Afterwards she wrote:
> Make friends.

These things, surely, added up to contentment. Madge, in times of trouble, had written lists and posted them up. Earn more money, spend less, stop Liffey picking her nose (or had it been worse? Liffey had a feeling that it was something far more sinister she had to be saved from) find lover, buy brown bread not white. Messages from her good lively self to her depressed self. Stop drinking, she'd even written, in the days when she did: when Liffey would come home from school and find her mother asleep and snoring on her bed. Or had Liffey herself written that one? She thought perhaps that she had. And Madge, as a result, had picked herself up and stopped drinking, and in so doing had given Liffey the encouraging feeling that life was not a gradual descent from good to bad, from youth to age, from health to decay, but rather flowed in waves, good times turning to bad, bad turning to good again. Wait, be patient, shuffle the cards.

Wait, Liffey; use your time well. Shuffle the cards. Write lists. If you fear loneliness, turn it into solitude and rejoice. Cultivate inner resources, wrote Liffey.
'There is nothing to worrry about,' Liffey told herself. 'So long as you are healthy and have money in the bank, there are no problems which cannot be solved.' She believed it, too.

Liffey composed a reasonable letter in her head to Mory and Helen, and wrote it out on a brown paper bag, having no writing paper, and then used it, by mistake, to re-light the Aga stove.

In the afternoon Liffey walked a mile and a half across the fields to the village of Poldyke, where there was a shop, a garage, and a post office, and a doctor came over on Wednesday afternoons from the big village of Crossley. At Crossley there were schools, and pubs, a greengrocer and a chemist. To get to Crossley, five miles away, meant a walk up the lane, past Cadbury Farm, and then along a stretch of main arterial road, where it narrowed alarmingly, and the lorries passed, and did not like pedestrians.

Liffey arrived at Poldyke one minute after the surgery was closed, in time to see the doctor drive off in his big new car. He was a small, desperate-looking man, with strained eyes in a dark monkey face, not so much older than Liffey: he drove off past her, both gloved hands gripping the wheel, hunched into a great coat, sunk into rich upholstery.

In the village shop Liffey cried out with delight over a rack of farm overalls, and bought one.

'For your husband? He'll be working the land up there, then?'

'No. For me,' said Liffey, before she could stop herself, and had to watch the look of puzzlement appear on Mrs. Harris's narrow face. Mrs. Harris worked the land behind the shop. Once or twice a day the shop bell would sound and Mrs. Harris would dust off hands and boots and come in to serve. 'She acts as if everything's toys,' Mrs. Harris complained to Mabs' mother later, 'not real things at all.'

Liffey was now eight days into her new, somewhat irregular menstrual cycle – the fourth since she had stopped taking the contraceptive pill, and her body was still recovering from a surfeit of hormones, as might a car engine flooded by the use of too much choke, and obliged to rest. She had not been made pregnant by Tucker, though who was going to believe a thing like that? And had had no opportunity of becoming pregnant by Richard.

Richard without Liffey

'The thing about Liffey,' said Bella to Richard that evening, 'is that she's so gloriously positive. Of course it can be a drawback. Well, look at you! Swept away on the powerful tides of Liffey's whims!'

'She's so wonderfully young,' said Ray. 'What a pity we all have to grow up.'

Richard badly missed Liffey, sitting there without her at Ray and Bella's table. He thought of himself as a tree with its main branch wrenched off, leaving a nasty open wound down the trunk, vulnerable to all kinds of disagreeable infections.

There were beans on toast and fish fingers for supper, prepared by Helga. Bella and Ray dined excellently in public, but meagrely at home. The dishes for their dinner parties were brought in by a deserted wife and mother of four who lived down the road. She also tested the recipes in the many recipe books which Bella and Ray devised together. Their speciality was fish dishes, but they knew a thing or two about edible fungi. She looked after Tony and Tina, Bella's children, on Helga's day off, but was now suffering from nervous exhaustion, so that Helga seldom could have a day off. Helga came from Austria, and worked for her keep, and pocket-money.

Ray and Bella lived busy lives. They had Marxist leanings. They applied their intellectual energies, every now and then, to the practical details of domestic life, so that the home ran smoothly on machinery and the labour of others. Tony and Tina picked up their own toys, lay their own places at table, washed up their own plates and cutlery when they had finished with them, plus one saucepan and mixing bowl each, and put their dirty clothes in the laundry basket and collected them clean from the dryer. They were quiet children. Other parents became quite disagreeable about them.

Richard had sometimes wished in the past that Liffey was more like Bella, and had a capacity for money-making and public-speaking. But Liffey devoted all her energies to the actual business of living, not doing, and that, he supposed, was that. And Liffey was restful, and Bella wasn't. And though Liffey, as Bella had pointed out, might be an emotional challenge, she was certainly not an intellectual one, and that was restful.

Richard found himself vaguely mistrustful of Bella and Ray's kindness in offering him, so readily, the use of Bella's sofa. He would have felt reassured had they suggested he baby-sat, but they had not. He told himself, over tinned peaches and custard, that he must not become paranoic.

That Mory and Helen's perfidy must not blind him to the essential goodness of others, and justness of the Universe. Business, after all, proceeded by trust, and the world, so far as he could see, was given over to big business.

Mory's 'shitsville, man' had been a shock, no doubt of it. The aggressions and hostilities that Richard had met, in his thirty-two years, had been of the muted, civilised kind; confined to office memos or gentle, if confusing, parental words. Richard, like Liffey, had learned early to placate, and smile, and turn away anger, and mix with others of a like frame of mind. 'If you didn't read the papers,' Liffey once said to Richard, 'but only looked about you, you'd really believe the world was a nice place.' And not recognising hate, spite or anger in themselves, and so not understanding how these things show their greater face in the dealings of management with labour, governments with governed, and so forth, could only look to communism or socialism, or facism, or any other available ism, as the source of conflict. Trouble, seen as coming from the outside, and working its way in, and not the other way about.

During the rest of the week Richard developed a whole assortment of fears and suspicions. He suspected that money was missing from his wallet, that taxi-drivers were cheating him by going the long way round, that his fellow employees were talking behind his back, that Miss Martin was going to make amorous advances, and that Liffey had organised his absence from her in order to be unfaithful. Such a thought as this latter had never crossed his mind before. He murmured it to Bella who only laughed and said, 'Projection, Richard,' which he did his best not to understand.

Miss Martin made call after call to Richard's solicitors. He confided in her now, and she in him. She seemed, marginally, in this new world of treachery, less dangerous than Bella.

Miss Martin was saving through a building society. In three

72

years she would marry her fiancé, then they would own their own house from the beginning. No rented accommodation for them. Richard marvelled at how well people of no ambition could run their lives. Miss Martin's boyfriend Jeff was finishing an apprenticeship as an electrical engineer. He would call for her, at the office, on occasion, and was a surprisingly handsome, tall and lively young man. Miss Martin was a virgin. She told Richard so. She believed in saving herself for marriage. She thought perhaps she was under-sexed, and hoped it didn't matter. There were more important things in life. Miss Martin was very capable. She never forgot things. She plodded around the office, thick-ankled and knowledgeable. The danger that she might turn into a seductress evaporated.

Liffey was more educated more cultured and sophisticated than Miss Martin, but Miss Martin would never have misread a timetable.

And Miss Martin would never expect her Jeff to drive six hours a day, just so that she could live in the cottage of her dreams. On the contrary, Miss Martin let herself be guided by Jeff's will in everything other than in sexual matters, where her will prevailed.

Lonely nights without Liffey.

Brave Liffey.

Richard had quite a lot to drink one night. Richard rang through to Cadbury Farm.
'Take a message to Liffey,' he said. 'Tell her I love her.'

The Underside of Things

Mabs and Tucker thought Richard was daft, wasting good money on such a call. There was a wistful look in Mabs' eye, all the same.

'Don't you start sticking pins in her,' said Tucker.
'Now why should I want to do that?' asked Mabs, virtuously.
'I don't know why women do anything,' said Tucker.

Once Mabs had made a model out of candle-wax to represent a farmer who had wronged Tucker and stuck a pin through its leg, and shut it in a drawer, and the farmer had developed thrombosis in his leg and gone to hospital. Just as well the pin had not been driven through the chest: Mabs had desisted from that obvious course because the farmer's daughter had once done her a good turn.

But Liffey was a different and difficult matter. It was Mabs' experience, and her mother's before her, that spells worked only upon angry and disagreeable people, and Liffey was neither. Moreover, if the spellbinder herself or himself was angry, then the spell could turn back like a boomerang. That was why a third party was so useful, to curse or spite for payment – in the same way as a psychoanalyst is paid, to receive spite and curses on behalf of others: sopping up the wrath turned away from cruel mothers and neglectful fathers and unfeeling spouses. The witch or spellbinder did more; and passed the evil on.

Mabs' mother, along with everyone else, said that spells were a lot of rubbish and she'd rather watch television any day; if you wanted to do anyone a bad turn these days all you had to do was ring up the Income Tax Inspector, or now, even better, the VAT man.

All the same, when Mabs and Carol had been little, they'd once nailed their mother's footprint to the ground – one damp day when she'd been hanging out the washing – and sure enough she'd developed a limp. That was a sure test of a witch.

'It's not magic,' their mother would say, limping, as she mixed her powders and potions, "it's medicine. Natural, herbal medicine.' And Carol and Mabs would listen, not knowing what to believe. She'd cured old Uncle Bob Fletcher of cancer. Everyone knew that. He'd gone on to ninety-nine, fit as a fiddle, and left her five hundred pounds and three acres in his will.

Dirty old man: some said Carol was his daughter; Carol and Mabs couldn't have come out of the same bag. One so small, the other so large.

Mabs went up to Honeycomb Cottage with Richard's message – Liffey was out walking so Mabs left a little note, and a bag of home-made sweets which Liffey didn't eat. She thought they tasted bitter.

Liffey, on the Tuesday of that week, organised a taxi to take her in and out of Crossley two days a week. She bought a new motorised bicycle at Poldyke garage, and on Friday a brand new Rotovator at Crossley. On Saturday she returned the bicycle. The engine was faulty. The village counted the cost of it all and marvelled.

Liffey's grandfather, Madge's father, had left Liffey a large sum of money, by-passing his daughter. What is the use, he asked her, bitterly, of handing wealth on to those who despise it? To those who would rather eat cheese sandwiches than steak au poivre? Madge had made nonsense of her father's life. She was as like as not to give away an inheritance to something she believed in – nuclear disarmament one year, save the whale or women's liberation the next. No, Liffey would have to have it. Liffey at least enjoyed spending money, and acted as most people did, on whim rather than principle. Liffey did not open bank statements. She put them straight into a drawer. Thus Richard's face was saved, and the illusion that they were living off his money preserved. Liffey would, from time to time, offer money to Madge, but Madge always refused it. Madge lived in a tiny cottage in a Norfolk county town, taught at the local school and ate school dinners, and now she had given up drinking whisky, was able to save most of her salary. Madge wanted nothing that Liffey could give. Never had, thought Liffey sadly. Not smiles nor gaiety nor prettiness nor money, which was all Liffey had to offer. Nothing of solid worth. Just what she *was* – nothing she had achieved.

At seven o'clock that evening Tucker came up to see if he could help Liffey with the Rotovator. Liffey's breath came short and sharp as she opened the door – but the tension between them had evaporated, and she was alarmed to see how ordinary he looked, and unattractive, and not in the least worthy of her. He stood in the kitchen, knowing more about her business than she cared to acknowledge, but no cause at all for erotic excitement. Grimy nails were just grimy nails, and not black talons of lust and excitement.

'I can manage,' said Liffey. 'I have the manual and am quite good mechanically.'

That was his cue to say she was quite good at other things too, but he didn't, so she knew it was over for him too, and was, when it came to it, relieved.
'My husband's coming back soon,' she said boldly. 'Stay and meet him properly,' which Tucker did, settling down in front of the Aga, easing off his working boots.

'Rotovator's no good for virgin land,' said Tucker. 'You'd need a tractor, your side of the stream. Bad soil, too. You'd be lucky to grow an onion. All right for cows but that's about all.'

Liffey was making mayonnaise. She squeezed in garlic.

'Strong stuff for eggs,' commented Tucker. 'Eggs are delicate.'

It had not all been rough and powerful: no. His fingers had been hard and calloused, but his mouth had been soft, and his tongue gentle.

No, Liffey, no. Enough.

Oh, lonely nights without Richard.

Richard arrived at seven minutes past eight, looking forward to his weekend. He was loving, cheerful and eager, and loaded with good things. Ray and Bella lived around the corner from the Camden Town street market, and Richard had bought aubergines and peppers, celeriac and chicory; and olives from the Greek shop, green and black, both, and fetta cheese and pitta bread: and whisky and a new kind of aperitif and good claret; and a joint of the best available lamb in all London.

Richard had resolved not to tell Liffey about the film he had seen the previous night with Bella and Ray, and how they had all gone off to a new fish restaurant afterwards, on expenses, for Bella and Ray were writing the place up for the column, or about the fun they had choosing the most expensive dishes on the menu, finding fault, and sending them back to the kitchen. The management had not seen it as fun, and Richard had wanted Liffey to be there, so he could discuss the whole thing afterwards, but where was Liffey? At the end of a muddy lane, a hundred and more miles away, which she loved more than she loved him.

Richard unloaded the good things on to the table, kissed Liffey, and was glad to see Tucker sitting there, since the presence of a stranger made the lie in his heart less likely to show in his eye.

How quickly Liffey makes friends, thought Richard. At least

he would not have to worry in case she were lonely, stuck away here by herself.

'Tucker and Mabs have been so helpful,' said Liffey.
'Until we get her driving, and get a telephone put in,' said Richard to Tucker, 'we're going to be dependent on your good services, I'm afraid. Sorry about the call the other night. Too much to drink.'
'That's what neighbours are for,' said Tucker.

Liffey had the uncomfortable feeling that Richard was in some way shelving his responsibility towards her, and handing it over to Tucker and Mabs.

Tucker suggested they both go over to Mabs for a meal, and Richard accepted with what Liffey saw as unseemly alacrity. 'But I've got supper waiting—' she began, but didn't finish. She moved the meat from the fast to the slow oven. They could eat it tomorrow.

Mabs saw the lights in the kitchen go out, and knew they were on their way up, and determined that Liffey should have an uncomfortable weekend. She could in no way see that Liffey deserved Richard's love as well as Tucker's attentions. Those who must be up and doing, as was Mabs, have little time for those who are content just to *be*, as was Liffey. And the need to be pleasant to her, for the sake of a pound here and 50p there, and an acre of free grazing, no longer seemed of pressing importance.

Mabs served a lamb stew from an enormous pot on the cooker. Liffey was given the gristly bits.
'Wonderful flavour!' marvelled Richard.
'It's because they're home-grown,' said Liffey. 'Everything here tastes wonderful.'
'No time to grow vegetables,' said Tucker. 'We do manage a drop or two of cider; come November you'd best be bringing your apples over for the pressing. You get quite a nice little crop off of some of your trees. No good for eating, mind. Not

if you've got a sweet tooth.' And he grinned at Liffey, and Liffey wished he wouldn't.

Liffey was well into her menstrual cycle. Some twenty-five or so follicles ripened nicely in her ovaries, one ahead of the others. In a couple of days it would reach maturity, and drop, and put an end to the generative energies of the rest. Nature works by waste.

There was apple pie and real cream for pudding, and afterwards Mabs handed round home-made Turkish delight. She pressed the mint-flavoured piece on Liffey. Liffey didn't think it was very nice.

Liffey and Richard walked home down the lane. The night was crisp and clear. The moon had a chunk out of it.
'Wonderful people,' said Richard. 'Real people; country people.'
'Those are my lines,' said Liffey.
'With none of the false romanticism about the country you get from townfolk.'
'Those are Bella's lines,' said Liffey.
They were, too.

Liffey was getting grumbling pains in her stomach. Her hand clenched Richard's.
'What's the matter?'
'Pains.'
'Ovulation pains?' asked Richard, knowledgeable.
'No, not like that.'
'What like, then?' He used the childish vocabulary that was their habit, and heard himself, and despised himself.
'Indigestion. Perhaps it was the stew.'
'Delicious stew. Why don't you make stews, Liffey?'
'Perhaps I will, now I'm in the country.'
'We're still going to have our baby, aren't we?'
'Of course!'

Bella had said that having a baby might be the making of Liffey. Responsibility might mature her.

'The Turkish delight tasted peculiar,' said Liffey. 'Why would a woman like Mabs make Turkish delight?'

Richard discovered that he was critical of his wife, that he jeered inwardly at her absurdities, and felt the desire to mock what had once entranced him. He blamed Liffey for the loss of his love for her. Richard had been to bed with Bella.

Full Moon

Mabs stared at the moon. The moon stared at Mabs. Tucker couldn't sleep.

Other people looked at the moon.

In Liffey and Richard's former apartment Mory lay in bed in the moonlight while Helen tweezed hairs from her chin. He had a sharp, pale face and a straggly beard which jutted above the bedclothes.

'No need to get uptight about anything,' said Helen, comfortingly. She was plump, pretty, dark and hairy. She was a freelance TV set designer, usually out of work. 'Liffey has money to burn. They can afford to live anywhere. We certainly can't.'
'I'm really hung up about Richard,' said Mory. 'I can feel my ulcer again. What sort of friend is he, writing solicitors' letters when he could just as well phone?'
'And there's Lally to think about,' said Helen.

Lally, Helen's sister, out-of-work model, and eight months pregnant, lay on foam rubber in the room next door, in the arms of Roy, out-of-work builder. If they married, her Social Security payments would cease. She was cold. She tossed and turned in the moonlight and presently decided the warmth was not worth the discomfort and told him to get the hell out of her bed, and build a fire. 'What with?' he asked.

'With that,' she said, and pointed at a Japanese bamboo screen of Liffey's and a little wickerwork stool. 'People before things,' she said.

'He's got it all ways,' observed Mrs. Martin, Richard's secretary's mother. She was a plump, busy little body, with a husband two years dead. She was ashamed of her widowhood, as if in letting her husband die she had committed a criminal offence – a feeling which the neighbours up and down the suburban street reinforced, by ceasing to call where once they had called, or even going so far as to cross the road when she approached. That they might have acted thus from embarassment, or from a primitive fear that misfortune might be catching, and so could hardly be any more responsible for their reactions than she was for her husband's death, Mrs. Martin failed to appreciate. She kept herself to herself, and studiously read the more profound of the women's magazines, scanning the pages for truth and understanding about wifehood, mistresshood, motherhood, never quite knowing what she was looking for, but feeling sure that one day she would find it; in the meantime she passed on to her daughter what she found out about the ways of the world.

'He's got it all ways,' she said now. 'Bachelor life all week, and country cottage at the weekends. Trust a man.'

'Oh no,' said Miss Martin. 'It wasn't his idea, it was her idea.'

'He'll be after you next,' said Mrs. Martin, 'in that case. You be careful. Men always cheat on women who organise their lives.'

'I'm not the type,' said Miss Martin, wishing she were. She felt cheated by life, which had taken away her father, and turned her mother into someone whose advice was based on reading, not on experience. Mrs. Martin thought it unwise of her daughter not to sleep with her fiancé Jeff; but Miss

Martin knew well enough that the only reason so handsome and eligible a young man as Jeff wanted to marry her, was that all the other girls did, and she didn't. He was a Catholic and divided women, in the old fashioned way, into good and bad. The good ones, Virgin Marys all, who had a man's babies by as near to an immaculate conception as everyone could manage; and the bad ones whom you loved, humiliated and left. Miss Martin saw all this quite clearly, and still wanted to marry Jeff. Mrs. Martin also saw it clearly, and didn't want her daughter to marry Jeff: her advice was directed, if unconsciously, to this end.

Their little white cat yowled to be let out. Miss Martin opened the back door and it darted out between her solid legs.
'Why should Mr. Lee-Fox choose me?' she asked.
'Because you're there,' said her mother. 'All a man needs is for a woman to be there.'

Miss Martin's boyfriend Jeff was on the Embankment doling out soup to vagrants and alcoholics. Once a week he did voluntary social work. 'There but for the grace of God,' he'd say. He took girlie magazines in his briefcase, to read in the early hours, when the flow of mendicants and suppliants dried up. Tonight the moon was so bright that he did not need his torch, and a shimmering mystery was added to an otherwise brutal reality, and he was glad. He put his trust in Miss Martin's virginity to cure him, in some magic way, of his unseemly lusts.

Bella and Ray lay far apart in their big double bed. Bella thought of the love of her life, who had been married for five years to someone else, and Ray thought of his hopeless love for Karen, schoolgirl. Bella and Ray held hands across the gulf which separated them, and felt better.

'Helga fancies Richard,' said Bella, with satisfaction. Bella lived in fear of losing Helga, for if Helga went, so would her own freedom from domestic and maternal duties. Au-pairs were becoming hard to find, and harder still to control. They demanded nights out, and lovers in their beds, and exorbitant wages. Helga had been showing signs of restlessness. A romantic interest in the house, in the form of Richard, would do much to keep her quiet and docile.

'So long as you don't,' said Ray, more out of marital politeness than any real anxiety.

'Of course I don't,' said Bella. 'He's much too simple for me.'

The moon, shining through the Georgian window, making shadow bars across the bed, made her think she was in prison, which in turn made her feel she could yet be free.

Helga, indifferent to a foreign moon, slept soundly in her box-room. She worked hard, too hard: she was always tired. She was a warm, rounded, sleepy little thing with busy hands, for ever cleaning and wiping and tidying. Sometimes she thought she would look for a new job with less work but there was never time. And if she went home, who would look after the children? They needed her. Those who responded to others' needs live hard lives, and go unrewarded. She knew it, but could do nothing about it.

Mabs' sister Carol, allegedly spending the night at Cadbury Farm, was in the back of Dick Hubbard's car. Later they would go to his office in the market square, letting themselves in when the pubs had closed and there was, they wrongly believed, no one about to see. While they waited, they indulged the passion that obsessed them both. It was true, the whole village agreed, that he was a better partner for her than her husband Barry, but she made her choice, and the village said she should stick to it. Carol was lean and dark as Mabs was broad and pale. Her limbs were silvery in the moonlight, smooth and slippery as a fish seen under water.

Dick Hubbard was worried because he had let Honeycomb Cottage when he should have sold, and allowed short-time interest to stand in the way of long-term benefit. He had recognised, long ago, that to act in this way was to doom himself to financial mediocrity. But still he let it happen.

'She bought a Rotovator,' he complained now to Carol.

'She'll soon get tired of it,' said Carol, comfortingly, 'and the weeds will be back.'

'She was even asking round for a builder.'

'Then have a word with the builder. You can pay a builder a fortune and the chimney will still come through the roof. What's the matter with you, Dick? Where's your spirit?'

'I don't know,' he said. 'The energy seems to have left my brain and gone down between my legs. I suppose that's how you like it.'

'I'll supply enough brain for both of us,' said Carol. 'You just supply the other.'

Mr. and Mrs. Lee-Fox lay under the moon and worried about Richard. He was their only son.

'Perhaps I brought him up wrong,' said Mrs. Lee-Fox.

'You did the best you could. Every mother does.'

It was their normal way of speaking – she agitating, he comforting. Now, in the middle of the night, it came like automatic speech.

'He should never have married her.'

'She's a nice, bright girl. His choice.'

'We'll never have grandchildren.'

'Give them time.'

'Our lovely apartment. And they've let the squatters in!'

'The law will get them out.'

'All our savings went to get him started.'

'And he is started,' said Mr. Lee-Fox. 'That's the way life goes. As his starts, ours closes in. We're left with the pickings of his takings. Once it was the other way around. You did it to your parents, I did it to mine. Now it's our turn.'

'I don't want it to be,' she said, as if he, like Superman, could turn the world the other way, but he just grunted and fell asleep. The moonlight cratered her skin as if it were the moon's surface, so she looked fifty years older than the modest fifty-three she was.

As for Liffey, the gripes in her stomach became worse. She spent the night groaning on the sofa or moaning on the lavatory seat. Liffey was not good at pain. Stoicism was her mother's prerogative. Madge, even if stung by a wasp, would manage to clamp her teeth before the involuntary scream could be fully released. Liffey, similarly stung, would shriek and jump and fling her arms about, breaking dishes and spilling food, giving easy voice to pain, shock and indignation.

Liffey was afraid of pain, as people often are who have endured little of it. She had never had toothache, never broken a bone, and had spent a healthy youth, unplagued by unpleasant minor illness. She avoided emotional pain by pulling herself together when nasty or uncomfortable thoughts threatened, and diverting herself conscientiously if she felt depression setting in. It could not always be done, but she did her best. Liffey was afraid of childbirth because she knew it would hurt. How could it not, if so large an object as a baby was to leave so confined a space? And the cries and groans of women in childbirth was part of her filmic youth: yes, that was pain, PAIN. And supposing the baby were born deformed? The fear would accompany her pregnancy, she knew it would. She could not say these things to Richard: women, though allowed to flinch at spiders and shudder at the thought of dirtying their hands, were expected to face pregnancy and childbirth with equanimity. Nor could she expect sympathy from Madge, who would see it as further proof of her daughter's errant femininity. And as for her friends – ah, her friends. Only a few days away, and she could scarcely remember their names or their faces. Liffey kept her fears to herself, and let others believe her reluctance to have a baby was, in the terms of an older generation, 'selfish', and in those of her contemporaries 'political' – namely, that she feared to lose her freedom and her figure, and sink into the maternal swamp.

Richard gave up waiting for Liffey to feel better and fell asleep at two-fifteen. He had had a long day. Up at seven, the strain of breakfast with friends, not family: then the office, a business lunch, a conference: then the long drive back to Liffey, then supper with the Pierces: and now poor Liffey groaning and clutching her stomach. He doubted whether he could have managed to make love to Liffey, even had she been feeling well, even had her pains been due to ovulation and she at her most fertile.

Richard slept. Liffey groaned.

It was not until after three that a cloud covered the moon: or, as Tucker felt, that Mabs let the moon go, stopped staring, and slept.

The cloud passed: the moon shone bright and firm again. In the morning, when the sun rose, it could still be seen as a pale disc low in the sky. Mabs waved to the disc as if to a friend, when she rose early to help with the cows. Lights flashed behind the Tor; she could not be sure why. She had noticed the phenomenon before.
'Something's going to happen,' she said to the moon, feeling a small excitement grow within her.

Mabs cast an eye over to Honeycomb Cottage and noticed that no smoke rose from the chimney, and presumed, rightly, that the kitchen range had gone out and that Liffey had had a bad night after the Turkish delight, and laughed.

Good and Bad

All the next day too Liffey moaned and groaned and shivered. The tiny bathroom was unheated, and there was no hot water, since the kitchen stove had gone out over-night.
'Oh, Liffey,' Richard reproached his wife, gently enough,

for she was a poor, weak, pale, shivery thing, 'it's one thing to live like this from necessity, but I can see no virtue in doing it from choice.'

'It would be all right if everything was working smoothly,' said Liffey, but she hardly believed it herself any more. She could see Richard was being brave and trying hard not to complain, and to enjoy what she enjoyed: and also perceived that he never would, and never could, had had to accept that though they were one flesh, yet they were different people, and that one or the other would have to submit. And that she had.

Richard cleared the flue with a broomstick and went up on the roof and extracted the matted twigs of jackdaws' nests which blocked the chimney. In one of the nests he found silver foil, bottle tops and a piece of Woolworth's jewelry, which he would have presented, ceremoniously, to Liffey, had she been in a fit state to receive it, or he, indeed, to give it. She was ill and he was dirty. He had to boil kettle after kettle of water before he could clean away the soot from his face and neck and the grime beneath his nails.

'But I like you dirty,' said Liffey. 'It's natural.' She was wrapped up warm and cosy on the sofa, and feeling a little better. She had been purged of her sin, her liaison with Tucker. 'What has nature got to do with us?' he asked. 'We've left the cave. Too late to go back.'

Outside, the trees were gaunt and bare against the winter sky, and snow clouds massed grey and thick behind the Tor. That pulled one way: Richard the other.

'Do you want to sell soup all the days of your life?' asked Liffey, 'live in an artificial world entirely?'

'Yes, Liffey I do. I want you to have babies and me to be their father and that's enough nature for me. I want to have light and heat at the touch of a button, and never to have to clear a flue in all the rest of my life. I find the country sinister, Liffey.'

It was an odd admission from him, who liked to deny the

existence of anything that science could not properly understand. 'That's because you fight it,' said Liffey. Smoke
puffed out of the chimney and made Richard cough, but
swirled round Liffey, leaving her alone. Liffey deduced,
wrongly, that nature was on her side. She was its pawn,
perhaps, but scarcely an ally. Mabs could have told her that.

'In the meantime,' said Richard, 'we shall make the best of it,
since we have to, and I will put up with being away from you
during the week, and you will put up with being separated
from me, and I promise not to look lustfully at anyone and
you must do the same.'

Now that Richard was with Liffey again he regretted his
sexual lapse with Bella. It had happened while both were
under the influence of drink, so much so that neither could
(or at any rate had the excuse not to) remember the details
the next day. Both had quickly resolved that it should not
happen again, or Richard had. In the clear light of Liffey's
gaze, he was happy enough that it should not.

Both had agreed, on marriage, that sexual jealousy was a
despicable emotion, and, while playing safe, and pledging
mutual fidelity, had taken it as a matter for congratulation
that neither was a prey to it. That it might more reasonably
be a matter for commiseration – inasmuch as neither offered
the other so profound a sexual satisfaction as to make them
fear the losing of it – did not occur to them.

Nevertheless, Liffey had certainly suffered a whole range of
unpleasant emotions – disappointment, pique, humiliation
and so on – over what Richard now thought of as 'The Office
Party Episode', and he did not wish her, or indeed himself, to
go through that again.

And he regretted even more than the physical infidelity, the
more subtle betrayal of Liffey of which he was guilty – the
discussion of her failings with others. Prying himself loose
from her, as if he was the host and she the parasite, he had let

in so much light and air, that the close warm symbiosis between them could never quite be repaired. They had been one: he had, in self-defence, rendered them two.

He could see, moreover, the threat to their happiness which their weekly separation entailed. He would see her, each weekend, more and more clearly. She, because she waited, would see what she expected. He, the one waited for, and for that reason the more powerful, would see reality. He feared that marital happiness lay in being so close to the partner that the vision was in fact blurred.

But it was a situation she herself had brought about. He could not be responsible for it, nor suffer too much on account of it. It was comfortable and convenient at Bella's, and exciting, too, in a way he would rather not think about.

'I'll bring down paint and wallpaper next weekend,' said Richard. 'We'll make everything lovely.'
'And guests,' said Liffey. 'Friends! Perhaps Bella and Ray would come?'
'They're very busy,' said Richard. And they went through their friends, and discovered that most would be too busy, or too frightened by discomfort, or too in need of crowds, or too quarrelsome, and in general too restless, to make good guests.

They made themselves think of Mory and Helen, although the subject upset them, and decided, or at any rate Liffey did, that Helen had fallen under the influence of her sister Lally, and that Mory was suffering from some kind of brainstorm consequent upon unemployment, and that it could not be concluded that there was anything disagreeable at all about the nature of human beings or the foibles of friends. It was, as it were, a one-off experience and should not embitter them. So said Liffey. Richard merely concluded, in his heart, that the business world and the personal world were pretty much the same, after all. Everyone behaved as well as they could afford to, but not one whit more.

'All the same,' said Liffey, 'let's just have you and me at weekends.' She suspected that was what Richard wanted: that after a week at the office and in Bella and Ray's home, he would be glad of peace and solitude at weekends. And he thought that was what she really wanted,. and was relieved.
'Money isn't important,' said Liffey, a little later. 'Money can't buy love.'
It was a favourite phrase, and one which came easily to the lips of someone who had never gone short of it.

Liffey's fortune, although she did not know it, was in fact down to seventeen pounds eighty-four pence. The cheque made out for the Rotovator, at present passing through the central banking computer, albeit at its slow Sunday pace, would overdraw her account by five hundred and thirty pounds and eight pence. Three years ago Liffey had instructed her bank to sell stock at will in order to keep her current account in balance, and this they had dutifully done. There was no more stock to sell. A letter to this effect had been delivered to her London home on the very day she left for the country. Mory and Helen had neither the will nor the inclination to forward letters, and this one now lay behind an empty beer can on the mantelpiece.
'If they want their mail,' said Lally, 'let them come and get it. I don't see why you should do them any favours!'

The apartment, which once had been warm with the smell of baking and the scent of the honeysuckle Liffey had managed to grow in a pot on the windowsill, and sweet and decorous with the music of Dylan and Johann Sebastian Bach, was now a cold, hard, musty place, stripped of decoration, echoing with righteous murmurings.
'Richard needn't think I'm going to pay him a penny rent,' said Mory. 'Because I'm not. I'm not the kind of person other people can send solicitor's letters to, with impunity. I give as good as I get.'
'It's not even as if we could pay the rent,' said Helen, 'as Richard knew perfectly well when he asked us in to caretake this dump of a place.'

'He's let this place run down,' said Lally's builder boyfriend, pointing out a damp patch in the ceiling, the blocked bathroom basin overflow, and the flaking plaster under the stairs. He pulled at a hot water pipe to demonstrate the rottenness of the wall behind it and the pipe broke in two and it was some time before anyone could find the stop cock of the water main. 'People who don't look after places don't deserve to have them,' he said, rolling another joint. He had given up building since meeting Lally. He referred to himself as Lally's piece of rough.

'I think Richard's got a nerve,' said Helen, the next day, pulling out the gas cooker to adjust a pipe so that the supply would bypass the meter, 'asking any rent at all for a place like this. Look at the wall behind the cooker. It's thick with grease! Liffey needn't think I'm going to clear up after her.'

'It's just a slum,' said Lally, feeding the fire with the remains of a bentwood rocker, 'everything in it's broken.' Liffey had left the chair, an original Tonne, under the stairs, while she found a responsible caner to re-do the broken canework.

'I say,' said Mory, uneasily, 'I think that might be rather a good chair you've been burning.'

'It was broken,' said Lally. 'Same as everything else in this dump.'

'Possession is theft,' said her boyfriend, going to sleep.

'All this antique junk,' said Helen, 'I really used to dig that scene, didn't I, Mory? Remember? Then I realised it was part of the nostalgia which keeps the human race dragging its feet. Chairs are things you sit in, not mementos to the past.' Mory said a little prayer, however, as the flames licked in and out the little bevelled squares of golden cane. Sometimes he wondered where the womenfolk were leading him: whether living by principle couldn't go too far.

During that weekend Mory and Helen took in a pregnant cat who settled in the linen cupboard and had kittens in a nest of Victorian tablecloths. Helen loved the kittens. Lally had pains from time to time, and thought she might be having the baby, but Helen looked up the *Book of Symptoms* and all decided she was not. They had given up doctors, who were an essential part of the male conspiracy against women, and were seeing Lally through her pregnancy themselves. At the very last moment, the plan was, they would dial 999 for an ambulance for Lally, who would then be taken to the nearest hospital too late for enemas, shaving, epidurals, and all the other ritual humiliations women in childbirth were subjected to, and simply give birth to the baby.

'I suppose you must know what you're doing,' said Lally's builder boyfriend, whose name no one could remember but which in fact was Roy, whose father had been a hard-line Stalinist, and who was fighting – at least they hoped he was fighting – a severe indoctrination in authoritarianism.

'There's a positive correlation,' said Helen, 'between the hospitalisation of mothers and infant mortality rates. We know what we're doing all right.'

Lally's pains were quite severe.

'That means it's not labour,' said Helen, 'it can't be. You don't have pains when you're having a baby, you have contractions. All that stuff about pain is part of the myth. Having a baby is just a simple, natural thing.'

Helen was excited by her new view of the Universe. Acid-tripping for the first time, six months previously, at Lally's instigation, had caused her radically to rethink her life and attitudes. If Lally showed signs of reneging, falling back into the accepted framework of society, Helen was there to prevent it.

Lally's pains stopped, and later she had diarrhoea and other symptoms of food poisoning, so Helen was vindicated. She put Lally on a water-only diet for two days. They clustered round the bamboo fire, which burned yellowly and brightly, and had a consciousness-raising session.

Were they all to be made homeless by the whims of the likes of Richard and Liffey? No. Would they fight for the roof over their heads: fight individual landlords: fight the system which denied them their natural rights? Yes. Would they join the Claimants' Union, just around the corner?

Tomorrow! All went to bed invigorated, cheerful and fruitful.

During Saturday night Liffey's pains returned, and when Richard moved his hand on to her breast, speculatively, she pushed it gently away. Liffey was worried. She thought it might have something to do with Tucker. Perhaps the introjection of his body into hers, so foreign to it, had started up some sinister chain of reaction? She worried for Richard's sake, in case something disagreeable of Tucker passed itself on to him, through her. It was nothing so crude as the fear of a venereal disease, but of something more subtle – a general degeneration from what was higher to what was lower. Tucker was mire and swamp; Richard a clean, clear grassy bank of repose. The mire lapped higher and higher. It was her fault.

Richard let his hand lie: they drifted off to sleep. Richard, to his shame, dreamt of Bella, and in the morning did not pursue his amorous inclination towards Liffey, but cleared damp leaves from the paths around the cottage, and missed his Sunday paper and the droney communal somnolence of the city Sabbath, and said nothing. The countryside did not soothe him. He felt it was not so much dreaming, as waiting. Its silence, broken only by a few brave winter birds, made him conscious of the beating of his breast, the stream of his own blood, and his mortal vulnerability. He could not understand why Liffey loved it so.

Mabs came over in the afternoon with home-made may-flower wine for Richard – which she claimed was unlucky for women to imbibe – and a dark, rich, sweet elderberry wine to soothe Liffey's insides.
'I don't know how you knew about my tummy,' said Liffey, gratefully sipping, and Richard wondered, too, how Mabs could know. Then they both forgot about it, as people will, when the penalty of unravelling truth is extreme.

Mabs carried Richard's wine in a brown carrier bag, and the

bottle was wrapped for safety in old magazines, which, inspected when Mabs left, turned out to be crudely pornographic. Liffey's little nose crinkled in mirthful disgust.
'Aren't people funny!' she said, sipping the sweet elderberry wine, which indeed soothed her tummy, and contained a drop or two of a foxglove potion with which Mabs' mother had dosed her daughters in their early adolescence, to keep them out of trouble. 'The things they have to do to get turned on.'

The thought came to Richard, after several glasses of the mayflower wine, which was dry, clear and heady, and contained the same mistletoe distillation which Carol put in Dick Hubbard's brandy and soda, that Liffey had never in fact been properly turned on herself, that her love-making, was altogether too light and loving and childish – a reflection, in fact, of herself – and that though he loved and cherished her, in fact *because* he loved and cherished her, he could never through her discover what lay in himself. The thought was quite clear, quite dispassionate, and final.

Richard put his arms round Liffey, but she moved away from him. Mayflower and elderberry do not mix – they belong to different seasons. They do not understand each other: any more than do foxglove and mistletoe, the one of the earth, the other of the air.

Carol was the next to call.
'Well,' said Richard to Liffey, 'at least you'll never be lonely here.' He thought that Carol looked at him with direct invitation, as she warned them not to spend too much on the house, as it would never be anything but damp, not to bother to try and grow vegetables, as the soil was poor, and to leave the roof alone, as it was so old that interference by builders would only make it worse.

It seemed to Richard that what Carol was saying, in effect, was that time and money spent on things was wasted: energy should be preserved for sexual matters. That the highest good was the union of male and female, and had Liffey not been in the room, and some scraps of discretion left to him, he would most certainly have made a sexual advance towards her.

Carol's lips mouthed words about damp-courses, potatoes and thatch but her eyes said come into me, and he could feel the warmth of her body even across the room, and it seemed to him that all the ingenuities and activities of the human race, and all its institutions – state, church, army and bureaucracy – could be read as the merest posturing; diversion from the real preoccupation of mankind, the heady desire of the male to be into the female, and the female to be entered by the male. He had another glass of mayflower wine. Liffey looked at him anxiously. He was flushed.

When Carol had gone, he kissed Liffey chastely on the brow. 'What's the matter?' she asked, puzzled.
'I'm glad I married you,' he said.

For those very qualities in Liffey which earlier in the day had seemed his undoing, he could now see as God-given.

Richard wanted Liffey to be the mother of his children. He wanted her, for that reason, to be separated out from the rest of humanity. He wanted her to be above that sexual morass in which he, as male, could find his proper place but she, as wife and mother, could not. He wanted her to be pure, to submit to his sexual advances, rather than enjoy them: and thus, as a sacred vessel, sanctified by his love, adoration and respect, to deliver his children unsullied into the world. It was for this reason that he had offered her all his worldly goods, laying them down upon the altar of her purity, her sweet smile. And he wanted other women, low women, whom he could despise and enjoy, to define the limits of his depravity and his senses, and thus explain the nature of his being, and his place in the universe.

Richard wanted Bella. Richard wanted anyone, everyone. Except Liffey.

95

Richard sat rooted in his chair.

'What's the matter?' asked Liffey, but he would not, could not speak, and presently said he would have to go back to London that night, instead of the next morning, which upset her and made her cry, but could not be helped. These cataclysmic truths had in some way to be properly registered in his mind through his actions, lest they become vague and be forgotten, washed away by the slow, slight, sure tides of habit and previous custom.

'Now have a good week,' Richard said, kissing Liffey goodbye. 'And look after yourself, and prune the roses round the door, and by this time next year we'll have a baby, won't we!' His breath smelt of mayflower wine, and she, redolent of its opposing elderberry, could not help but be a little pleased that there had been no opportunity for love-making that weekend.

'You didn't put anything in that wine, I hope,' said Tucker to Mabs.

'Why should I do a thing like that?' asked Mabs. 'None of that stuff works, in any case. Or only on people who're stupid enough to believe in it.'

'You can't change people,' said Audrey, Mabs' oldest daughter, listening when she had no business to. 'But you can make them more themselves.'

'What do you know about it, Miss?' Mabs was angry, and surprised that one of her children should have a view of the world and contribute it to the household.

'Only what Gran tells me,' said Audrey, putting a table between herself and Mabs. She had her father's protection, but that only made her the more nervous of her mother.

Mabs looked at Audrey and saw that all of a sudden she was a young woman with rounded hips and a bosom, and Mabs' raised fist fell as she felt for the first time the power of the growing daughter, sapping the erotic strength of the mother. She was quiet for a time, and felt the more pleased, presently, that she had dosed Liffey to keep her off Tucker, and Tucker off her; and dosed Richard so that he should pay Liffey out properly while away during the week; and hoped again that she herself was pregnant, and still young.

Solitude

During the next week the wind turned to the north and rattled through the cottage windows, and the sky was grey and heavy, and the Tor hidden by cloud and mist.

Liffey cleaned and painted and patched and repaired by day, and shivered by night. She came to know the pattern of wind and rain around the house, as she lay in bed listening, hearing the wainscot rustle with mice, and the thatch with restless birds, and further away the hoot of an owl or the bark of a fox, and when all these noises for once were stilled, the tone shifts in the silence itself, as if the night were breathing. Once she heard music, faintly, on the wind, and was surprised to remember that the night world had people in it, too.

Liffey was lonely.

Liffey admitted defeat in her heart, and that she had been wrong, and not known what she had wanted, like a child, and not cared what Richard had wanted, like an unhappy child: and wanted Richard back the sooner to apologise. As soon as Mory and Helen were disposed of, she would join Richard in London.

Liffey walked to the Poldyke pub one evening, in search of companionship, and the host of friendly young couples whom she had come to believe inhabited every corner of the world, but found instead only old men drinking cider who stared at her in an unfriendly way. She walked back home in the dark, stumbling and groping, without a torch, having forgotten how black the night could be. Wet trees behind her whispered and gathered.

Liffey was frightened.

Mabs came up once or twice for coffee and a chat, and Liffey was grateful.

Liffey wrote a change-of-address letter to her mother. It did not mention loneliness or fear, merely hopes fulfilled and desires gratified. She had always found it difficult and dangerous to confide in her mother, and was accustomed to prattling on, instead, filling silence as now she filled the space on the page. Madge read the letter and recognised its insincerity and screwed it up and put it in the fire, and thereafter had no record of her daughter's new address.

Liffey walked to the telephone box at Poldyke to call friends, but once there lacked the courage to put in coins, and speak. It seemed as if she were having to pay for friendship, and she was humiliated. She walked home over the icy stubble of the fields and in the shadow of herself that the low sun cast in front of her, perceived a truth about herself.

She was someone shadowy, inhabiting a world of shadows. She had not allowed the world to be real. She had been accustomed to sitting beside a telephone, and summoning friends up out of nothingness, dialling them into existence, consigning them to oblivion again, putting the receiver down when they had served their purpose. She had no friends. How could she have friends, who had never really believed that other people were real? It was her punishment.

And if Mory and Helen were real, not cut-out figures set up by Liffey in the play of her life, to flail about for a time in front of paper sets, then perhaps they could not be manoeuvred and manipulated: perhaps they could not be got rid of.

Liffey cried.

She wondered whether Richard was real, and whether she wanted him to be real. Her life since she had left her mother's house had been a dream. And still her mother would not write to her. Perhaps, thought Liffey, I am as unreal to my mother as everyone except her is unreal to me. A child might very well seem unreal to the mother. Something dreamed up, clothed in flesh and blood, which sucked and gnawed and depleted.

Liffey cried some more.

The north wind grew stronger and came through the missing roof tiles in sudden cold gusts.

Liffey walked to Poldyke again and made herself telephone friends and talk and invite them down, but they were all too busy to talk much, or thought the winter too cold to come and stay, and though all were polite and friendly, Liffey sensed the displeasure of those who remain, towards the one who had wilfully absented herself: and marvelled at how out of sight could so quickly become out of mind, not from carelessness or malice, but from a desire to preserve self-esteem.

Liffey ran out of butter and walked all the way into Poldyke again, and saw six tins of loganberries on Mrs. Harris' shelf, and loving tinned loganberries, bought all six, thus leaving none for Mrs. Harris' other customers, and nearly breaking her arm as she carried loganberries and butter back.

Liffey thought, I must get back to civilisation quickly.

Liffey rang Richard from Cadbury Farm to tell him all these things, but Miss Martin who answered said Richard was in a meeting, and would not fetch him out of it.

The grey sky groaned and heaved: dark, lonely days drifted

into darker, lonely nights. Liffey wanted Richard again. She dreamed he was making love to her and she cried when she woke.

There was no sign of Tucker.

Inside Liffey (4)

Although all was not well without, all was very well within. Liffey's uterus had settled down nicely after its recent state of confusion. It lay like an inverted pear, settling upon the upper end of her vagina, narrowing into the cervical canal, finished off (where in a pear the stalk would be) by the cervix itself. This, on a good day, could be detected by Richard's engorged penis as a hard knob, and by a doctor's hand as a firm, dome-shaped structure. The walls of Liffey's uterus were some half an inch thick, and composed of a whole network of muscles, some up and down, some oblique, some spiral, all extraordinarily flexible, and all involuntary – that is, uncontrollable by the conscious Liffey. The blood supply, simple, ample and good, came from the main blood vessels in Liffey's pelvis; and the nerve supply, anything but simple, enabling as it did the muscle to contract rhythmically during menstruation and more dramatically during labour, would only send messages of discomfort when uncomfortably stretched. These nerves could be cut or burned or ulcerated and Liffey would be none the wiser.

Now, as the fifty-first of Liffey's potential ova for the month ripened, the walls of the uterus lined themselves richly and healthily in preparation for its fall and fertilisation. Liffey's fallopian tubes (the pair of ducts attached to the outer corners of the uterus) waited too, secreting from their own mucous membrane the substances which nourished all visiting sperm, and, more rarely, any fertilised ovum. Of the four hundred million sperms which Tucker had released into Liffey the week before, on the sixth day of her cycle, some forty million had reached her cervical canal, but only a few dozen had survived the quick, forty-five minute journey up the uterus and along the fallopian tube. Here, in spite of the warm, sugary, gently alkaline environment which did its best to preserve and nurture them – and Tucker's were good strong sperm – all had inevitably perished, since no ovum arrived within the forty-eight hours of their life span. All died, but surely, surely, some molecular vestige of Tucker remained within Liffey?

One way or another, like it or not, we are part of more people than we imagine: one flesh.

Be that as it may, on the fourteenth day of Liffey's cycle, now nicely re-established at twenty-eight days, an ovum released by Liffey's left ovary, and swept up by the fimbriae, the little fingers of tissue where the fallopian tubes curl round to meet the ovary, swam into the healthy canal of the tube itself.

Ins and Outs

Liffey knew nothing of all this. She gave these matters even less attention than a car driver might give to his car. All she knew was that it was Friday night, and that she was looking forward to Richard's return: that dinner was cooked, candles lit, and everything in order. She wore a swirly skirt, a blouse instead of a T-shirt, and scent. Everything in fact was ready and prepared – an outer symbol of an inward state.

In the conscious and the unconscious world alike, this is the pattern. Things are made ready, offerings are prepared, fulfilment is hoped for, and sometimes occurs. The cosmic soup prepares for life, birds prepare nests, men prepare for

war, wombs prepare linings, priests are prepared for ordination. Friday washing and ironing prepares for Saturday
Sabbath. It was not surprising, then, that Liffey prepared
for Richard, and found pleasure in it.

Things get ready, then burst into life. Nature, like its
subsidiary processes of love, and friendship, and learning,
proceeds by halts and starts.

Reverently, Richard made love to Liffey. She found him
gentler and more considerate than ever, and although this
should have gratified her, she found it oddly irritating.

Richard was not gentle with Bella, nor had been with the
motorway whore he had picked up on the journey away from
Liffey, back to London, the previous Sunday night. They
were the users-up of surplus seed, not of intended seed; they
were instruments of his anger, inasmuch as a man who has
conscientiously decided to respect and adore his wife, to
project rather than to incorporate his resentment of her –
must find something to do with his anger, and the erect penis
can be used to punish and destroy, as well as to love and
create. So can soft words.

These were the five women Richard had made love to, since
his adolescence. Mary Taylor, a forty-year-old barmaid,
whose habit and pleasure it was to seduce sixth-form boys
from the local boarding school.
Liffey, his wife.
His secretary, on the occasion of a drunken office party.
Bella Nash, his friend and landlady and best friend's wife.
Debbie, a fifteen-year-old delinquent, who travelled the
motorways.

His encounter with Debbie of the unknown last name,
precipitated by fate and the emotional tumult brought about
by sudden self-knowledge – or else a physical irritation
induced by Mabs' mistletoe and mayflower – and his on the
whole unvoiced resentment of Liffey's recent behaviour,

had gratified and satisfied him. To use, pay, and forget a more than willing girl hurt, so far as he could see, no one. It did not interfere with his uxorious love of Liffey, his more complex and imaginative lust for Bella, or his work.

If Richard was saddened by anything, it was by the new knowledge of years of sexual opportunity lost – a common enough sadness in those whom circumstance or conditioning have prevented from making full use of youthful sexuality. Richard resolved that while he could, he would: that Liffey's living in the country, though adventitious, would in the end help them both. It would help him, Richard, to know himself and by knowing him, to love her, Liffey, better, and in the end, surely, as they both grew older, to love and want Liffey alone. He could see fidelity as something to be travelled towards, achieved in the end; and the journey there could surely be made as varied and exciting as possible.

Mabs the while, lay in bed with Tucker and laughed out loud.
'Now what?' He was nervous.
'I don't know,' she said. 'I just feel things are going the way I want.'
'Up at Honeycomb Cottage?'
'That's right.'
'Leave them alone,' he begged. He should never have let himself be pushed by her, right into Liffey. She'd done it to him before once, with a former schoolfriend she'd come to envy.

'That Angie,' Mabs had deplored, with sudden savagery, 'what's she got to be so stuck up about, anyway?' And Tucker had been sent over before Angie's big wedding, and Angie had ended up with an arm mangled in a hopper, and a drunk for a husband, and one single stone-deaf child, big wedding or not. It was as if he, Tucker, had been sent in to prepare the way: make an entry through which Mabs could pour ill-wishes.

But these were night thoughts. In the morning, he knew,

Mabs would be just another farmer's wife, in Wellingtons and head scarf.

He rolled over her, as he could feel her needing, as he knew controlled her, if only for a while. Mabs was a sweep of forested hill, of underground rivers, and hidden caves, and dark graves and secret powers. Liffey was a willow-tree, all above ground. He liked Liffey. He would do what he could to protect her.

'Well,' thought Liffey, lying there, revered by Richard, 'at least he loves me. He won't get into trouble in London.' For she saw now that sexual opportunity is more powerful than sexual discrimination, and that by and large those who can, will, and there was Richard, by himself in London all week, and a young and handsome man: although of course Bella would keep an eye on him for her, and what's more it had all been her doing.

'I miss you and love you,' said Richard, as they lay together, wind and rain swirling around the chimneys outside, snug and warm beneath a hundred per cent eiderdown quilt from Heals, and it was true. He missed her and loved her. She was his wife.

She missed and loved him. He was her husband.

Inside Liffey (5)

Meanwhile some forty million of Richard's sperm were starting their migration from the vault of Liffey's vagina to the outer part of her fallopian tubes. Her orgasm or lack of it, made no difference to their chance of survival. The sperms had been formed in the testicles suspended in the scrotum beneath Richard's penis. Here, too, the male hormone testosterone was formed. Richard's testicles produced perhaps a little less than average of that particular hormone, rendering him in general kind and unaggressive, not given to using force to solve his problems, and needing to shave only once a day, not twice: but not so little that he did not berate Mory over the telephone and feel the better for it. It was some months since Richard's sperm had been so plentiful. The electric blanket he and Liffey loved, and which now Mory and Helen delighted in, had overheated his testicles, and moreover the tight underpants Liffey so admired had overconstricted the overheated testicles, thus causing a degree of infertility. But now, deprived of the electric blanket, wearing more comfortable pants, the sweat glands of his scrotum were once again able to maintain the testicles at their correct temperature and enable spermato-genesis to occur. The sperms, once produced, were stored in the slightly alkali, gelatinous fluid produced by his prostate gland, which lay at the base of the bladder at the root of the penis.

Richard ejaculated four millilitres of seminal fluid, each containing one hundred million sperm, well within the normal sperm count (which can vary between fifty and two hundred million sperms per millilitre and be ejaculated in quantities between three and five millilitres). Each sperm was about one-twenty-fourth of a millimetre long and consisted of head, neck and tail. The head of the sperm contained the chromosomes required to fertilise the ovum. The neck contained the mechanism which moved the tail. The tail propelled the sperm forward, at a rate of one millimetre every ten seconds; not bad going for an organism so very small. If it came up against a solid object it would change direction, like a child's mechanical toy. So doing, a sperm would even get by a cervical cap; or the vinegar-soaked sponge Liffey's grandmother used to trust, before she had Madge. Liffey's cervical canal was that day receptive and benign to Richard's sperm: the mucus there, mid-cycle, had become transparent and less viscous than normal. As the hours passed, so the sperm moved, readily and more plentifully than Tucker's before them, up into Liffey's fallopian tube.

Conception

Saturday morning came, and lunchtime, and then it was time for supper.

Mabs suddenly and unexpectedly leaned forward and slapped Eddie for slurping his tea. He cried. She slapped him again and snatched away his bacon and baked beans. All the children snivelled. They were having a late tea. Earlier, Tucker had taken Mabs to the pictures.
'What's the matter with you, then?' asked Tucker. 'Can't you just leave the children be?'
But she couldn't. Something had gone wrong. She knew it had.

Baked beans fell from Mabs' fork on to her tweed skirt. Audrey ran for a damp cloth.
'Little creepy crawler,' said Mabs to Audrey, but she took the offered cloth, and darted Tucker an evil, glinting look as she wiped, as if it was all his fault. He knew she was thinking about Liffey.
'You sent me up there,' said Tucker. 'It was what you wanted.'

Mabs strode about the kitchen, her face distorted. Tucker nodded sideways to the children, who slipped away quickly.

'Calm down,' said Tucker. He was frightened, not knowing which way Mabs' anger was to turn. Mabs stood at the window and looked at the Tor, and he could have sworn that as she did the clouds that hung above it swirled and churned in the moonlight.

'How funny the clouds look, above the Tor,' said Richard to Liffey. They stood side by side on the stairs, leaning into each other, dreamily.
'They often look funny,' said Liffey. 'It quite frightens me, sometimes. But it's just air-currents.'

Richard's sperm, now in Liffey's left fallopian tube, had there encountered a fully-fledged ovum, some five hours old and in good shape. By virtue of the enzymes that they carried, en masse, they liquefied the gelatinous material that encased the ovum, enabling one of their number to penetrate the ovum wall, running into it head first, leaving its tail outside.

And there, Liffey was pregnant.

'I do love you,' lied Richard.
'I love you,' said Liffey.

'Calm down,' said Tucker to Mabs, once again, and surprisingly, she calmed down. She moved away from the window.
'It's her I blame,' said Mabs, smiling at Tucker, 'not you. Did she wear a bra?'
'No,' said Tucker.
'Well, there you are,' said Mabs, as if that explained everything. And then, 'What's bad news for some is good news for another.' It was something she often said, and her mother too. Dick would say it to Carol, sometimes, referring to Carol's husband Barry, as a counter-point to their lovemaking, making Carol laugh.
'Tucker,' said Mabs. 'What size shoe does she wear?'
'Little. Three or four, I should say.'

Mabs looked down at her own large feet and sighed. She scraped all the children's teas into the pig-bin, yelled down the corridor for them to get to bed, and she and Tucker went to their bedroom together, like an ordinary couple, and she not at all hooked up to the hot lines of the Universe.

Inside Liffey (6)

Liffey slept. The female nuclei of the ovum and the male nuclei of the sperm, each containing the chromosomes which were to endow her child with its hereditary characteristics, both moved towards the centre of the ovum, where they fused to form a single nucleus. The nucleus divided into two parts, each containing an equal portion of Liffey and Richard's chromosomes. Liffey's brown eyes: Richard's square chin. Her gran's temper: his great grandfather's musical bent. And so on.

That was Friday night. By Sunday night, as they listened to Vivaldi on Richard's cassette player and toasted their toes by the wood fire, the two cells had divided to make four, eight, sixteen – by early Monday morning, when Richard left for London there were sixty-four, and could be termed a morula. The process was to continue for another 263 days; and 266 days from the time of conception, when the specialisation of different tissues was complete – some that could see, others that could hear; some to breathe, others to digest, stretch, retract, secrete; some to think, others to feel, and so on – and then when all were ready a baby would be delivered, weighing seven pounds or so. If Liffey's nature and physique were such that she would not abort the child, by accident or on purpose, or die from the many hazards of pregnancy: if Richard's were such that he could protect it until it was grown; if the combination of genes that formed the child allowed it health and wit enough to survive – a naked, feeble creature in a cold world, with only mews and smiles to help it – and then fulfil its designed purpose and itself procreate, successfully – the human race would be one infinitesimal step forward.

Nature works by waste. Those that survive are indeed

strong, but not necessarily happy. Auntie Evolution;
Mother Nature; bitches both!

Inside Richard's Office

Offices do, for some, instead of families: and for others, more
prudent, as a useful supplement to them. Bosses are as
parents, subordinates as offspring, and colleagues as sib-
lings. For entertainment there is the continuing soap opera
lives which brush past each other, seldom colliding, seldom
hurting.

It does not do, of course, to mistake office life for real life.
For if a desk is emptied one day by reason of death, or
redundancy, or resignation, or transfer, it is filled the next,
and the waters close over the departed, as if they had never
been. In offices no one is indispensable; in real life people
are.

Mother dies, and is gone for good. The Personnel Officer
dies, to be reborn tomorrow.

It does not do, either, to mistake office sex for real sex, least
of all carry the fantasy into the outside world. Secretaries
marry bosses, it is true, but must remain secretary and boss
for the rest of their lives, hardly man and wife. He parental:
she childish. And colleague may marry colleague, but the
quality of comradeship inherent in the match, of fraternal
common sense and friendliness, keep them for ever like
brother and sister, hardly man and wife.

Miss Martin was in love with Richard. Why should she not
be? He was young, he was pleasant, he was good-looking, he
was forbidden; above all he was there. He had come to
confide in her. She was sorry for him too, regarding Liffey as
a bad wife, who could not even consult a railway timetable

accurately, and who rang the office at inconvenient times, distracting Richard when he most needed to concentrate, intruding and interfering in a world which was none of her business.

Miss Martin knew that hers was a hopeless love. She could place herself quite accurately in the world. She was sensible, but dull. She had a solid, pear-shaped figure which no amount of dieting would make lissom. She preferred to serve rather than be served. She was deserving, so would never get what she deserved. She did not understand her fiancé Jeff's regard for her, and rather despised him for it. If he loved her, who was not worth loving, how could she love him? He seemed lively and handsome enough now, but would soon settle down, and be as dull and plain as she was.

Miss Martin, in fact, following the death of her father, was in a sulk which might well last her whole life. She was consumed by spite against the Universe, which had spited her, and taken away the object of her love. She would find no joy in it. The determination glazed her eyes, dulled her hair and skin.

In the meantime, Richard would do to be in love with. The passion, being forbidden and unrequited, would serve as its own punishment. It made her heart beat faster when he came into the room, and her hand tremble when she handed him his coffee, and her typing perfect, and her loyalty fierce. It was a secret love. It had to be. It would embarrass Richard to know about it. The love of the socially and physically inferior is not welcome, especially if the object of the love is male. Miss Martin, in other words, knew her place.

She knew it, as it transpired, better than he did.

On Monday Richard arrived in the office, and hung his coat upon the hook provided. (Later, Miss Martin would re-arrange it, so that it hung in more graceful folds.) She had waiting for him upon his desk a list of the day's appointments. There was mud upon his shoes, and she tactfully remarked upon it, so he could attend to it before encountering his boss.

'That's country life,' said Richard. 'All mud and stress. But Liffey loves it. Have you ever lived in the country, Miss Martin?'

'I'm a suburban sort of person,' she replied. 'Neither one thing nor the other.'

'I need a nail file,' he remarked, and she provided it. She did not find these attentions to his physical needs in any way humiliating. They set him free to attend to matters which by common consent were important – the making of the decisions which kept them all employed. She could have made the decisions as well as he, of course, but nobody would then have believed they were important, let alone difficult.

Messengers came, telephones rang and files were circulated. Currently obsessing Richard's department was the maximising of the salt content of a particular brand of chicken soup, and the growing conviction that some kinds of salt acted saltier than others, a fact verifiable by common experience, but not scientific experiment. Pleasing the public palate is not easy.

'Of course Liffey would have everyone keeping their own chickens and boiling them down for soup,' said Richard. 'She's not a great one for packets.'

'I wouldn't have the heart,' said Miss Martin. 'Poor chicken!'

Before lunch Richard took out an unlabelled bottle of white wine.

'All this talk of salt has made me thirsty,' he said. 'Will you have some, Miss Martin? It's home-made. A neighbour of ours made it. Mayflower. It's supposed to be unlucky for women to drink it, and Liffey won't, but you're not superstitious, are you?'

'No,' said Miss Martin, drinking too. Richard noticed the

stolid fleshiness of her behind as she bent to a filing cabinet, and found himself rather admiring it. Liffey's buttocks proclaimed themselves to the world, moving in open invitation, cheek by cheek beneath tight jeans. Miss Martin had something to hide. But what? He took another glass.

'I love you,' said Miss Martin, two glasses later. The love induced by the mistletoe, parsley, and mystery ingredients in the wine was of an elemental, imperative kind, and overrode inhibitions induced by low self-esteem.

Richard flinched, as if physically assaulted, but quickly recovered. Miss Martin was an excellent secretary, he liked her, and for some reason pitied her, as he pitied certain kinds of dogs, who look at humans with yearning eyes, as if able to conceive of humanness, but know they can never aspire to it, and are doomed to creep on four legs for ever.

'That's just the wine talking,' said Richard more truly than he knew. 'You'd better not have any more.' But he poured her another glass, even as he spoke.
'I don't see why I shouldn't love you,' complained Miss Martin. 'No skin off your nose.'
'Well,' said Richard, 'since it's sex that makes the world go round—'
Miss Martin felt argumentative. She often did, but was accustomed to keeping her arguments to herself.
'I'm not talking about sex,' she said, 'I'm talking about love.'
'You're only not talking about sex,' said Richard, 'because I suspect you know nothing about it.'
'I'm a virgin,' she said.

Miss Martin rang up the colleague with whom Richard was supposed to be lunching, and said he had been delayed by a crisis, and they went off to lunch together, oblivious to those who saw them. He strode on long, cheerful legs, and she trotted alongside on her little dumpy ones. It wasn't right. He was a kestrel; she was a sparrow doomed to pick at leavings. In nature everyone knows their place.

Mabs would have been pleased at the un-rightness brought about by her mother's potion, and would certainly have thought it served Miss Martin right. Mayflower wine is unlucky for women to drink, and she had been warned.

'I think,' said Richard, blindly, 'I would be doing you a kindness in saving you from suburbia and a life of proper propriety.'

And in a room at the Strand Palace Hotel, after lunch, for her sake rather than his, or so it appeared to him, he did not so much as save her from these things, as make them intolerable to her for ever.

By five o'clock both were back in the office: Miss Martin was pale and stunned and at her typewriter, and he was trying to catch up with his work. Neither could quite believe that it had happened, and Richard certainly wished that it had not.

Miss Martin told no one. There was no one to tell. 'I was drunk,' she told herself. 'You know what home-made wine is.'

Justifications

Richard quite wanted to tell Bella about the astonishing episode of himself and Miss Martin, but prudence forbade it. She would have laughed at him, from her lordly position, sitting astride him on the study sofa, exacting response from him, payment, this pleasure for that, as if she was the queen and he the subject. Boadicea. Knives on the wheels of her lust, cutting into self-esteem.
'I took her virginity,' he could have said. 'It seemed my right, even my duty. She certainly expected me to.'

'Took her virginity,' Bella would have sneered. 'A poor Victorian dirty old man, that's all you are at heart.'

But he knew there was power in it. That he would never be forgotten: thus his life lasted as long as hers. He would keep that to himself.

'Don't you worry about all this?' he asked Bella. He had to ask her something. She demanded rational conversation until the very last minute of their love-making, and question and answer seemed the least troublesome means of providing it.
'Why should I worry?'
'In case Ray finds out. He might come home early.'
'Ray never comes home early.' She was bitter, but he could see her logic. Bella was doing what she was because Ray came home late: it was the grudge she bore against him. It circled and circled in her mind – words rather than meaning. Ray Comes Home Late. Ray could not, therefore, come home early, or she would not be doing this. He could see that the logic might well apply to Bella, making her husband inaudible and invisible if he returned early from his visit to the nubile Karen and her homework problems – perhaps taken ill, or overcome with emotion – but would hardly save him, Richard, from Ray's anger and upset.
He said as much.
'Ray wouldn't be angry or upset,' said Bella. 'Why should he?
He likes me to enjoy myself. And what else can he expect, the way he never comes home until late. And you're a friend after all.'
'You don't think this is an abuse of friendship?'
'It might be a *test* of friendship. Whenever I go away my friend Isabel sleeps with Ray. She and I are still the best of friends.'
'I expect you compare notes,' said Richard, gloomily.
'Of course,' said Bella.
'I don't want you to talk about me,' said Richard.

She sighed and raised her eyes to heaven, revealing an amazing amount of white.

'I don't think Ray treats you very well,' said Richard.

'In what way?' Bella was interested.

'The way he talks about other younger women in front of you. And complains about your tits.'

'That's just his insecurity.'

'He calls you "the old bag".'

'He projects his fear of ageing on to me,' said Bella, 'that's all.'

'Well,' said Richard, 'I do feel bad about doing this, in spite of what you say.'

'Of course you do. It's the only way you can get it up.'

He found her crudeness horrific and fascinating, and was unable to continue talking.

On evenings when Richard did not accompany Ray and Bella on some gastronomic jaunt, or was keeping Bella company on Ray's late nights out, he ate simply enough, with the family. The staple food of the household was fish fingers, baked potatoes, and frozen peas. Food, except on special occasions, was regarded as fuel. Tony and Tina, the children, watched television and read books while they ate. 'Today's children have no palate,' mourned Bella.

The Nash household was for the most part quiet, as if saving its strength for uproar, or recuperating its strength from the last outburst. Helga the au-pair washed and cleaned and fried fish fingers and ironed: the children did their home-work, Ray wrote in the attic, Bella and Richard silently worked or studiously made their secret love.

Sometimes it reminded Richard of his parents' home: the semblance of ordinariness, of kindness and consideration and warmth, as passions gathered and dams of rage prepared to burst.

Married to Liffey, in the little sweetness of their love, he had forgotten all that. He had learned, as a child, to smile and please and be out of the way when storms broke. Liffey had learned the same lesson.

Richard would do things with Bella as he believed debased the pair of them.
'No such thing as a perversion,' Bella would say, 'so long as both enjoy it.'
But Richard knew that she was wrong: that in dragging the spirituality of love down into the mist of excitement through disgust, he did them both a wrong. He would never do such things to Liffey. She was his wife. But he had to do them with someone, or be half alive.

All Bella's doing, thought Richard. Bella's fault.

Or he could have lived with Liffey for ever, in the calm ordinariness of the missionary position, as had his mother and father before him, and known no better.

Miss Martin had trembled and moaned so much he'd simply got it all over as soon as possible.

Richard could see that Miss Martin too might come to enjoy it. Perhaps it was his duty to ensure that she did: to bring her to the enjoyment of sex, before casting her back into the stream of life from which he had so tenderly fished her? The more Richard contemplated the notion, the more attractive and the more virtuous such a course appeared.

There were, Richard thought, three kinds of women, and three kinds of associated sex. Liffey's kind, which went with marriage, which was respectful and everyday, and allowed both partners to discuss such things as mortgages and shopping on waking.
Bella's kind, which went with extra-marital sex, and self-disgust, and was anal and oral and infantile, and addictive, and so out of character that nobody said anything on waking if only because the daily self and the nightly self were so divorced.

Miss Martin's kind, which involved seduction: the pleasure of inflicting and receiving emotional pain: in which the sexual act was the culmination not to physical foreplay – for orgasm was in no way its object – but of long, long hours, days, weeks, of emotional manipulation.

It would not be possible, nor indeed desirable, Richard thought, to find these three different women in one body; he could never satisfy his needs monogamously. Could any man?

On Wednesday morning Richard said to Miss Martin, whose hand shook more than ever when she handed him his coffee, whom he had had to reprove more than once for carelessness in typing, and who was now wearing her hair curled behind her ears – 'I like your hair like that.'

It was the first personal remark he had made to her since their return from the Strand Palace Hotel.

Miss Martin blushed. Later he asked her out to lunch. He knew she would not refuse: that she would make no trouble for him: and make no demands. She was born to be a picker up of other people's crumbs. Well, he would scatter a few. She needed the nourishment: and the more wealth that flowed from him, the more there would be to flow. Richard knew that in sexual matters the more you give out, the more there is to give.

Nature

Inside Liffey, a cystic space appeared in the morula of her pregnancy, which now could be termed a blastocyst. It grew sprout-like projections, termed choriomic villi. It drifted down towards the cavity of the uterus. So each one of us began: Nature sets us in motion, Nature propels us. It is as well to acknowledge it.

And by Nature we mean not God, nor anything which has intent, but the chance summation of evolutionary events which, over aeons, have made us what we are: and starfish what they are, and turtles what they are: and pumpkins too, and will make our children, and our childrens' children what they will be, and an infinitesimal improvement – so long, that is, as natural selection can keep pace with a changing environment – on what we are. Looking back, we think we perceive a purpose. But the perspective is faulty.

We no longer see Nature as blind, although she is. Her very name is imbued with a sense of purpose, as the name of God used to be. God means us. God wills us. God wants for us. We cannot turn words back: they mean what we want them to mean; and we are weak; if we can not in all conscience speak of God we must speak of Nature. Wide-eyed, clear-eyed, purposeful Nature. Too late to abandon her. Let us seize the word, seize the day; lay the N on its side and call our blind mistress Ƶature.

On Thursday night the calm of the Nash household was disturbed. Ray and Bella had a row. Both thought they behaved as rational people do when provoked beyond endurance, and both were in error. Ray and Bella acted as people act when their metabolisms are disturbed, as Ƶature works its terrible, its integrating changes in the body, and the messages received from the outside world are both distorted and distorting.

Bella wept. Ray shouted. Ray said he was in love with Karen because she was sixteen, had a mass of red hair and a tiny mouth.
'It isn't love,' cried Bella. 'It's lust.'
'It's love, Bella, love,' he shouted, and the volume of his voice made African objects d'art, lean mahogany phallic things, tremble on the pine bookcase.

'But she's a fool. How can you love something that's less than you.'

'Perfectly well,' he shouted.

'What do you mean by love?' she yelled.

'What any teenager means.'

'You're not a teenager. You're a poor impotent old man.'

'And you're a jealous old cow.'

She snatched up a sharp fruit knife and advanced upon him and he was frightened and fled, and in the bedroom Helga reading Tina and Tony their bednight story, raised her voice and tried to protect her charges from the noise of adult life.

Bella, having taken up her knife and wielded it, felt better. She was indeed jealous. Σature had rendered her jealous, thus giving her children (or so Σature thought, living as she does so much in the past) a better chance of survival. Even as Bella was ashamed of the emotion, so did acting upon it fulfil and satisfy her – as to act upon all the major impulses which Σature dictates – whether they be aggressive, defensive or procreative – fulfils and satisfies.

If it feels right, it is right, according to Σature, but not, alas, to man. At the same time as feeling better, Bella felt ashamed, and upset, and confused.

The voice Bella gave to confusion, grief and resentment was the more violent inasmuch as her unused ova – laid down, waiting for delivery, when she herself was still in the womb – were beginning to atrophy with age, and her cyclic production of oestrogen and progesterone was at a critically low level. She was suffering, as the months went by, from an increase in premenstrual tension, and from mild indigestion. She was forty-four – an early age for such symptoms of menopause, the average being forty-eight point five – but such things happen. Though by and large, those whose periods begin early, continue late. In sexual matters, to those that hath, is given more.

The voice that Ray gave to anger and despair was the more

violent, inasmuch as his supply of testosterone was uncomfortably diminishing, leaving him prone to sulks, moods, depressions and outbursts of rage. Karen, being young, even tempered, clear of complexion and of spirit, seemed the more enchanting. He felt that youth was infectious, and it was true enough that by stimulating his sexual appetite, Karen might stimulate his supply of testosterone, and make him better tempered, for a while. In the meantime, his tongue was acid and his moods were black.

Presently their parents stopped shouting, crying and stamping, and Tina and Tony slept. Next morning Helga swept and cleaned with a set face.

'I only stay because of the children,' she said. It was her theme song. She ironed Richard's shirts, beautifully.
'How can I thank you?' he asked.
From her look, he could tell. He wondered why he had suddenly become so desirable to the opposite sex, and concluded it was because he had become available.

Richard, observing Helga, suspected that there was perhaps a fourth kind of woman, and a fourth kind of sex.

Helga, and sex-as-payment. Helga would iron his shirts, and then demand to be brought to orgasm. She would work as busily and concentratedly on that as she did his shirts. As the iron was to the shirt, so would his penis be to her satisfaction.

He did not wish to put his theory to the test. Later, perhaps. Bella was upset enough as it was.

'You know,' said Bella on Friday night, after he had sent Liffey a telegram to say he'd been delayed at a meeting, and would return on Saturday morning. 'You're terribly angry with Liffey.'
'Why should I be angry with Liffey?'
'Because she won't let you be a man. She wants you to be a little boy, so you can romp hand in hand with her through green fields, for ever.'

'I'm not angry with Liffey,' he repeated.
'Yes you are. That's why you're doing these terrible primitive things to me. I'm her stand-in.'

Richard wished Bella would leave the inside of his head alone. There were a thousand motives which could be attributed to every act, but none of them made the act any different.

He had been angry with Liffey. Now, he was not. Or so he believed.

Inside Liffey (7)

By Saturday morning the fine hairs of the blastocyst inside Liffey had digested and eroded enough of the uterus wall to enable it to burrow snugly into the endometrium and there open up another maternal blood vessel, the better to obtain the oxygen and nutrients it increasingly required.

This implantation, alas for Liffey and her doctors, occurred in an unusual part of her uterus – in the lower uterine segment. Too far down, in fact, for safety or comfort. Perhaps this was a mere matter of chance – perhaps, who's to say, it was a matter of Mabs' ill-wishing? If prayers can make plants flourish, and curses wilt them, and all living matter is the same substance and thought has a reality, and wishing can influence the fall of a dice, and kinetic energy is a provable thing, and poltergeists can make the plates on the dresser rattle, why then Mabs can curse Liffey's baby, and Liffey protect it, as bad and good fairies at the christening.

Liffey looked up at the sky and thought it was beautiful, and the blastocyst clung where it could, not quite right but not quite unright, and growth continued and the so-far un-differentiated cells began to take up their specialist parts, some forming amniotic fluid, some placental fluid, and some becoming the foetus itself. The degree of specialisation which these later cells would eventually achieve would be rivalled nowhere else in the Universe, enabling their owner to read, and write, and reason in a way entirely surplus to its survival.

Σature intends us to survive only long enough to procreate. We have other ideas. Ask any woman past the menopause, withering like a leaf on a tree, and fighting the decline with intelligence, and oestrogen. Ask any man, reading *Playboy*, whipping up desire. These extras, too, Σature gave us. Why? Are we to assume Divine Intent, and fall on our knees, set the Σ the right way up, go back to Nature, and retreat to God? Never!

Liffey's child was to be male. Liffey contributed her share of twenty-two chromosomes plus the X chromosome which was all she could, being female, hand over. Richard handed over twenty-two chromosomes, plus as it happened, a Y sex chromosome. Forty-four plus an XY makes a male. Had Richard handed over an X sex chromosome – and there was a roughly fifty per cent chance that he would do so -- the forty-four plus an XX would have made a female. The sex of the child was nothing to do with Liffey – who left to herself could only have achieved a girl – but was determined by Richard.

The ratio of male to female babies conceived is some 113 to 100 but by the time of delivery has dropped to 106 to 100, since the male embryo is marginally the more likely to perish. So Liffey's baby, being male, and placed too low in the womb for maximum safety, already had a few extra odds working against its survival. Neverthless, it had survived a few million obstacles to get this far, and if there is such a thing as a life-force, a determination in the individual of a species, as distinct to the group, not to give up, not to perish, not to be wasted, why then Liffey's baby had that determination.

Marvels

On Sunday morning Tucker and two of his children, Audrey and Eddie, came round to visit.

'You didn't go to church, then?' enquired Tucker.

'We're not really believers,' said Liffey.

Tucker looked amazed.

'Somebody had to make it all,' said Tucker.

While their elders talked about the weather, crops, and cider apples, Audrey wandered and Eddie leaned, and fidgeted. They were not like Tony and Tina. They did not believe the adult world was anything to do with them.

Audrey wore platform heels, three years out of date, a short skirt, holed stockings, and a shiny green jumper stretched over breasts which would soon be as robust as her mother's. Her large eyes followed Liffey, making Liffey nervous, but sometimes she would look sideways at Richard, and smile. She sidled round the perimeter of the room, as if her natural habitat were out of doors.

Eddie leaned against the wall, and shuffled from foot to foot, and fidgeted. His face was pale and puffy, his little eyes were sad, he had cold sores round his mouth, and coarse stringy hair. If Audrey looked as if she were biding her time, Eddie, at the age of eight, looked as if his had run out. His nose dripped a thick yellow mucus, which from time to time he would sniff back up his nostrils.

Eddie, fidgeting and fumbling, pushed a glass ashtray from a shelf and broke it.

Slap, went his father's hand across his cheek, and slap again.

'Oh don't!' cried Liffey and Richard in horrified chorus. 'Oh don't! It doesn't matter.'

'He's got to learn,' said Tucker, surprised, slapping again. Eddie snivelled rather than cried: as if life, already despaired of, was now merely continuing on a slightly more disagreeable level.

Liffey, half horrified, half fascinated, by this exercise of power, of parent over child, strong over weak, raised her eyes and found Tucker looking straight at her.

Tucker hadn't forgotten. She knew he would be back.

Liffey retreated to the kitchen to make real lemonade for the children, from whole chopped lemons, blended and then strained, and sweetened with honey. Audrey followed her in.

Audrey spoke.

'I've had nothing to eat all day,' she said, 'and won't till the end of it, that's according to my Mum. I was cooking bacon and eggs for all our breakfast, the way she told me, but then she changed her mind and made me make the beds and when I came back breakfast was cold, and I said don't make me eat that I'll be sick, but she did make me, so I ate it, and then of course I threw up over everything and she made me wipe it up and then she made me go to my room but my Dad made her let me out.'

Liffey did not believe Audrey. Mabs loved children and wanted more. She often said so.

'Would you like a sandwich?' Liffey asked, all the same, but Audrey refused, having taken a look at the brown wholemeal bread. 'I only like white sliced,' she explained, and then, as if in apology, 'you be careful of my Mum. She's got it in for you. You only see the side of her she wants you to see. You don't know what she's like.'

It was a clear warning, and Liffey disregarded it. Nobody nice, ordinary, and well-meaning wishes to believe that they have enemies, let alone become the focal point of energies they do not understand. Liffey had assumed a discretion and secrecy in Tucker that did not exist: and that Mabs could have instigated the seduction did not even occur to her and that the same convulsions which animate a mindless cluster of single cells – of division and multiplication within, and incorporation and extrojection along the outside perimeter – applies to the whole of existence, from galaxies to groups of human beings, she did not know. She could not see the dance of the Universe, although she was part of it.

'You'll feel better about your mum tomorrow,' said Liffey, and offered Audrey some of her lemonade, but Audrey, preferring the bottled kind, only distantly related to the lemon, declined to drink.

Richard went back to London. Liffey waited for Tucker to call, and was relieved when he did not. She locked the door at night, and was placating towards Mabs, whose bulky figure she would see, at odd times of the day, trudging over the fields, making Liffey feel both secure and anxious. On Thursday Liffey expected her period to start, but it did not. Her pituitary gland, out of its accustomed season, was producing extra progesterone: too much for menstruation to begin. The inner surface of Liffey's uterus had, in general, become highly secretive and active, and thus would continue until the end of her pregnancy, whether this ran to term or otherwise.

A week passed. Two weeks. Richard came and went. They agreed that they loved each other and that a little absence made the heart grow fonder, and that there were things about the Universe which could be learned singly, and which could not be learned together. That these things included, for Richard, sexual knowledge, did not occur to Liffey. He gave an account of his days which included Bella and Miss Martin, and she knew that Bella was old and his best friend's wife, and that Miss Martin was stodgy and plain, and why should he anyway, since he had her, Liffey, and Friday,

Saturday and Sunday nights – on a good weekend – were three nights out of seven.

Liffey dug the garden. Dick Hubbard came over to inspect the roof and told Liffey not to bother with the garden since the soil was so poor it was a waste of time. There were prowlers about, and the local prison was where they sent sexual offenders and the security was shocking and there were always break-outs, hushed up of course, and Honeycomb Cottage was on the direct escape route, over the fields, from the prison to the main road.

But Liffey, who wished to harm no one, feared no harm.

Mabs came over with seeds for the garden and talked of the prison working parties too, describing the prisoners as without exception harmless and amiable.

Liffey started a compost heap, having read that artificial fertilisers were the ruin of the soil. Richard scoffed, and marvelled at his wife's capacity of handling what to him was better churned up as quickly as possible in a waste disposal unit. Mory and Helen failed to answer solicitor's letters, pay rent, or answer the door when Richard knocked upon it.

Illegal, his solicitors said, to knock down your own front door.
Wait, wait.

The other side of the door Lally's pains came and went. Her legs swelled. Spots swam before her eyes, and she had headaches.
'You don't think I should call a doctor?' she would sometimes say, plaintively. But Helen said no, doctors would only interfere with the course of nature.
'I think the baby's overdue,' Lally ventured one morning. The flat was almost bare of furniture now. Bedding could not be burned, conveniently, as it filled the rooms with a choking smoke.

126

'How can a baby be overdue?' asked Helen. 'When a baby's due it comes out,' and Lally was obliged to admit that that was so. Helen was her elder sister, and had known best from the beginning.

Neither Mory nor Roy liked to interfere. Helen had a determined and positive nature: once given over to the winning of Pony Club rosettes and hockey colours; since her conversion equally determined to bring about the New Society. She smoked less than the others, as they smoked more and more, which gave her, if only by default, definite qualities of leadership.

'I suppose the wicked weed doesn't do the baby any harm,' murmured Mory.

'It stops me feeling the pains,' said Lally, who had never at the best of times been prepared to sacrifice comfort and entertainment in the dubious interests of the baby ('all these dos and don'ts are just punitive – part of the male plot to make the pregnant woman miserable' – Helen) and at the moment felt happiest in a stupor.

The apartment became increasingly damp, dirty and uncomfortable. Helen declined to make Roy's coffee, Lally could not, and Mory did not. There was no cooked food, and Roy felt bad without at least one dish of meat, potatoes and vegetables a day. He started doing sums on pieces of paper, and concluded that he could not be the father of Lally's child and moved out, taking Helen's amber beads and all their supply of marihuana with him. Helen wept: Lally groaned and started to haemorrhage. Mory ran into the street and stopped a police car who called an ambulance. Lally was taken to hospital where the next day the baby was still-born, of placental insufficiency, the baby being six weeks beyond term.

'Liars, murderers,' sobbed Helen, 'you should never have called them in, Mory.'

But he had lost his faith in her, and threw about a great deal of Liffey's blue and white Victorian china.

Lally went back to stay with her mother, 'Just for a time,' she said.

'Traitor,' stormed Helen. 'Don't give her my love, whatever you do.'

The doctors said that Lally's fertility might be henceforth somewhat impaired, but Lally did not mind, at least for the moment.

The bank wrote another letter to Liffey, and Mory and Helen failed to pass it on. But Mory made telephone calls to Argentina, in the weeks before the Telephone Company acted on Richard's instructions to disconnect the telephone, where he had heard of a job, and where truly creative architects, artists in concrete, were appreciated. Helen said it was an impossibly reactionary and oppressive society, and they were not going to such a place, not even for a week, and Mory said he was, he didn't care about her.

Still Liffey's period did not begin. Three weeks late! She felt a little queasy and put it down to some vague virus infection: and was sick one morning, and her breasts were tender – but so they often were just before a period – and she had to get up in the night to pass water, but put this down to a chill on the bladder.

No, no, thought Liffey, I can't be pregnant. Not this month. Not while Tucker might be remotely connected with the event. Which surely he wasn't, because surely—

Liffey discovered she knew next to nothing about pregnancy, or what went on inside her, and really had no particular wish to know. It is hard to believe that the cool, smooth, finished perfection of young skin covers up such a bloody, pulpy, incoherent, surging mass of pulsing organs within: hard to link up spirit to body, mind to matter, ourselves to others, others to everything. But there it is, and here we are. Hearts beating, minds running; fuel in, energy out.

Liffey, trembling on the edge of a train of thought which

would both enhance and yet debase her, make her ordinary where she had thought herself special, special where she had believed herself ordinary, was pushed by guilt and trepidation to go into Poldyke and buy the one paperback book on pregnancy that they had in stock.

News quickly got back to Mabs.

Mabs stood and stared at the Tor. It was very cold that day, and deathly still. The cows stopped rustling in the fields and the birds waited in the trees. Tucker stayed out of the house and sent the children to Mabs' mother.

'No reason to think it's mine,' said Tucker, to the trees.

To Mabs, Tucker said, 'Just because she's bought a book, doesn't mean she is.'

But Mabs did not reply, and both knew, as surely as one knows a death before it's verified, that Liffey was indeed pregnant.

Liffey wondered: Mabs and Tucker knew.

Everything Mabs felt, but gave no voice to, partly because she scorned to, partly because she did not have a vocabulary to express the complexity of the things she felt: fear of ageing, fear of death, loss of father, fear of mother, hate of sister, resentment of her children (who, once born, were not what she had meant at all), jealousy of Tucker, sexual desire towards other women, pretty women, helpless women; resentment of women who spread their possessions, their homes, delicately around them and stood back in pride: envy of brainy women, stylish women, rich women, women who could explain their lives in words: all these things Mabs felt, surging up in a great wordless storm, on knowing that Liffey was pregnant.

She, Mabs, could stump about the fields, and put her

powerful hands before her, and spread her fingers wide, and the whole power of the Universe would dart through them – but what use was that to Mabs? It could not make her what she wanted to be.

Mabs, pregnant, felt the fury of her unconscious passions allayed, and could be almost happy. And, so, pregnant, became ordinary, like anyone else, and used her hands to cook, and clean, and sew, and soothe, and not as psychic conductors.

Mabs knew, too, that there are only so many babies to go round, and that if Liffey was pregnant, she would not be.

Mabs thought all these things, and since she could not voice them, then forget them; she knew only that she liked Liffey even less than before, and that the answer to her dislike was not to keep out of Liffey's way. No.

The air grew warmer: the cows rustled in the fields; the birds found the courage to leave the trees and look for food in the thawing ground: clouds passed easily over and around the Tor.

Tucker fetched the children back. Tucker liked the idea of Liffey being pregnant. It was as if Mabs had barred the light of the world, eclipsing it, and suddenly he could see round her, and all this time she had been hiding wonderful things.

Liffey was in her fifth week of pregnancy. The baby was two millimetres long, and lay within a newly formed amniotic sac. It's backbone was now beginning to form.

Liffey felt her tender breasts, and thought no, no, surely not. She was not ready to have a baby. She had not grown out of her own childhood: a baby was something which would grow at her expense: which would diminish her: which would bring her nearer death. It seemed bizarre, not natural at all.

130

She said nothing about it when Richard came home the next weekend. And he told her that he thought Bella was a repressed lesbian, and that Miss Martin had announced her engagement in the local papers, and they both laughed a little, but kindly, at the hypocrises of the one and the modest aspirations of the other.

'As for Helga,' said Richard, 'she's the original Hausfrau! The three Ks. *Kirche, Küche, Kinder*. I thought women like that went out with the dinosaur. Of course she's the size of one.'

But Richard's shirts were clean and ironed, and he brought no washing home for Liffey. She was glad of that. She was feeling a little tired.

She felt an increase in her sexual desire for Richard. She wished to try new positions, but Richard seemed embarrassed so she quickly desisted, marvelling at herself. It was as if her body, no longer needing to insist on procreation, had at last found time for its own amusement. Richard went back to London on Sunday night. She hoped her conduct in bed had not driven him away early.

On the Monday morning Liffey was sick, and on the Monday afternoon went into Crossley and bought, with some embarrassment, a pregnancy testing kit and by Tuesday mid-day, having dropped some early-morning urine into a phial, adding the provided chemicals, and putting it to set, soon knew that she was pregnant.

A certain elation began to mingle with her fear. The sick feeling, which might have been brought on by anxiety, and uncertainty, lessened a little.

Liffey went round to Mabs.

'I'm pregnant,' she said. 'Can I use the telephone to ring Richard?'

'But that's wonderful!' cried Mabs, and insisted that they open a bottle of blackberry wine to celebrate, and delayed Liffey getting to the telephone until well after one o'clock, by which time Richard had gone to lunch.

Or so Miss Martin said. In actual fact Richard had just kissed her gently on the eyes, to kiss away her tears, and she had had to break away from his embrace to answer the telephone. The tears had come after a full office week in which Richard had ignored her except for sending letters back for re-typing and reproving her in front of other people: she thought, she hoped, that the cause of his unkindness was her having announced her engagement to Jeff, but how could she be sure? She knew that tears irritated him, but by Tuesday lunchtime could no longer hold them back.

And instead of shouting, he kissed her.

'Who was that?' asked Richard.
'It was only your wife,' said Miss Martin, and he had to stop himself from striking her. *Only* Liffey! He knew that Jeff, poor Jeff, would end up beating her. She invited it, mingling tears with acts of hostility.
'But it was your lunch-hour,' Miss Martin put in her feeble excuse, 'you said you didn't want to be disturbed in your lunch-hour.'

He made her ring back Cadbury Farm, and get Liffey on the line. But Mabs answered. Her broad accent rang thick and strange in the quiet office.
'Your Liffey's here tippling with me,' said Mabs, 'and she's got something important to tell you. She's pregnant.'

There was silence. Mabs had the receiver away from her ear.
'I'll bet that shook him,' she said, aside to Liffey.

Liffey took the phone. There were tears in her eyes. She felt that a moment had gone, lost, never to be recaptured. It was one in which she might have lost her fear of having the baby, and in Richard's spontaneous pleasure learned how to accept it.

'Are you sure?' Richard was saying. 'Liffey, are you there? You're sure you haven't made a mistake?'

The telephone went dead, and although Miss Martin, sobbing, denied that it was her doing, and did her trembly best to re-establish the connection, Liffey at the same time was trying to get through to Richard, and by the time she did he had indeed gone off to a meeting.
'Is there any message?' asked Miss Martin, who had recovered her composure, and blamed Liffey because she had lost it in the first place. 'I'd ask him to ring back, but he is so busy this week, and we're expecting a call through on this line from Amsterdam.'

Liffey put down the phone.
'I don't like the sound of that secretary,' said Mabs. 'She sounds for all the world like a wife.'

Suppositions

Knowledge of pregnancy comes early to modern woman, perhaps too early, before body and mind have settled down into tranquillity.

Liffey, all alone, trembled and feared and cried. She thought her life was over. She thought that to be pregnant was to be ugly, and that afterwards her body would be spoiled; she would have pendulous breasts and a flabby belly.

Her mother Madge had strange creases over her stomach, flaps of ugly skin, for which she held Liffey responsible. 'Stretch marks!' she would observe, making no attempt to

hide them. Madge viewed her body as something functional:
if it worked that was all she cared about. But Liffey loved her
body and cherished it: she feared maturity, she wanted to be
looked after, for ever; to be placed, physically, at a point
somewhere between girl-child and stripling lad: hips and
bosom all promise, waiting for some other time, but not now,
not now. Not yet.

Richard wanted a boy-wife, she knew it. She knew it from
the way he groaned at biscuits and moaned at buns and
worried in case she grew fat.

On the way home from Cadbury Farm Liffey slipped and
fell, and lay for a moment, stunned and shaken, with the
world slipping and sliding about her.

A face loomed over her. It was Tucker. Tucker helped her
up and set her on her feet, calmly and kindly.
'You look after yourself,' he said. 'And don't go drinking too
much of Mabs' wine. It isn't good for you.'

Liffey ran home, as quick as she could over slippery ground,
for light snow had been falling, and locked the door. During
the night more snow fell, fine and light and driven by strong
winds, which in the morning left a blue, washed sky. And
such a brilliant tranquillity of white stretched across the
plain to the Tor, broken only by the sketched pencil-lines of
the half-buried hedgerows, that tears of wonder came to her
eyes, and she felt better.

Richard woke on Bella's sofa to the sight of Bella's books: the
works of Man, not nature, and found it reassuring. The news
of Liffey's pregnancy had come as a shock. He was glad, but
not altogether glad.

If Richard was to be husband and father, how could Bella
continue his education? How could he in all conscience
continue to lie on his back with Bella on top of him, wresting
from him any number of degrading pleasures?

How could he discover what it was in Miss Martin that made her cry when she lay beneath him, as if she had the key to all the sorrows of the Universe?

How could he discover the nature of Helga's being, which he now passionately desired to know?

But to be a father! There was pride in that, and pleasure in looking after Liffey, and wonder in the knowledge that a man was not just himself, but so stuffed overfull with life that there was enough to pass on – and here in Liffey was the proof of it.

Richard decided to give up Bella and Miss Martin and concentrate on Liffey.

It was a decision he was to make frequently in the following months, as a dedicated but guilty smoker decides to give up smoking.

Six weeks. The limb buds of the foetus began to show and the tail to disappear. The heart formed within the chest cavity and began the activity which was to last till the end of its days. Blood vessels formed in the cervical cord. Parts of the stomach and intestine formed.

Liffey wondered how to be rid of a baby she did not want, without telling anyone that she did not want it.

Richard wondered how to subdue in himself that part of his being which did not dovetail with his nature as husband and father.

Liffey thought she was growing a malformed baby, which would have a lolling head and tongue, and flippers for arms, finished off by Tucker's black fingernails. Liffey was guilty, in other words, and believed that no good could come out of her.

Mabs walked about the hills and fields, and the rain poured

out of the heavens so hard it stirred up the ground where she trod, and there was little to choose between heaven, or earth, or her. The Tor vanished altogether, obscured by water, fog and cloud, in which occasionally, sheets of lightning danced. Earth, water, fire and air no longer retained their separate parts.

Seven weeks. Budding arms and legs, and little clefts for fingers and toes. Blood vessels throughout, and the liver and kidneys forming. A spinal cord, and a well-shaped head with the beginnings of a face, and a brain inside. It was not, all the same, conscious. It was an automota, as the jellyfish are, and the whole kingdom of the plants, and mucl. but not all of the insect world. It was not yet truly a mammal. Mammals have the gift of consciousness: decision can over-ride instinct, and often, but perhaps not as often as we assume, does.

'You are looking poorly,' said Mabs, and made Liffey a brew of ergot and tansy tea; a rich abortificant, which had, fortunately for Liffey but unfortunately for Mabs, no effect on Liffey or her baby beyond giving the mother slight diarrhoea. 'This will do you good.'

Liffey had become a little frightened of Mabs, and drank whatever she suggested, for fear of offending her.

Richard succumbed to loneliness, vague resentments of Liffey, various worries connected with the varying saline content of the water flow at the soup works, and fornicated as much as possible with Miss Martin and Bella.

'I shouldn't,' whispered Miss Martin. 'Not if your wife is pregnant.' But she did, and even left out her own contraceptive cap, once, and fortunately did not get pregnant, an episode which led her to believe she was infertile, and did nothing for her self-esteem. She knew nothing about ova, where they were, or how long they lasted. All she knew was that her very being cried out to have Richard's baby, if Liffey did: and her conscious mind, that glory of the mammal kingdom, did very little to protect her.

'Live as much as you can while you can,' said Bella. 'Before life and Liffey close in.' Bella was old, by nature's standards, and her conscious mind had less trouble over-riding her instinctive drives. All that remained of naturally rivalrous behaviour was her current irrational dislike for, and impulsive disparagement of, Richard's pregnant wife Liffey.

Mabs' period began, staining oyster silk underwear. Mabs scrubbed away, hating Liffey, and focused her ill-will. And in London Helen looked up and saw the letters to Liffey on the mantelpiece and said, 'I suppose I'd better post those,' and did, and Mabs at once felt better and actually baked a cake for tea.

Liffey opened the letters and understood that she was no longer rich, that she was to live as the rest of the world did, unprotected from financial disaster; that she was pregnant and dependent upon a husband, and that her survival, or so it seemed, was bound up with her pleasing of him. That she was not, as she had thought, a free spirit, and nor was he: that they were bound together by necessity. That he could come and go as he pleased; love her, leave her as he pleased: hand over as much or as little of his earnings as he pleased; and that domestic power is to do with economics. And that Richard, by virtue of being powerful, being also good, would no doubt look after her and her child, and not insist upon doing so solely upon his terms. But he could and he might: so Liffey had better behave, charm, lure, love and render herself necessary by means of the sexual and caring comforts she provided.
Wash socks, iron shirts. Love.
And that to have been unfaithful was a terrible thing. That financially dependent wives are more faithful than independent wives. That she must go carefully.

Liffey thought of all these things for the space of three days.

'You're looking worse,' said Mabs, and offered Liffey more ergot and tansy tea, which Liffey pretended to take, but emptied instead into a pot plant which was altogether dead two days later. Had Liffey known this she might indeed have drunk the tea.

On the fourth day Liffey ran up country lanes, and over rough ground, fleeing her past, and her present, and her mother, and trying to shake her baby free. But the baby barely noticed any change to its environment. How could it?

Annunciation

The wind sang in Liffey's ears, and told her she was wasting effort and energy: that all things were destined, that she was what she was born, and would never change: would for ever be the girl without a father who wished she had no mother; and that though she ran and ran she would never escape herself. As Liffey ran, so antelope run over the African plain, and kittens across the domestic lawn, frightened by themselves, seeking refuge in flight, running as likely into danger as to safety. Her muscles ached: her energy drained. Liffey stopped running.

Liffey looked about her. The rain, which had poured and poured for weeks, had stopped, and the sky was washed and palest blue. She could still see the Tor, but now from a different angle, so that its slope was less acute, and the tower on top was clearly man-made, not eternal. It was friendly: scarcely nuministic at all. It had been weeks, she felt, since she had looked about her and noticed the world in which she lived. She saw that the leaf buds were on the trees, and that new bright grass pushed up beneath her feet, and that there was a sense of expectation in the air. All things prepared, and waited.

Liffey sat on the ground and turned her face towards the mild sun. She felt a presence: the touch of a spirit, clear and benign. She opened her eyes, startled, but there was no one there, only a dazzle in the sky where the sun struck slantwise between the few puffy white clouds which hovered over the Tor.

'It's me,' said the spirit, said the baby, 'I'm here. I have arrived. You are perfectly all right, and so am I. Don't worry.' The words were spoken in her head: they were graceful, and certain. They charmed. Liffey smiled, and felt herself close and curl, as a sunflower does at night, to protect, and shelter. The words dispersed, and the outside sounds came in. Birdsong, traffic, distant voices.

'I have been blessed,' said Liffey, to herself, walking carefully and warily home, eyes inside and misting from time to time. She did not say it to anyone else, for who would believe her?

'Richard, I felt the baby's spirit arrive. It was the soul that came. I know it was.'

No.

'Madge, mother, did you know I was pregnant? No? Well, I am and what's more the Holy Ghost, or something, descended and now inhabits me.'

?

No.

'Mabs, friend, you know how I slept with your husband, Tucker, well you don't, but I did, except it isn't his baby; well, I just *know*, because the baby's said so—'

?

No.

'Mr. and Mrs. Lee-Fox, your daughter-in-law speaking, the flimsy one who trapped your only son into marriage: the never-quite-accepted, never-to-be-accepted one, who tried to charm her way into your hearts but failed, who now says just to have Richard's child isn't enough, but has to have an Annunciation instead, as if Richard was some Middle-Eastern carpenter and she was Mary—'

?

No.

'Bella and Ray, Liffey speaking. You know, Richard's wife, your lodger's wife, who chose to live in the country and apart from her husband and is now pregnant and poor but compensating with quasi-religious experiences—'

?

No.

Liffey made up the fire and polished the windows to let every scrap of light in, and settled down to cherish the baby.

Growth

Richard, told of the loss of Liffey's wealth, frittered away on pretty things and useless things and delicious things, was first irritated, then relieved, and then filled with a great sense of protectiveness and love for Liffey, as if by her very helplessness she solicited something from him which she hitherto had not. He moved through the world with an added weight and dignity, so that presently his colleagues remarked to one another that Richard had changed.
'He's older than one thinks,' somebody said, and at meetings his voice was listened to, and not just heard.

Richard resolved to give up Miss Martin and Bella, and kept the resolution for a full week.

Then Bella got him drunk, on free champagne at a restaurant opening, and if he did with Bella, then why not Miss Martin?

And Helga was sulking slightly, as if thanks were not sufficient recompense for her ironing of his shirts, and the folding of his socks in the neat Continental way, not the angry convoluting inside out way the English had.

Eight weeks. The baby's heart beat strongly now. The inner ears were growing fast, although they still showed no external part. The face had nostrils and a recognisable mouth, and black pigmentation where the eyes were to be. Elbows, shoulders, hips and knees were apparent. The spine moved of its own volition, for the first time, although fractionally. The length of the foetus was two point two centimetres. There was no apparent room within for the soul which gave grace to its being.

Mabs, or so she thought, knew everything there was to know about Liffey. She certainly knew about Liffey's new poverty. Liffey used Mabs' telephone, having none of her own; and if she wished to be private had to walk a mile to the public call-box at Poldyke – a manual exchange, where it so happened that the operator was a friend of Mabs. Letters to and from Liffey were left at Cadbury Farm, for the postman would not walk up the track, and Mabs was not above steaming open any she thought interesting. Shop assistant friends gave an account of what Liffey purchased, and the doctor's receptionist, also a friend, passed on details of her health.

'She's having to learn to live like anyone else,' said Mabs smugly, observing that Liffey now bought groceries much as anyone else did, and that her order at the butcher's was for mince and sausage, no longer fillet steak and stewing veal. 'Her Richard won't like that!'

And it was true that Richard did not like it very much. The euphoria of his compassion and tenderness faded; difficulties, so bravely anticipated and overcome in principle, remained in detail to plague and depress him. With the merest suspicion in the mind that Liffey's skinny, shabby clothes might be chosen because they were cheap, she stopped looking chic, and looked dowdy instead. Her cooking – when she was obliged to use inexpensive ingredients, and deprived of the cream and brandy she liked to add to everything, from soup to stewed apples – was not as seductive as before. And what Richard had construed in Liffey as sexual delicacy, now seemed rather more like sexual limitation – for without a doubt what had occurred to Liffey had occurred to Richard too – that once a wife is financially dependent, she is sexually dependent too. Richard felt by that token the more in a position to criticise.

He cherished Liffey, of course he did, but no longer quite as an equal. He was almost sorry for her; he came down at the weekends because he ought, not because he wanted to. Nothing was said: the movement in their relationship was slight: too slight to find voice, but both sensed it.

Now he was rich, and she was poor.

Mabs knew it, and she was glad.

Mabs knew everything about Liffey except what she could not know – that Liffey's baby had spoken to her; settled clear and bright inside her and promised that everything would be all right. That Liffey, now, had powers of her own: that Mabs could no longer have Nature all her own way: that forces worked for Liffey too, and not just Mabs. Winter winds were on Mabs' side, and frost, and lightning and storms. Liffey loved sun, and breeze, and warmth; and they loved her. And spring was coming.

Danger

Tucker put the cows on Liffey's side of the stream field. One of them was pregnant. It bellowed and groaned one misty evening. It lay down: it shuddered: it jerked its limbs and arched its neck. It rolled its eyes in a terrifying manner, showing an expanse of red-veined white. Could any eye on earth be so large? A single leg, Liffey was horrified to see, stuck out from under its tail. A single leg, a calf's leg, in a frozen wave to the world, as if a frame of a film had been frozen. Blackish mucus gushed out around it, even as Liffey looked, and with it came a stench strong and disagreeable. Liffey looked and gasped and ran, crying for Mabs and Tucker.

Tucker was out. But Mabs was in the kitchen, watching television. She took a long time deciding what to do: whether to wait for Tucker or call the vet, and then finally came herself, pulling on a long pair of rubber gloves. Together they set off back up the lane. Liffey wanted to go back inside the cottage but Mabs wouldn't let her.

'Why don't you watch? It's always nice to watch animals being born.'

But it wasn't. The calf was dead when Mabs pulled it out by its emergent leg, tugging and grunting, while the cow lowed and moaned. When the calf's head came out, it was putrid; pulpy and liqueous. Then the cow heaved and groaned and died.

'Three hundred pounds down the drain,' said Mabs, furious. 'At least she wasn't a good milker or it would have been nearer four.'
And she left cow and calf lying there, and walked back to the

cottage with Liffey. Liffey composed herself as best she could: she felt sick and wanted to sleep, but Mabs wanted to talk, it seemed.

'So you're going through with your baby,' Mabs said.
'Of course,' said Liffey, surprised.
'I'd have thought you'd have waited until you and your Richard are more settled.'
'Why?'
Mabs just shrugged, and Liffey felt, for once, wary, and as if forces she was not quite in control of were abroad, and dangerous. Supposing what happened to the calf happened to her baby? She wished she had not seen it.

Liffey feared the contagion of ill-fortune, as pregnant women do. Oh, show me no bad sights: sing me no harsh songs: let good fairies only cluster around the baby's cradle.

'Nothing to a termination these days,' said Mabs. 'Girls I know have it done in order to get away on holiday in peace. They don't mind a bit, up at the hospital. Funny thing, that cow that just died. Her fourth calf, and still something can go wrong. We mostly lose them first time round. Just like people. First babies are always the trickiest. Longer labours, that's what does it.'

Liffey folded her mind around the baby, to guard it.
'I couldn't possibly have a termination,' said Liffey.

Mabs did not like the firmness of Liffey's response. Liffey's baby, she began to feel, might be harder to get rid of than she had imagined. She felt it more and more acutely as the supplanter of her own, product of some process set up by Tucker and so stolen from her: she despised Liffey for a fool; she despised the baby for choosing where it had to grow. She smiled warmly at Liffey, dispelling most of Liffey's doubts, but not all. Liffey, for once, had noticed Mabs' ill-will.

'You'd better get up to the doctor soon,' said Mabs. 'You look a little peaky.'

'I'll wait a bit,' said Liffey, and spoke gently, and smiled, as people do when they sense danger, and know better than to aggravate it, and went inside her cottage.

Mabs stood, still in bloodied rubber gloves and thick muddied Wellingtons, and stared after her for a little, and then moved off towards Cadbury Farm.

The lane was very, very old. The hedges were so high that in summer they would form a tunnel of green. Earthworks and barrows stood at the summit of the hill above the Cottage. Here the people of the Bronze Ages had lived, and died, worked their magic and honoured their dead, until the Iron Age invaders had arrived, and driven them out, and lived off a past which was none of their own. Once messengers had hurried up and down the lane, with good news and more often bad, and mothers, at their coming, had clutched their children to them, and fathers wondered how to turn ploughshares into swords, and stood there wondering too long.

Liffey stood in the kitchen and watched Mabs plod away, and wondered why she was afraid, and realised, of course, it was the dead calf and the dying cow which had upset her. Unreasonable to blame Mabs for what was Nature's fault.

At about the same time as Liffey witnessed the death of the cow, Richard was obliged to rescue the Nash's cat from the gutter, where a passing car had flung it to die. In the end he could not nerve himself to pick the animal up, fancying its dead eye was glaring at him, and while he was hesitating Helga, with alarming speed, came running out of the house, scooped the remains up into a plastic bag and dumped them into the dustbin, and got back to her cleaning as if nothing had happened. Richard was sick.

Liffey rang her mother and told her the news.

'I suppose you know what you're doing,' said Madge. 'Is it what you want?'

'Yes.'

'Why?' asked Madge, disconcertingly.

'I suppose because it's natural,' said Liffey, brightly.

'So are varicose veins,' said Madge.

'It's not as if I had a career,' said Liffey tentatively, over the crackling line to her mother far away. 'It's not as if I was good at anything else. I might as well use up my time having a baby. I might even be a born mother.'

'Not if you take after me,' said Madge, which might almost have counted as an apology. 'Aren't you too frightened? You know what you're like about pain.'

Liffey realised at that moment that she would never, ever, receive her mother's whole-hearted approval. Marks would be given, but marks would always be taken away. Six out of ten for overcoming cowardice: three out of ten for indulging her own nature and having a baby: and there she was, with an average four-and-a-half out of ten, when a pass-mark to mother's love was five.

So we live, as daughters; and, as mothers, are astonished that we elicit the same sad anxiety from our progeny. It was not how we meant it to be, when we dandled them on our knees.

'So you're having a baby in the country,' said Madge, 'while Richard works in London. Is that wise?'

'It's what has to be,' said Liffey. 'Not what I want. As soon as Richard gets Mory and Helen out of the apartment we'll be together again.'

'You could afford something else,' said Madge. 'What's the matter with you?'

Liffey did not want to hear the note of relish in the mother's voice when she explained about the money; she put it off. 'I like it down here,' said Liffey, and a ray of sun broke through the clouds, and she knew that it was true. Only that some danger lay across the land like a sword.

Madge hiccuped on the other end of the line, and Liffey wondered if she were drunk again, and along with the dreary everyday feeling that she had failed to live up to her mother's expectation of her, there now travelled another strand, sharply painful: of anxiety for her mother's welfare. The fear of the child, back from school, whose footstep hesitates at the gate of the house, wondering what's to be found within. Liffey remembered that, too. Her heart beat faster: her hand trembled: tears started in her eyes.

'It's all right,' said the baby, suddenly and unexpectedly. 'All that is past. Be calm, be still.'

And Liffey was, and Mabs, listening in on the extension, knowing only what was available to her to know, wondered why the tone of her voice changed.

'Why don't you come down and stay?' asked Liffey. 'It's going to be so lovely now spring is coming.'

'I was never one for nature,' said Madge, presently, cautiously, 'or for family either. But I suppose it is the kind of thing a mother is expected to do. Once you're given a label you never escape it. I'll come down presently if I can find the time.'

Liffey, to be hung for a sheep as well as a lamb, telephoned Richard's parents.

'A baby!' cried Mrs. Lee-Fox, 'how wonderful.' But in her voice Liffey could hear shock and despair. Now Richard and Liffey were married for good, for ever: they had joined not as children join, for fun and games, but as man and wife, together, as parents, to face trouble and hard times. Mrs. Lee-Fox was in danger of losing her son.

Liffey wondered if she had always heard the other voice, the tone that lies behind the words and betrays them: and if she had heard, why she had not listened? Perhaps she listened now with the baby's budding ears? And certainly this disagreeable acuity of hearing diminished within a week or two: perhaps because Liffey could not for long endure her new sensitivity to the ifs and buts in Richard's voice when he assured her he loved her: perhaps because the matter of hearing was, once properly established, less in the air so far as the baby was concerned.

147

Mrs. Lee-Fox handed Liffey over to Mr. Lee-Fox, who repeated his wife's enthusiasm, and the phone, following a misunderstanding as to who was actually to talk to whom, went down rather abruptly. Liffey did not telephone back.

Mabs put down the extension and called Liffey into the kitchen for a cup of tea.

Later in the week Mabs sent Tucker up with some new-laid eggs from her hens. Tucker smiled at Liffey in a friendly and ordinary manner, and did not outstay his cup of tea and biscuit.

Liffey used two of the eggs for breakfast the following day. On the mornings she did not feel sick, she felt extremely hungry: with a kind of devouring, none-selective hunger, as if already feeling the need to stock up now for hard times ahead. This was one of the hungry mornings, when she was glad Richard was not about to witness her greed.

The first egg plopped perfectly out of its shell into the pan: the ball of orange yolk held firmly in a strong white. The second fell out in a runny, smelly, thin flow, yolk and white already mingled, leaving the inside of the shell stained a yellowy green, and spread across the bottom of the pan with unbelievable speed, so that the first egg was contaminated.

Liffey's heart beat: her hand flew to her mouth. She knew beyond doubt that Mabs had sent a message of ill-will. Her earlier doubt of Mabs had been transitory: had been washed away by civility, smiles and cups of tea. And as Richard had pointed out, to ask a barely pregnant woman to witness the delivery of a dead calf may be tactless, but can hardly be called a conspiracy. And he had laughed, and Liffey had tried, and managed, to laugh too.

The reasonable part of Liffey told her that she was being absurd, that an addled egg sent by a neighbour is a mistake, not an attack; she assured herself that Mabs had no reason to dislike her, that what had passed between her and Tucker was over, secret, and of no consequence; and that Mabs was truly the friend she seemed. The other unreasonable part of Liffey cried out in wild alarm, and would not be pacified. Her sins would find her out.

Liffey was not accustomed to being unfaithful. She did not suffer, as did many of her married women friends, from sudden overwhelming sexual passions for this inappropriate person or that. She was not practiced, as they were, in the arts of forgetting, and self-justification and mendacity. Liffey tried to forget, and could not. She tried to justify and failed. She wanted to tell Richard, but the longer the time that passed between the event and the confession, the more difficult that became: and the more occasions on which she and Richard, Mabs and Tucker were in the same room, sharing the same conversation, the same meal, the more implicit deceit there must be in her silence, and the more difficult it was to break.

It came to Liffey that she and Mabs were linked, through Tucker, in the mind, in a more compelling and complex way than ever she and Tucker had been in the flesh. It flitted through her consciousness that this was perhaps what Mabs had intended, but so fleetingly the notion did not take root, did not settle, did not open itself up for contemplation. Liffey continued to feel uneasy, as people do, when clues are offered, and in the interests of peace of mind and self respect, ignored.

Liffey walked to Poldyke and rang Richard from the phone-box there; and Miss Martin graciously allowed them to speak.

'Richard,' said Liffey, 'do you think Mabs could be a witch?'

Now Richard was in a meeting with a marketing man who wanted money to set up a feasibility study on the subject of community salinity centres, which he, Richard, could not recommend. When Liffey asked her question he already felt much practised in patience, and answered politely and quietly.

'No, Liffey, I don't. What are your reasons for suggesting it?'

'She sent up some rotten eggs this morning, saying they were fresh.'

'Liffey,' said Richard, reasonably, 'it is hard, even for a farmer's wife, to know what is going on inside an egg.'

Liffey accepted Richard's version of events; she was a stay-at-home wife: she had already begun to believe he knew best. She looked at the weather from out of her window: he journeyed into strange places, and knew many things, and understood them all. 'If you don't mind, Liffey,' he said. 'I am rather busy,' so she put the telephone down, and he reproved Miss Martin mildly for putting through a telephone call while he was in a meeting. Miss Martin wept secretly because he had reproved her, but her heart leapt at this rebuff of Liffey. Perhaps, she thought, he was at last beginning to see Liffey for what she was. Foolish, empty and useless.

Carol, in the telephone exchange, dialled through to Mabs to report.

Later in the morning Mabs came up to Liffey and said she did hope the eggs had been all right; one of the hens had been laying outside the nesting box and Audrey had found the cache and not told her until after Tucker had come up with them.

Mabs smiled and chatted about husbands and elm trees and babies and said it was high time Liffey went to see the doctor, wasn't it, and Liffey agreed, and realised she was being silly about Mabs, who was a good friend, just sometimes tactless.

'What was all that about witches?' asked Richard at the weekend.

'Just a silly idea,' said Liffey. 'One gets silly ideas when pregnant.'

Mabs asked them over for supper.
'Let's not go,' said Liffey. 'We haven't really got all that much in common.'
But Richard wanted to go.
'You wanted to live in the country,' said Richard. 'I would have thought you could find plenty in common. It's not as if you were the greatest intellect in the world, Liffey.'

He had come home on Friday, resisting the temptation to stay over with Bella for a smoked salmon festival, because he had been a little worried by his brief and surprising exchange with Liffey on the telephone. Now, since she seemed perfectly well and cheerful, he resented having made the sacrifice. He found it difficult to wind down on Friday evenings; he found himself looking round for people to confide in, or chivvy, or engage in argument or sexual provocation, while Liffey wanted him to sit quietly and stroke her hair, as if they were some still-life of a young married couple: by Saturday he wanted to do nothing but sit, and recover, while Liffey wanted him to be out mowing or digging and painting, and on Sunday he waited for the evening, passing the time with the Sunday papers, so that he could return to London, and real life.

It would be better, he told himself when Mory and Helen were eased out of the apartment and Liffey and he were together again. He would not need Bella or Miss Martin then. He would not have to justify his infidelities by finding fault with Liffey. He could still see some kind of future for them both – even a rosy one – it was just the present he found difficult, and in particular Friday evenings.

'You're never at your nicest on Fridays,' observed Liffey.
'I'm tired,' he said.
'But not too tired to go up to Mabs and Tucker?'
'No,' said Richard.

There was something different about Richard these days, thought Liffey. A kind of snap of power; a glint of ice behind the boyish eyes: she saw that he might indeed become something significant in his organisation. She was not sure she wanted that. They were to have roamed together, hand in hand for ever, through the long tangled grasses of life.

She sat at Mabs' dinner table and felt frail, and rather ill, and tired, while Richard and Tucker talked about fertilisers, about which Richard was surprisingly knowledgeable, and milk yields, and Mabs urged Liffey to eat up the gristly, fatty lumps of pork in her plateful of meat stew. Richard thought how peaky Liffey looked, and had a sudden longing for Miss Martin's solid plumpness. He caught Liffey's eye, and she smiled at him, and there was a quality of sadness in her smile, as if she mourned a lost innocence.

Resolutions

'Bella,' said Richard, later in the week, 'all this is getting on top of me. It has to stop. It's not as if it were love.'
Bella just laughed. It was not easy to hurt Bella. She sat on top of him, breasts full and firm, swaying backwards and forwards calmly and slowly and smoking a cigarette, which he supposed was ridiculous but nevertheless appealed to him.
'If it were love,' said Bella, 'I wouldn't be doing it. Love hurts. This is just sex.'
Richard's feelings were wounded. He thought she ought to love him. He thought that her not loving him might be dangerous, making him more inclined to love her. He would wait until she loved him and then, having given her back a whole range of feelings she had forgotten that she had, would quietly and gently leave. That was what a man could, and did, do for an older woman.

He could wait until Miss Martin was out of love with him,

and then quietly and gently leave her. That was what a kindly man did, when the object of someone else's unrequited love. Richard wanted to do his best for everyone.

Mr. and Mrs. Lee-Fox rang Richard and said they'd pay for Liffey to have her baby as a private patient, so she didn't have to go through the ordeal of a public ward.

It was a light, friendly, easy telephone conversation: one parent on each of two telephone extensions. Richard knew it had taken them a good week of urgent, desperate, anxious conversation, planning and sleeplessness, to achieve this ease, and unanimity. So major decisions had always been dropped into his life. First closed doors, raised voices kept determinedly low: the feeling of agitation and argument in the house, then bombshells presented like grapenuts at breakfast. You're going to boarding school. We're going away: you're to stay with Aunt Betty. We've written to your school: you're having extra tutoring.
'Not in front of the child,' the Lee-Foxes had agreed on their honeymoon – both having been the victims of naked parental conflict. Never in front of the children. Our child, as it turned out to be. Had it been children, such resolutions might have been abandoned.

Richard, at his office, was a great protagonist of open decision making. His every thought, his every conclusion, his every action was recorded by Miss Martin, and circulated throughout the department. Never, thought Miss Martin, was there an office from which streamed so many memos and minutes.

'We'll hide nothing from our child,' Richard said to Liffey on one of the rare occasions he spoke about their coming baby. 'We won't let happen to it what happened to me.'

He passed on the news of his parents' offer to Liffey.
'Have it privately?' Liffey was unenthusiastic, thus surprising Richard. 'No. I'd rather have it like anyone else. I don't want to be thought special. I'm not.'

So then Richard had to ring his parents back, and in refusing their offer sound both ungracious and ungrateful.

'No,' said Bella, darkly, nibbling Richard's ear. 'I don't think this is the dawn of social conscience in Liffey. I think it is self-interest. In private wards you bleed to death by yourself. At least in the public wards there are other patients there to help you.'

'You're not at all nice about Liffey,' complained Richard. 'You should remember I'm married to her and be more tactful. Don't you feel in the least guilty about her? You are taking what is hers by rights.'

'No man is the rightful property of any woman, and vice versa.'

'But you're liberated. I thought Liffey was supposed to be your sister.'

'So she is. She is welcome to Ray any time she likes. Perhaps she would like to come and stay for the weekend?'

'I don't want Liffey anywhere near this house,' said Richard with some passion, but Bella curled her tongue around his, and although the texture of her flesh between his thighs did not have the resilience of Liffey's or the firm solidity of Miss Martin's, it had a kind of practiced feel, as if sexual impulses travelled a well-worn, easy path, coming and going with conviction, and marvelling at this, he stopped worrying about Liffey.

Miss Martin was not so outspoken when it came to her feelings towards Liffey. She confined her comments to ums and wells and I sees, but timed so that Richard would begin to see Liffey as Miss Martin saw her – as someone damaging to his professional, emotional, financial and physical well-being. I am one of the world's givers, said Miss Martin, by her very lack of sexual response, lying beneath Richard in hotel, or board room, or cloakroom; I am not one of the world's takers. Not like Liffey.

Liffey, whom she had never seen. Liffey, the boss's wife. Above her in status: the marriage partner, not the concubine. Concubines travel through the house by night, with long needles to plunge into the hearts of wives. They kill if they can, through love, spite and anger mixed.

Investigations

Eleven weeks. Liffey's baby had eyes beneath solid eyelids, a nose and rudimentary hands and feet. It weighed two grams. It lay safely in a sac of amniotic fluid. It rocked as Liffey walked.

Liffey felt that her baby was sufficiently rooted in the world to stand a little classification and investigation, of a scientific and medical nature, and made an appointment to see Dr. Southey on his weekly visit to Crossley.

Mabs kindly drove Liffey in, but mistook the time of the doctor's first appointment, and did not wait to check that the surgery was open, so that Liffey had to wait in the cold and rain for nearly an hour.

Dr. Southey, the same young man who had once nearly run Liffey over, in a car which appeared too big for him, was serious, kind and well trained in psychosomatic medicine.

When he reproached Liffey for not having attended earlier she made no reply, and he took her reluctance – how could she say that she had not wanted the baby frightened away – as a sign that she was unenthusiastic about her pregnancy. And the fact that she was cold to the touch reinforced his sense of unease. She was at first reluctant to be examined internally, and he suspected that she was neurotic.
'Why did you have to do that? What did you discover?' she demanded, afterwards.
'That your dates are about right, that there are no tumours,

or abnormalities of your pelvis, no major infections, no ulcers on your cervix, and that the size of the pelvic cavity, and its outlet, are reasonable.'
'You mean I have minor infections.'
He sighed.
'Giving information to pregnant women is impossible,' he said. 'All I mean is, if you have minor infections, I cannot detect them.'

She looked at him, strong chinned and mutinous, and he decided that he liked her. But that she was too thin.
'I want all the information you have,' she said. 'It's my body and my baby, and I'm not a fool.'
'I daresay not,' he said, 'but that won't stop you going into a grey depression because you misunderstood what I say. Better, in my experience, to say nothing. I took a cervical smear while I was about it.'
'What makes you think I have cancer?' she demanded, and he laughed, thinking his point well made. Presently she smiled, too, and after that they got on better.

He took blood from a vein.
'What's that for?'
'To see if you have syphilis.'
'Is it going to be like this all the time? One indignity after another?' she asked presently and he replied yes, that having babies was not the most dignified of processes. It was, he added, the ultimate triumph of the body over the mind.
'And of desire,' she said, 'over common sense.'
He thought she meant sexual desire, but she did not. She meant the overwhelming desire, of which she was now so conscious, to be part of the world about her: to be a woman like other women; to feel herself part of nature's process: to subdue the individual spirit to some greater whole. When, now, she knelt in the flower beds and crumbled the earth between her fingers to make a softer bed for a seedling, she felt she was the servant of Nature's kingdom, and not its mistress. And what sort of common sense was that?

He asked her what she did all day.

'I wait for my husband to come home at weekends,' she said. 'I wait for the baby to grow. I garden, I think, I listen to the radio. I walk up to see Mabs, my friend. Sometimes I'm sick, and then I wait to feel better. I do a lot of waiting.'

It occurred to him that she might have invented the husband, away in London; when she had gone he wrote a memo for the social worker to check.

Liffey Lee-Fox, whom everyone had envied, now the object of compassion and concern! Mabs, hearing about the social worker from Ellen, the doctor's receptionist, felt both gratified and annoyed. She asked Richard and Liffey over for Sunday lunch and added mistletoe-tansy to Richard's glass of nettle wine, and a distillation of pure ergot in Liffey's elderberry.

Audrey, the previous autumn, had searched the heads of rye stalks for the violet-black grains with their fishy, peculiar odour, where the ergot fungus had attacked the grain. She had done well, and her grandmother had been able to prepare quite a quantity of fluid ergot, and told Audrey to tell her mother to use sixty drops if she wished to abort a baby. Audrey wasn't listening properly and told Mabs to use six drops and the dose had in fact a beneficent effect on Liffey's system. She was twelve weeks pregnant; her period would in normal times have been due; she was suffering from a slight hormonal imbalance, and on the verge of losing some of the uterine lining – a process which, once started, can continue until all the contents of the uterine cavity, baby and all, have been lost. The few drops of ergot caused the uterus to contract, but mildly, and Liffey's condition being marginal, the bleeding stopped. Had her elderberry wine been fractionally more strongly dosed, the uterine contractions would have been powerful, and Liffey would have miscarried.

Richard, his entire system agitated by mistletoe poison, and mistaking his general restlessness for sexual ardour, wanted to make love to Liffey as soon as they arrived home, but she refused. Intercourse can be dangerous during pregnancy at the time of a threatened miscarriage; one contraction, as it were, leading to another, although at all other times in pregnancy is perfectly safe; an hour before the baby is born; an hour after.

Liffey, refusing Richard again! It made him angry. He went home on Sunday evening – he now thought of London as home – and went to Bella's bed, not she to the sofa in the study. Thus he defied the last of the proprieties. But where was Ray? At a discotheque with Karen – with one ear pierced by a silver earring. Bella had lost single ear-rings by the dozen over the decades – and could never bring herself to throw away the one remaining. Now Ray, following male teenage fashion, made good use of them.

Mabs waited, and waited in vain, for Liffey to come running with news of blood and disaster. She could not understand it. Mabs looked at another full moon, and at the Tor, riding the skies beneath it.

'I suppose it looks like a woman's breast,' she said to Tucker. 'And the tower on top is the nipple. Perhaps all those hippies are right, prancing about mother-naked up there. Do you think so, Tucker?'

Alterations

Tucker was not feeling so frightened of his wife. Mabs minded about his going with little Liffey, who was anyone's for the asking, and being able to make Mabs mind made Tucker powerful.

Mabs had noticed the change in Tucker and gone to her mother, who was already compounding a mixture of belladonna together with the bark and twigs of the Virginia Creeper which grew above Carol's door, to ensure Barry's fidelity and sobriety. But Tucker was not to know that.

Carol's husband Barry was as unaware as Tucker of the changes in his nature brought about by his wife. It was Carol's habit to mix foxglove pollen into the egg of his daily sandwiches, thus sparing herself from his sexual attentions. She herself took an infusion of lignum vitae – a hard and rare wood much imported from the West Indies in the nineteenth century and used for the axles of horse-drawn vehicles – dissolved in whisky, the better to respond to the advances of Dick Hubbard. The blacksmith at Poldyke had a few old lignum vitae timbers left, and in exchange for a kiss and a pinch and the promise of more was happy enough to let Carol scrape away at the black, hard, heavy wood. He could not see how it harmed him, let alone benefited her.

Carol and Mabs' mother was now teaching Audrey her skills and sometimes Mabs wondered if it was Audrey's doing that she did not get pregnant, in spite of the infusion of coca which she, Mabs, took daily, and which made her, sometimes, visionary; so that Glastonbury Tor swam towards her through the sky. Perhaps it was the coca, too, which gave her frequent rages a force which superseded the ordinary rules of cause and effect, and sent her perceptions a little beyond the ordinary, piercing extra deeply into the crust of reality.

Inside Mabs (1)

But coca or not, visions or not, Mabs did not become pregnant. Tucker's sperm swam obediently to meet her monthly ovum, and fertilised it well enough; the ovum dutifully developed the required choriomic villi with which to embed itself into the waiting uterine wall, but then proceeded with too laggardly a pace along the fallopian tube, arriving in the cavity of the uterus eight days after fertilisation instead of the required seven, and by that time had ignobly perished, for lack of a suitable foothold, or villihold.

It would require a very special drug to meet such a specific need, and the drug was not coca.

Inside Liffey (8)

Thirteen weeks. Liffey's waist thickened. She had to tug at her jeans to do them up. Her uterus was distending: the amniotic sac within measured four inches in diameter and the foetus was three inches long. The baby's face was properly formed: its body curled in an attitude of docility; resting, waiting, listening, growing. What it most needed now was time, which Liffey, by her love and caution, must supply.

Twenty-seven weeks to go. The most dangerous days were over, for the baby's organs had properly formed and no major congenital abnormality had become apparent – nor, now, were likely to – which might lead to miscarriage. Although the baby could still, of course, be expelled if the mother body for some reason or other rejected it – even though there was nothing in the baby's own ordination, as it were, to lead to this sorry conclusion. But any drugs or infections introduced into the mother's body would now have the barrier of the placental wall to cross and could harm only in extreme circumstances.

And there was, of course, the one great hazard to this baby's survival, still undiagnosed by the outside world, in the fact that the placenta, now fast forming, had lodged in the uterine wall beneath the foetus instead of to one side of it. For here the choriomic villi of the fertilised egg had clawed and stuck and now, where they had first attached, were developing with vast speed, into the complexity of the placenta, linking itself with arteries to the foetus, separating the mother's circulation from the baby's, selectively transfering to the baby oxygen, carbohydrates, fatty acids, proteins, amino acids, vitamins and essential elements, removing excreted products, carbon dioxide and urea for the mother to dispose of through her own system – but also, alas, by virtue of its unusual position, blocking the baby's eventual path to the outside world.

It was as if the fertilised egg, on its way out of Liffey's uterus, had grabbed its last chance: clung where it could and not where it ought. A lucky, hopeful, still surviving baby.

Upsets

Richard wrote to Liffey in the middle of the fifteenth week.

It's ridiculous, we really ought to get a telephone. I've been promoted and I can't even ring you to tell you! £60 extra a month! Of course tax will take £30, but never mind. When the baby comes at least we'll get an allowance for that. Only another six weeks, when the summer train services begin, and I'll come down mid-week as well as weekends.

Liffey cried. She had expected that Richard would commute every day once the summer came. So had he, once upon a time. But circumstances changed.

'I'm now Junior Product Manager on Beesnees Soup,' wrote Richard, in a letter which was delivered by Audrey, and bypassed Mabs:

It's a real challenge: the salinity factor has yet to be solved. It means a certain amount of travelling, to factories, sales conferences and so on, but at least all in this country. The jet-set life comes later! Darling, I'm afraid I have to be in Edinburgh this weekend, so do look after yourself. And please try and make some friends: you keep yourself much too much on your own. Shall I ask your mother to come down? I hope you're seeing something of Mabs and Tucker: they're real friends to you: you mustn't get all funny about them, the way you sometimes do. I'm enclosing £20 for food and so on. Now be careful and write down what you spend. You know what you're like. Love, in haste, Richard.

'Isn't Richard coming home this weekend?' asked Mabs that Saturday morning, bringing round a drop of cider for Richard to try. She and Tucker did not drink cider themselves, finding it a sour and disagreeable drink, but they knew that Richard delighted in it, detecting species of apples and vintages as he drank, with an interest and knowledge that country people seldom displayed.
'Richard's away on business. He's been promoted. Isn't that wonderful?'
'But what about the cider?' Mabs seemed quite disappointed.
'I'd like to try it,' offered Liffey.
'It wouldn't do you any good,' said Mabs, 'in your condition.'
But Liffey insisted, and tasted it, there and then, and presently, quite liking it, drank a glass or two more, and later that night had an uprush of sexual desire which disconcerted her. Had Tucker put in an appearance, she would have unlocked the door to him, but Tucker did not: Mabs entwined her long legs around Tucker's middle and held him fast.

While Richard, in and out of Miss Martin, passed through the wilds of Cumberland on the way to Edinburgh, Bella and

Ray went together to a newly opened fish restaurant in Fulham.

'There's nothing wrong with what I feel for Karen,' said Ray. 'I don't want you to think that, Bella. I don't want to upset you.'

'The only thing that upsets me,' said Bella, 'is your taste. Why don't you fuck her and get it over?'

Bella rose and left the restaurant, but not before slipping twelve oysters into a plastic bag.

'Where are you taking those?'

'Home to the children.'

Bella forgot to put the oysters in the refrigerator when she got home and left them on the kitchen table. The cat, an instant replacement of the one run over, ate them and was found ill to the point of death the next morning, and had to be taken by Helga to the vet. It was a journey of two miles but Bella would not let Helga take a taxi. She had to walk.

'The vet's bill's going to be bad enough, let alone a taxi!'

'Don't think I'm going to pay the bloody vet's bill,' said Ray to Bella, but absently, without acrimony. Really, he could think of little else than Karen: her long, somehow unformed legs, her plump, smooth face, still unmarked by woe and indecision: her little hands: the way she moved about the world, choosing between one happy option and the next: living by choice and not necessity.

The cat died in the carrier bag on the way to the vet. Helga did not cry, but Tony and Tina did, when they heard the news.

'Supposing it had been us?' asked Tony. 'The oysters were meant for us.'

Everything seemed upset that weekend. Routines were altered and not for the better.

That Saturday night Carol told her husband that she was going over to Mabs, and made him a nice cup of tea before she went. He did not drink the tea, since the shepherd's pie she'd made had g.ven him indigestion – the onion was still raw, the mince lumpy and the flour thickening barely cooked – and as a result did not fall asleep over Match of the Day. He heard mice nibbling and rustling and rang Mabs to ask to speak to Carol, and Tucker answered and said no, Carol hadn't been round. Funny, thought Barry, but quite soon Carol came back and said she hadn't gone up to Mabs after all but had stopped by her Mum's, who was having trouble with a bee swarm. The fright, or suspicion, or unease, or whatever it was which had churned round in his heavy, kindly, trusting mind, stirred him strangely, and he paused in the middle of his swift, embarrassed, usually silent love-making and asked his wife if she loved him.

'Of course I do,' she said.

'Idiot,' said Mabs to Tucker, when she finally got back to bed. 'I had to run all the way down to the estate office. Haven't I got enough to do?'

'I'm not going to tell lies for anyone,' said Tucker. 'Especially not for your sister, who is a married woman but having it off with Dick Hubbard.'

'She fancies him,' said Mabs. 'She can't help herself. And Dick Hubbard's more use to us than Barry ever will be. Thank your lucky stars it's you I fancy, Tucker.'

'It'd better be,' said Tucker, 'or I'd knock his bloody head off, whoever he was. Yours, too.'

He would have, as well.

In other rooms at Cadbury Farm Mabs' children slept, uneasily. They were left-over children; out-grown their usefulness as Mabs' babies, left to get on with their lives as best they could. Eddie, of all of them, wouldn't accept his fate. He would sidle up to his mother and muzzle into her crutch, as if trying to get back in. All it did was disgust her. She disliked him for his soppy ways, his running nose, his watery eyes and the dull reproach therein. The others were tougher, or more sensible, and kept their distance and grabbed the baked beans, and shut their eyes and minds to night-time visions of strange people who belonged to long ago. There had been a farm on the site when the Romans came, and uncooperative people there who had to be killed to be quieted, but still weren't quiet.

To Tucker, the children were part of the landscape, like the cows and the farm, and the dogs. He hoped that when the boys grew bigger they would help on the farm. He did not see how the girls could be much use to him. Cattle were fed a carefully calculated amount in terms of cost and nourishment, in order to return a profit in milk and meat yield. Sometimes it cost too much to keep the animals alive, and then it was best to slaughter. You knew where you were with animals. But the girls just ate and ate and grew and grew and what return was there in that? Some other man would presently have the benefit of them. To nurture girls seemed to Tucker an absurd philanthropy.

Mabs slept. Tucker couldn't.
Better, thought Tucker, Mabs dreaming beside him, to satisfy the pleasure of begetting via some other man's purse – Liffey's body; Richard's income. Richard was a good enough man on a fine day in a rich season, but not much use when the cold wind blew. In the meantime there was something to be learned from Richard – the fresh wind of new ideas. He could feel them ruffling the surface of his mind. And such was Tucker's sense of mastery, via Liffey's body, Liffey's baby, (which he had come to assume, if only from Mabs' attitude, was his) that he could condescend to Richard, secretly; while Richard condescended to him, openly. Tucker thought he would visit Liffey again, before long, so she did not forget.

Tucker grew sleepy. He saw the world was composed of virgin ground: of furrows waiting to be ploughed. Seed to be dropped, watered, nourished: then to grow. That was the wonder of it. Perhaps if Mabs was to have her baby, visiting Liffey again was not a good idea. Perhaps a man used his fertility up: burying himself too often in already fertilised ground might weaken his capacity. Tucker would resist the temptation, which was, after all, not the temptation of the flesh, but the temptation of laughing at Richard. Who spoke well, wrote well, thought well, earned well, dressed well, but could not look after a wife.

Tucker laughed and slept.

The sun, rising in the east, sent streams of early light westward and caught the Tor in brilliance, beneath lowering dawn clouds.

Sixteen Weeks

The baby weighed five ounces and was six inches long. It had limbs with working joints, and finger and toes, each with its completing nail. It was clearly male. It lay curled in its amniotic sac, legs crossed, knees up towards its lowered head, which it sheltered with little arms. Its lifeline, the umbilical cord, curled round from its stomach and into the nourishing placenta. The baby stirred, and moved, and exercised, according to its own will and not its mother's: a little being within a greater being, grown out of it, and from it, but now itself, no longer part of the greater whole. It moved, but Liffey could not detect the movements: she would have to wait another month or so for that.

It was time to see the doctor again. Liffey remarked on it to Mabs.

'You look healthy enough to me,' said Mabs.

'They like you to have a check-up every month,' said Liffey.

'They like to claim their various allowances,' said Mabs, 'and keep their clinics open and their files full of forms, and if they're men they like peeking up your insides. Is it Dr. Southey you have? Tucker won't let me see him. They got him for indecent assault up in London. That's why he's working down here.'

The baby laughed, amused. Liffey heard.

'And when you think of that thalidomide business,' said Mabs, 'I think it's best to keep out of their way. Those poor little babies with flippers. Baby kicking yet?'
'Not yet.'

All the same Liffey used the telephone to make the appointment and Mabs was annoyed. Liffey was proving more difficult to control than she had thought possible. The way to bring her back to heel, of course, would be to send Tucker down again, but that was now out of the question. Mabs felt hollow and cold in her insides. She missed the movement of the kicks and shruggings of an unborn child. Tucker filled her up a little, from time to time, but it was not enough. And if Tucker went to Liffey, ploughed about in those already warm and packed places, she might find herself trying to kill the baby by killing the mother. And that she recognised would be wicked. The baby, being Tucker's was hers to kill. Liffey was not.

Mabs offered to drive Liffey into the surgery.
Liffey declined.
'The walk will do me good.'
'Suit yourself,' said Mabs, and Liffey felt she had behaved ungraciously. Liffey felt it was important to stay on the right side of Mabs. She now looked to her, as a pregnant girl will to an older and more experienced woman, for advice, company and reassurance. She recognised that the advice was often bad, and the reassurance marred by a blunt tactlessness, but she did not doubt Mabs' good will.

All the same, if she could help it, she did not travel in Mabs' car. Mabs' driving frightened her, and the way she was jolted over the rutted tracks made her worry for the baby, and there was something about the car itself which worried her. She thought it was haunted.

Cadbury Farm, too, was haunted, but in a more positive

way. It was suffused with a sense of activity, both past and present. It had sprung out of the ground two thousand or so years ago, had fallen down, been raised again, been added to, a new beam put here, a rotten one replaced there, the generations passing the while; children born, others dying, genes shifting and sorting all the time within, languidly, but to a steady, beating, almost cheerful purpose. But the Pierce's car had none of this richness. It sopped up the energies of its occupants – Tucker's fixed and narrow will, Mabs' flourishing discontent, the children's sly and secretive passions – and all to no purpose, except the eventual disintegration of plastic upholstery and the rusting of metal parts.

Dr. Southey thought Liffey looked puffier and heavier than she ought. She seemed tired and anxious.
'Wouldn't you be better off back in London, with your husband?'
'There are problems about that.'
'What sort?'
'Oh, just practical. Not matrimonial.' She believed it, too.
'Anyway I love the country.'
'In what way?'
'It makes me feel more important.' She had the capacity to surprise him. He looked forward to her visits.

She lay on the couch, her stomach bare. Her uterus, normally hidden away in the pelvis, had now risen to a point halfway between her pubic mound and her umbilicus. His hand felt it out. He thought her dates were correct: the uterus was at the expected height for sixteen weeks.
'I have pains in my side,' she said, 'low down.'
'They'll go away.'
'What are they?'

The pains were caused by the shrinking of the corpus luteum of her ovaries – no longer required to produce the progesterone which had inhibited the shedding of the uterus wall during the first months of her pregnancy. The placenta had taken over the task. It was a sign that all was well, not bad. He said as much.

'You're sure it's nothing wrong?' she insisted.
'Of course it's not.'
'I do worry about it. I'm not used to worrying. I used to leave it to Richard to do the worrying. He always worried about his parents, if there was nothing else. Now he seems to have stopped and I've started.'
She laughed, rather nervous and embarrassed, reminding him of a hen gone broody, changing its nature from something greedy and silly, into something prepared to die rather than expose its eggs to harm, looking out at the world with a stubborn, desperate wisdom. And for what? To lead ten fluffy chicks back into the hen coop – and forget them a week or so later.
'Is there any treatment?' Liffey asked.
'The passage of time,' he said. 'Come and see me next week if you're still worried.'

Liffey went home.

The pains went. Others came. Liffey's ovaries were enlarged and developed a series of small cysts, which may have accounted for some of the fleeting pains. Her vaginal secretions increased; she passed water frequently.
'Yes, but why?' she made a special journey to ask him.
'I don't know,' he said, impatiently, 'these things just happen to pregnant ladies.'
He was busy: he had two patients with terminal cancer. He wished he could keep his respect for pregnant women. They seemed to him to belong so completely to the animal kingdom that it was almost strange to hear them talk.

The weather turned cold. A wet west wind blew day after day and took the blossom from the trees.

Liffey's body, which normally contained ten pints of blood, now had some twelve pints coursing through it, the better to supply her uterus and markedly swelling breasts, but diluting the concentration of red cells therein. Liffey became anaemic.

Mabs knew Liffey was anaemic because Carol's friend worked in the laboratory at Glastonbury and did the blood counts. The doctor prescribed Liffey iron tablets, and she took them, although they gave her indigestion.

Mabs felt that time was working for her. Mabs comforted herself with the thought that perhaps all she need do was wait, and the baby would leave of its own free will, and natural justice would be served.

'Why are you hiccuping?' Richard asked.
Sometimes he worried for Liffey's health, in case the punishment of the Gods was diverted from him to her. He was having altogether too good a time.
'It's the iron pills. I don't think I'll take them any more.'
'Don't be irresponsible, Liffey. You ought to be thinking of the baby, not yourself.'

Richard had a few bad weekends after that. His skies clouded over, for no apparent reason. Nothing had changed, of course, except his attitude to them. He was concerned for Liffey and her baby, and now his concern afflicted him. There were enough things in the world to worry about, surely, without the gratuitous addition of another? Parents, job, income, the car, accommodation; worries heaped in upon him one upon another: wives, surely, were meant to decrease the load of anxiety, not increase it with anaemia, with hiccuping, and puffy eyes, and the threat of the thing within? Miss Martin implied as much, all week. Hard to throw it off, at weekends.

The curse of the irrational, moreover, descended upon him. He dug the garden, he planted peas and beans; he hammered and painted when he meant to do nothing but rest and relax and compare cider and home-made wines with Tucker. He saw that the chains of fatherhood were already around him: he was preparing for the baby. As well be a humble cock-sparrow lurching to and fro, to and fro, straw in the beak for the nest: exhausted, bored and foolish, helpless in the face of his nature. Richard pulled a muscle in his back, and blamed Liffey.

Bella sent him to an osteopath, who made it better, and the next Friday Richard returned to Honeycomb Cottage with a car loaded with food and drink, and was loving and kind and considerate.

'We can't go on living like this,' he said. 'We don't see nearly enough of each other. But, oh, Liffey, London is such a terrible place.' And he reeled off tales of vandalism and violence: a colleague's wife mugged on her way home; someone's daughter's friend raped: someone else's apartment burgled: lead pollution in the air: the pale faces of children: the grey look of the elderly.

Liffey's words, once upon a time. Now Richard's.

Mabs and Tucker came over for a drink. Richard sat with his arm round Liffey, and Liffey, blooming in his new-found protection, wore a smock and looked really pregnant.

'You are looking well,' said Mabs. 'How's the anaemia?'
'Much better,' said Liffey.
'Wonderful,' said Mabs. 'It's the elderberry wine's done that.'
Mabs gave Richard a bottle of nettle wine to take back to London.
'Give some to your secretary,' said Mabs. 'Perhaps it will sweeten her.'
'Take more than drink to sweeten Miss Martin,' said Richard automatically.

Richard kept his second appointment with the osteopath, and the back pain returned. He decided to spend the next weekend in London. Ray had gone off to Brussels on a free fish-tasting excursion for two, but taking Karen with him instead of Bella, who had a dentist's appointment she couldn't miss. Bella was left at home, angry, which meant sexually extremely active: and Miss Martin's Jeff was also away for the weekend at an Encounter Therapy course, which meant that Miss Martin was free all Friday night, and her mother staying with relatives, so there was an empty house available for their love-making. Richard told Bella that he was with Liffey on Friday night, Miss Martin that he was with Liffey on Saturday night, and Liffey that he was at a weekend conference on permitted saline additives. Unfortunately, as often happened when he stayed away from home, his potency was unaccountably diminished and both Miss Martin and Bella were disappointed. Moreover Miss Martin had looked forward to making him a proper English breakfast, with bacon, eggs and sausages, and not the bread and jam and coffee with which Bella and Liffey apparently fobbed him off – but Richard only toyed with the plateful, and left the sausage altogether, and she felt he found her home rather ordinary and suburban. But of course he had hurt his back, and that clearly affected his enthusiasms – sexual, culinary and aesthetic.

Richard blamed the osteopath.

Trouble

Mabs thought she might be pregnant. Her period was late. She felt heavy. She brought the children home iced lollies, and took Eddie to the dentist and let him sit on her knee in the waiting room.

Then her period started.

Storms clashed and banged around the Tor. Tucker laughed and Mabs' eyes flashed. Mabs went out with her mother before dawn and gathered wild arum, cherry laurel and henbane, in the grey light. Or rather Mabs pointed and her mother picked; Mabs was bleeding and wasn't supposed to touch. In any case old women make better herbalists than young. Mabs' mother chanted Hail Marys as she picked.

'Do shut up, Mum,' complained Mabs. 'That's the wrong sort of mumbo-jumbo.'

'It'll do,' said Mabs' mother. She didn't look like a witch, any more than did her daughter. She had a round, lined face and open features and wore spectacles which swept up at the sides in the fashion of thirty years ago. She was proud of her straight stature and good figure, wore tweed skirts and ironed blouses and went to Keep-Fit classes.

'And what are you up to, anyway,' she asked of her daughter, 'that the Blessed Virgin wouldn't like?'

Mabs smiled.

'Just putting a few things right, Mum,' she said.

'Because if you want to get pregnant,' said Mabs' mum, 'this is the best way I can think of, of making sure you're not. And what do you want more children for? You don't look after the ones you've got, and you're too old anyway. Now stop snivelling, or I'm going straight home back to bed.'

And indeed, Mabs stood up to her large knees in the long grass of the graveyard and snivelled, because her mother was being unkind. She might have been anyone's daughter.

Mabs persuaded Audrey to do the distillation, and added a whole half-glassful to a bottle of the previous year's elder-berry wine, and gave it to Tucker to take over to Honeycomb Cottage. Liffey would not be the only one to drink it, but she was beyond caring.

The six or seven drops of the distillation which Liffey swallowed did indeed lower her blood pressure, but without harming the baby. Her blood pressure, as the pregnancy advanced, and the level of progesterone in her body dimin-ished, was returning to normal. She no longer felt so faint, nor so disinclined to stand for long in one position, as the circulation of blood through her various tissues proceeded more normally, although the blood vessels were not quite so relaxed as before. She was, in fact, beginning to feel well. Her complexion was smooth, her eyes glowed, her hair shone; she moved more lightly: she flung her arms around Richard; she bubbled and burbled and overflowed; she drank the glass of elderberry and felt obliging and friendly.

'How was she?' Mabs asked Tucker on his return.
'Looking better everyday,' said Tucker.
'Country air, country food, and country wine,' said Mabs. But he did not trust her.
'Mind you be nice to her,' Tucker said. 'She's done you no harm.'

Mabs was heating up hen food on the stove, and a musty smell filled the kitchen. The hens were off-lay again, and warm food for a day or two often started them off again. He came up behind her and ran his hands up her sides.
'She's pregnant and I'm not,' said Mabs, not looking at him. It was a confidence, and a question, and contained no threat.
'It might be,' said Tucker cautiously, 'that you're your own worst enemy when it comes to that. Takes a soft and gentle woman to have a baby, not one full of hate.'

She thought he might be right, and resolved to try leaving Liffey's baby alone for a while. Liffey was mid-pregnancy in any case, and the baby harder to shift now than at any time, and she could always return to the kill later on, if it did not work.

Time passed. Liffey had to use a safety pin to do up her skirt. She had gained twelve pounds: she had lost weight, as many women do, in the first three months of pregnancy, but the change in her diet from expensive protein foods to cheap carbohydrate bulk, had more than compensated. The extra twelve pounds, of course, included the weight of the foetus, the placenta and the amniotic fluid, and the increase in the circulating blood. Liffey could expect, through the course of the pregnancy, to add about twenty-eight pounds to her normal weight. Now, at four-and-a-half months, she had added eight pounds more than Dr. Southey thought proper, but on the other hand her colour was better, her face less strained and the quiet life she led for five days of the week did her more good than the two weekend days with Richard could do her ill.

Richard's solicitor, in the meanwhile, wrote three more letters to Mory, which Mory did not even see, as Helen now destroyed all letters as they came through the letterbox. The kittens loved playing with paper shreds. Richard's solicitor, moreover, was having domestic troubles, his files were in confusion, and migraine headaches sometimes kept him away from his office for weeks at a time. He was a friend of Richard's father, had once known Richard's mother well and felt headaches coming on whenever he stretched out his hand to Richard's file, thus considerably delaying Richard's cause.

'Everything's under control,' he would say, whenever Richard rang, or Miss Martin, asking for news, 'these things can't be hurried. Tenancy disputes always take time.'
'Is that what we're in?' Richard asked, troubled. 'A tenancy dispute? I thought they were in illegal possession?'
'I know what I'm doing, young man,' said Richard's solicitor, merrily enough, but with a hint of asperity behind the merriment, putting Richard properly in his place. And when Liffey asked Richard if he trusted his solicitor, Richard replied, 'I know what I'm doing, Liffey. Tenancy disputes always take time. And he's an excellent solicitor. My father swears by him.' So that Liffey, in her turn, was put in her place.

Mory's application for a job in Argentina went unanswered.

Miss Martin's mother read an article aloud to her daughter, over tea. Its title was 'The Sticky Snare of the Married Man', and Miss Martin was worried enough to say to Richard, 'This can't go on.'

'What can't go on?' he asked, blankly, and she felt at once that she had been presumptuous, and fell into silence, and was the more easily manipulated afterwards.

She did suggest to Jeff, however, in desperation, that if he really wanted it, she would sleep with him before their marriage. But he said he wanted their married life to begin properly, and that he valued her purity very much, and explained what she had not known before, that his mother had been a 'wild' woman and disgraced the family very much, and he was determined to have as a wife someone who would not repeat that sordid pattern. So she apologised, and felt even more guilty than before, and interpreted that emotion as a new flux of love for Richard.

Mabs sat at the kitchen table, and glowered. The room was cold, although outside the sun shone. The cows went off milk, the hens stopped laying again, one of the mangy dogs lay down at the end of his chain and died. Mabs dragged the body inside the house, and wept with pity and frustration mixed. She laid it upon the kitchen table, considered it, rang up her mother to ask if she had any use for a dead dog, and her mother said no, but Carol might; and Carol sent Barry over in the van to fetch it back. Before he came Audrey stole a few of the coarse hairs from beneath its tail and taped them across Eddie's ear, which had started discharging as a result of Mabs' frequent cuffs.

Mabs contemplated the nature of a world which could kill a dog she loved, but keep Liffey's baby, whom she hated, safe.

Mabs decided that being good was no way to become happy, let alone pregnant.

Visitors

Madge came to visit Liffey. She thought it was expected of her. She came by taxi from the station, and fretted at the extravagance. She thought the thatch was unhygienic and the rooms damp, but grudgingly admired the view. She said that Liffey should not be pregnant, in as much as she had no job, no training, and now no likelihood of getting one.
'Richard will look after me,' said Liffey.
'I'm sure I don't know where you get it from,' said Madge, sourly.
'Get what?'
'Naïvety.'
'It isn't naïvety. It's trust and love.'
'There's always Social Security,' said Madge, 'when the money runs out, which I suppose it will soon. Do you keep check?'
'Of course,' lied Liffey.

Madge conceded that Liffey looked well; she advised her not to eat fish, which contained a great deal of cadmium and other poisons, and asked her if she were not worried about fall-out from Hinkley Point, a nuclear power station some twenty miles distant.
'I used to worry about that kind of thing,' said Liffey. 'Not any more.'

Mabs came round with damson wine, which Madge at first refused. Then she accepted, and sipped the deep red, sticky mixture.
'It hasn't fermented out yet,' said Madge, firmly. 'It has a bitter edge which will soften in time.'
And she poured her glassful back into the bottle and did the same for Liffey's.

'I see you're not drinking any yourself,' she said to Mabs.
'Doctor's orders,' said Mabs, vaguely.

'I think you're very foolish to drink that stuff, Liffey,' said
Madge, when Mabs had gone. 'Goodness knows what it does
to the baby.'
'I'm afraid you offended her,' said Liffey, reproachfully.
'She's my only neighbour and I'm dependent on her, and
she's very proud of her home-made wine.'
'I didn't like her and I didn't trust her,' said Madge. 'I get
girls like her at school sometimes. Wherever they are, there's
trouble. Heavy girls with good legs. They cheat at exams and
steal from cloakrooms and if they offer you chocolates, you
can be sure they're stale.'

But Liffey took Madge's advice in the wrong way, and felt
that her mother, far from trying to protect her, was
attempting to upset and worry her. She did not wish to be
told bad news, only to hear good news. It was a tendency
apparent enough in normal times, but emphasised now that
she was pregnant. Disaffection made her bold.

'Mother,' said Liffey, startling Madge. 'Will you tell me who
my father is?' It had been laid down between them long ago
that Liffey did not enquire into the circumstance of her
birth. Enough, Madge's look had always said, that I had you;
that I introduced you into the world, with considerable
difficulty, and without any great pleasure to myself.
'It's only natural to want to know,' said Liffey, into Madge's
silence.
'It might be better for you not to,' said Madge, filling Liffey
with instant fear, that her father had been monstrous or
deformed, or that she was the result of rape and that her child
would inherit criminal tendencies. She had told Richard, for
lack of any other way of accounting for herself, that her
father had been a student friend of her mother's, who had
died in an accident shortly after her, Liffey's, conception:
and Richard had amended that part of it to 'shortly after the
wedding' for his parent's ears.

Lying, which had once seemed an essential part of Liffey's life; the very base, indeed, on which it was founded – though a changing, shifting base, the consistency of an underfilled bean bag – now seemed inappropriate. The baby gave her courage: compounded the reality of her existence. She could not be wished away, or willed away.

'I want to know,' persisted Liffey, and heard the baby murmur its approval, and leap in delight. She put her hand on her stomach. 'The baby moved,' she said to her mother. 'Moved for the first time.'

'I expect it's indigestion,' said Madge, but Liffey knew it wasn't. The flutter came again.

'He was an actor,' said Madge. 'He assured me he was infertile. He'd had mumps when he was sixteen. When he made me pregnant he refused to believe it, thought I was trying to pull a fast one, and wouldn't have anything to do with you or me. Mumps in men makes only a very small minority infertile, of course, but you know what men are. They believe what they want to believe, and expect you to do the same.'

'What sort of actor was he?'

'Shakespearean.'

'Was he a good actor?'

'He certainly thought so. I didn't. He was the sweet-faced, curly-haired kind. Heterosexual, but who'd have thought it. He was very charming, and very boring. You know what actors are.'

'How old was he?'

'Twenty-five.'

It seemed strange to Liffey to have found a father who was younger than she was.

'You didn't want to get rid of me?'

'I did,' said Madge brusquely, 'but it was illegal and expensive and dangerous, so I didn't.'

'Could I get in touch with him? If he didn't want a child, he might want a grandchild.'

'I doubt it very much,' said Madge. 'He went to Canada to avoid a paternity suit.'

Madge left on the Friday afternoon – missing Richard by a few hours.

'Much as I'd love to see him,' she lied, 'I have a pile of examination papers waiting. I must get back. And they may have forgotten to feed the cat.'

Liffey knew that the minute she was out of sight she would be out of her mother's mind: she realised that children do not forget mothers, but that mothers forget children. That Madge had done her duty by her: had manfully taken the consequences of misfortune, had seen them through, and then put the whole thing from her mind – in the same way as, year after year, she would put a whole Upper Sixth out of mind, as it passed from the school into adult life, and out of hers.

Liffey waved her mother goodbye and knew that the parting was for ever. They would see each other again, no doubt, but that small part of Madge which had been mother, had been firmly swallowed up by the rest, and ceased to be mother.

Movement

Eighteen weeks. The doctor laid a stethoscope to Liffey's swelling abdomen, and she heard the beat of her baby's heart. 160 a minute.

Liffey, listening, wore on her face an expression of satisfaction, gratification and calm.

'What are you so pleased about?' asked the doctor. 'Anyone would think it was your doing. All you have to do is just exist. The baby uses you to grow. You don't grow it.'

Liffey knew better. She hugged her baby in her heart. Ah, *we*: we have done it. We are doing it. It is all going to be all right. Listen to the heart; there it is, the pulsing of the Universe. It never stops. It is available to those who listen.

'I felt the baby move,' she said.
'Indigestion,' he said. 'It's too early.'

Richard brought his washing home every weekend. Bella had told Helga not to do it any more.
'Liffey has nothing better to do,' said Bella, 'and you have, Helga.'
Bella's jealousy was spreading: ripples from the central pool of her feelings towards Karen. She did not mind Helga's eyes so often upon Richard, but objected to Richard's upon Helga.
'Women are so wonderful, so extraordinary,' Richard would keep saying. 'All so different.'

'We are half the human race,' snapped Bella, but he failed to get her point, and she ruthlessly sorted through the washing baskets and hauled out all Richard's underpants and sweaters and vests and shirts and socks and jeans and shoved them in a pillowcase and sent them back to Liffey.

Liffey washed them lovingly, treated them with softener, and dried them in the wind and sun, and ironed them and folded them; and presently Miss Martin, Bella and Helga were all to admire her handiwork. Miss Martin the whiteness of his shirt as he divested it, Bella the softness of a sock, and Helga the smoothness of vest.

Liffey looked in the mirror and was surprised. She was darker than she remembered. The increased pigmentation which accompanies pregnancy was more noticeable in her than it would have been in a fairer person. Freckles, moles, nipples, all became darker; and the hair on her legs, usually so light as not to need removing, had become darker and more plentiful. Liffey noticed them with alarm, as she took off Richard's safety-pinned jeans and lay on the doctor's couch, knees up, legs apart, at the twentieth week.

He put on a fine rubber glove to perform the examination, and did it, as before, with a cool professionalism which belied any notion that it might count as a sexual assault. 'Do you have to do this again?' Liffey asked the doctor and he replied, 'Yes, mid-term.' But offered no further information and she did not ask. She had accepted his part in her pregnancy: the father's part.

Ellen, the doctor's receptionist let slip to Mabs how well Liffey was doing. The next day Mabs brought Liffey round a tonic, made, she said, with honey and rosemary, but containing also dried mushroom powder, which she did not mention. Liffey took a tablespoon every morning.

Twenty weeks. The baby moved, there could be no doubt of it. A pattering, pittering feeling, like the movement of butterfly wings. Extraordinary. She walked all the way to Poldyke to tell Dr. Southey.

But listen, doctor, we have the whole world here inside!

Liffey told him, too, that her mouth felt oddly dry. That he could not explain, nor did he understand it. Her haemoglobin count was high, yet she complained of listlessness, she was pale, and her eyes were dull. The doctor sent the health visitor up to visit Liffey. Mrs. Wild, a competent lady in her middle years, reported a quiet, clean, orderly household. No, there wasn't much food in the cupboards but then it was a long way from the shops. The husband worked away, but then so do many in rural districts. He came home at the weekends. Most weekends. The garden was beautifully tended. No phone, but neighbours were close at hand. Nothing to worry about.

The doctor worried about her, all the same. He would have asked her over to supper at home, but Liffey had no transport, and he could not find time to collect and deliver her himself, and his wife could not drive. Besides, where would it end? The world was full of listless young women.

He did not have the strength to give them all the kiss of life. Nevertheless, he did what he could for her. He persisted: he asked Mrs. Wild who the neighbours were.

'Tucker and Mabs Pierce,' said Mrs. Wild.

'Eddie's mother?'

'Eddie's just accident prone,' said Mrs. Wild, defensively. He did not comment. He studied Liffey's card.

'I know what it is,' he said, laughing. 'She's overlooked. Mabs Pierce is one of the Tree sisters.'

Tales of old Mrs. Tree filtered through to the surgery. She was reputed to have dosed her husband to death with a cure for rheumatism; to have made horses limp and hens go off-lay. A woman whose son had jilted Carol had lost her hand in a food press the day after news got out – crushed to a pulp, and injuries by crushing were, as everyone knew, witch's doing.

'Because the mother's a witch doesn't make the daughter one too,' said Mrs. Wild, who had been born in Poldyke, although trained elsewhere.

'I hope you don't believe in witches,' said the doctor, surprised.

'Of course not,' she said, saving herself.

'Just as well,' he said, 'or they might have power over you. Those who don't believe in them can't be harmed by them, and Liffey Lee-Fox is not the kind to believe in witches. So let's rule out overlooking, and find another reason why someone with a high haemoglobin count – up in the mid-eighties – should be pallid and listless.'

'Marital troubles,' said Mrs. Wild.

'Quite so,' said Dr. Southey.

He asked Liffey to come to the surgery every week, instead of every two weeks: the two-week arrangement was a measure of vague unease about her: the one week of something nearing anxiety. A visit a month is the normal arrangement in mid-pregnancy.

'He must be worried!' said Mabs, when Liffey told her. 'And

you're not looking very well. I hope you're taking your tonic?'

'Oh yes,' said Liffey.

'Well, make sure you do. It's honey and rosemary. Best thing in the world if you're poorly.'

'It certainly tastes delicious,' said Liffey, and it did.

Tucker noticed the change in Liffey. He was angry with Mabs. He defied her.

'You stop doing whatever you're doing to her,' he said. 'Just stop doing it. What's bad for one is bad for all.'

'She's taken what's mine,' said Mabs.

'That's where you're wrong,' he said. 'There's always more than enough to go round.'

'But there isn't,' said Mabs. 'How can there be? If one has it, another one hasn't.'

It was a deep doctrinal point: a profound rift. Tucker had a vision of continual creation, streaming outward: Mabs of a fixed state Universe, of strictly limited riches. Her children felt it, dividing up the fixed and miserly amount of her love, and starving.

'Anyway,' said Mabs, 'what makes you think it's me who's harming her? More like the doctor's poisoning her with his iron pills. I know of a child who died, taking them out of his mother's bag and thinking they were sweets. If they'll kill a child, they can't be good for the mother. Someone should tell her.'

Tucker took Mabs, all dressed up, to the Farmers' Ball. She wore real sapphires and a green silk dress and they went in the new Rover they kept in the barn for special occasions. They had bought it with the help of a government grant for the purchase of farm machinery. He wore a suit and a tie. Dressed up, they looked quite ordinary: almost negligible. But they were pleased with themselves and took the Rover down the track to show themselves off to Liffey.

Liffey looked pathetic and wan, standing on the path outside Honeycomb Cottage, waving. The garden, beyond Liffey's energy now to control, was overgrown and tangled, and the evening light sombre. Liffey herself was too fat in parts, and too thin in others. Mabs, secure in green silk, thought she could afford to be kind.

Tucker put it to her another way.
'If you want to get pregnant,' he said, 'you'll have to do as I say. A man has to be boss in his own house. Look around you.'
And looking round, Mabs saw the force of his argument, saw, as he did, a natural order in the world about her, of male dominance and female receptivity: saw the behaviour of hens around the cockerel, the cow submissive before the bull: the bitch accepting the dog, the little female cats yowling for the tom.

Mabs even contemplated leaving the mushroom powder out of Liffey's tonic, but she talked the matter over with Carol who snorted and said, 'What are you talking about, Mabs? People aren't animals. Tucker talks like that because it suits him, not because it's true.'

Richard said to Bella, 'Liffey's looking awfully ill.'
Bella said, 'I don't want to hear about your wife, Richard.'

Richard rang up Mr. Collins, his solicitor, in the hope that there would be news of the apartment, and the routing of Mory and Helen, but only an answering machine replied, taking a message and promising a return call. No return call was made.

'You don't really want your wife to come back to London,' said Miss Martin, sadly. 'You're having the best of both worlds, the way things are.' That was, according to her mother's magazines, the way men were, and she believed them.

And even while Richard worried for Liffey, Richard knew that what Miss Martin said was true. His duty lay towards Liffey, but no longer his inclination. And what was a man to do about that?

Liffey, on her next visit to the surgery, accepted a lift in Mabs' car. She did not think she had the strength to walk. The rutted path was baked in the sun, and the car jolted and jerked fiercely.

Dr. Southey looked quite shocked when she came into his surgery.

'You're taking your vitamin supplement?'

'Yes. And Mabs next door makes me up a tonic.'

'What's in it?'

'Only honey and rosemary. I take it every morning.'

'Then don't,' he said, and added, on impulse. 'You're not still being sick?'

'Yes, quite a lot. Isn't that normal? You said not to worry about it, just to put up with it.'

'For God's sake, woman,' he shouted, 'where's your common sense?'

Where indeed? Out the window, along with independent judgment. The pregnant woman leans upon her advisor; no longer thinks for herself. He had heard it often enough at the ante-natal clinic. 'I feel like a cabbage: I look like a cow.' Large-bellied women, sitting in their stolid rows, legs apart, for comfort's sake.

Liffey looked quite startled.

'I meant not to worry for the first three months,' he said, more gently, relieved to have discovered the cause of her trouble. He prescribed some tablets, and Liffey fetched them from the chemist – as Mabs discovered from her friend the girl in the dispensary, but too late to do any switching – but in fact did not take them, memories of thalidomide in her mind. But she did stop taking Mabs' tonic and instantly felt better, and stopped vomiting. But she did not make a connection between the two events.

Dr. Southey assumed that the cessation of vomiting was due to the anti-histamine drug he had prescribed.

Mabs watched Liffey grow plump and bloom again. She

186

burned the bottoms of saucepans out, and slammed doors and hit Eddie and shook her fist at the sky, which provided a flash of lightning and a crack of thunder but little more.

Glastonbury Tor looked black from a distance, like a coconut cake covered by flies. It swarmed with tourists and hippies, and little knots of people trying to focus cosmic energies down from the skies with one device or another. It was a shoddy place this time of year, Mabs felt, its powers divided amongst too many purposeless people: covered with litter. She felt displaced. Liffey, on the other hand, felt merry and bright and companionable and more like other people. Ramblers came past the door, and mushroom hunters, and Mrs. Wild called again, and Audrey would come up and talk, and sometimes Eddie would just come and stand and stare.

'I hope you're taking your tonic,' Mabs said to Liffey.
'Oh yes,' lied Liffey, to save embarrassment and trouble. So she had lied to her mother, when asked if she had brushed her teeth, or done her homework. She had not quite given up lying, for it is a hard habit to break; it was to her advantage, now as then: she lied convincingly, and Mabs believed her, as had Madge before her.

Inside Liffey (9)

The baby was unharmed by the general depletion of Liffey's energies. The placenta took priority over the normal demands of Liffey's system. Liffey, as she vomited, suffered from lack of calcium, vitamins, proteins, fats and carbohydrates – but the baby did not. Liffey's fat deposits were broken down, as necessary, to provide what was needed.

Liffey was now seven months pregnant. Her heart was

enlarged. Its workload had increased by some forty per cent, it beat at a rate of seventy a minute – nine more than was its custom before she was pregnant. Her heart was, little by little, pushed further up her chest by her enlarging uterus. All this was normal, if extraordinary and uncomfortable. Liffey's lungs too, were working at considerable disadvantage, being pushed into a smaller and smaller area within her chest: her ribs were having to spread sidewise to accommodate them. She took large breaths from time to time: she was comfortable only on high chairs, sitting straight. If she slumped, she felt she could hardly breathe at all. She started piling up the pillows behind her at night. Just as well, perhaps, that Richard was only with her, now, on Saturday nights. He pleaded pressure of work on Friday evenings, and on Saturday took the early morning train to the country, and the one back to London on Sunday night. The local station was open again now, and had been for some months, but the notion of Richard being a daily commuter had long been abandoned.

He made love to Liffey reverentially, and she wished he would not. She had developed, through her pregnancy, a marked interest in sexual matters, and a desire for sexual experiment, and an almost seedy interest in pornography, as if her body was anxious to keep her in practice and her genitals lubricated. She did not understand it, and did not like it, finding herself searching through drawers for the sex magazines Mabs used to wrap her offerings of this and that, and which she had meant to burn but never got round to. She told no one, feeling ashamed: and as Richard seemed shocked if she wanted to change her position from that gentle one of nesting spoons, which was the most sedate her pregnant shape would allow, Richard felt uneasy and embarrassed. Sex with Liffey, for Richard, was an expression of affection and a mark of dedication, not of need fulfilled, or passion gratified, or desires sated.

Liffey suffered now from vague aches and pains. Her ligaments, in particular those in her pelvis, became softer and liable to overstretch. A group of moles on her forearm enlarged. The hair on her legs were so dark and so obvious she took to shaving her legs with Richard's razor. Her skin became rather dry and she itched and scratched a good deal. The veins in her legs, now slightly varicose, irritated. Her vulva did too, for the same reason. She developed thrush and painful little ulcers as a result, but they responded at once to fungicidal pessaries prescribed by the doctor.

'Thrush!' she cried in horror. 'But I'm so careful to be clean.'

He explained that the thrush fungus flies through the air, and that there is nothing it likes more than a warm, moist, pregnant vagina. Liffey, he said, was lucky not to have developed piles, or they would be irritating too.

In the City, in the Summer

In the city the streets baked, drivers and pedestrians alike were bad tempered, dog turds withered where they lay, sight-seeing buses held up the traffic, exhaust fumes hung about the unhurried air, and were breathed in by the foreign visitors, who sat outside cafés on makeshift tables, holding up the city's flow of business.

Mory and Helen kept the windows wide open: the electricity supply had been cut off so there was no refrigerator, and the butter melted before it could reach the bread: they had no money for the launderette – or rather none they were prepared to waste on it – and dirty clothes lay in heaps upon the floors. Helen would not wash by hand, and Mory could not. They seldom left the apartment together, fearing that if they did someone would nip in when they were away and bar the door against their re-entry. For these misfortunes they blamed Liffey.

On one of these hot days Helen recognised the writing on an

envelope, and saw that it was addressed to her, and refrained from destroying it and opened it. It was from her younger sister Lally, accusing her of murdering Lally's baby.

You always hated me, [wrote Lally] because I was so much prettier and brighter than you, and could walk and talk before you, although I was ten months younger. And then you married Mory and thought you were one up because you were married before me, but then I got pregnant without even bothering to marry, so you had to have your revenge. I know all this because I am in treatment with a wonderful man who has explained it all to me.

Helen screamed and cried and grew purple and Mory thought she would choke.
'We can't live like this,' he moaned. 'What's gone wrong with our lives?'

Helen took a whole lot of sleepers and when she woke, said, 'It's this place. Everything's gone wrong since we came here. We've got to get out.'
'How?' asked Mory.
'Write to Richard,' said Helen, 'and say we'll get out if he gives us a thousand pounds to find somewhere else. Then we can have a holiday, get to the sun and out of this dump.'

Richard received the demand, and telephoned his solicitor, who was not there.
'You can't respond to threat and blackmail,' said Miss Martin, righteously.
'You haven't got a thousand pounds,' Bella pointed out.
'Your wife would suffer if you moved her now,' Helga pointed out. On those rare evenings when both Bella and Ray were out together Richard now joined Helga in her little attic room. He had been right about the exacting nature of her sexuality: he interpreted her neglect of his washing as a reproof, concluding that he failed her in some way. Indeed, he was so nervous of discovery by Bella, as to be unduly hasty in his performance with Helga.

Richard thought that Miss Martin, Bella and Helga judged the situation rightly, and said nothing to Liffey about Mory's offer. Pregnant women, he knew, should be spared undue worry. He had looked through the letterbox, in any case, on one or two occasions and seen the filth within, and wished Liffey to be spared the sight.

Richard felt inadequate in his dealings with Mory and Helen. He had been emasculated by the law; his instinct was to break down the door and snap Mory's neck, and throw Helen down the stairs, and regain both his territory and his pride, but these things were illegal and uncivilised. Nor could he find the courage to hurt his family's feelings by changing his solicitor. Frustrated in his masculinity in these respects, he felt obliged to reassert it by taking Miss Martin, Bella and Helga to bed: and inasmuch as it was Liffey's doing that Mory and Helen featured in his life at all, accounted her responsible for its general current unquietness.

He found his weekends at home increasingly unsatisfactory. Liffey was not so active about the house as she had been. There were dead spiders in his toothmug, and she put food on the table in saucepans, instead of dishing up properly. And there were no napkins. He had become accustomed to napkins, in the restaurants he frequented. But in his heart he knew that the trouble lay not in Liffey, but in his own guilt. He would find fault with her in order to justify his conduct: and the worse his conduct was the more he would diminish her. Liffey fails me in this respect, and that: therefore it is only reasonable for me to find consolation elsewhere.

He could not look her in the eye. He would rather be in London, compounding his offences, than face her trust.

Ray made matters worse by confiding in him.
'What am I going to do about Bella,' asked Ray, 'now that I have Karen? It isn't just the infatuation of a middle-aged man for a young girl – it is more like an appointment made by

destiny. Of course I'll wait. She's only sixteen. I shan't sleep with her until she's nineteen. It wouldn't be right. And then of course we'll be married. But that's three years pretending to feel husbandly towards Bella when I'm waiting to marry someone else.'

'So long,' said Richard cautiously, 'as Karen feels the same in three years time.'

'Karen's one of nature's innocents,' said Ray, with confidence. 'I wouldn't dream of presenting her with my feelings: she would be shocked and alarmed. But I just catch her looking at me sometimes – those pure green almond eyes beneath the long blonde hair – and I *know*, and she *knows*, and she'll wait for me—'

'Of course Bella might find someone else.'

Ray looked startled.

'I hardly think so,' he said. 'She's far too old in the tooth for that. Besides I trust her implicitly. It's just one of nature's cruel tricks – to keep a man attractive long after a woman is past it.' 'Quite so,' said Richard.

Complications

In the thirtieth week of Liffey's pregnancy Mabs went out into the night with a dead candle, and melted it down, and moulded the soft wax into an image of Liffey, stomach bulging, and drove a pin through its middle. An owl flew out of a hedge just as she struck, hooting and flapping, and quite scared her.

And then when she went back into the house to put the image into a drawer she found Audrey at the kitchen table, complaining of stomach pains. It quite took Mabs aback. She took the pin out, and in the morning Audrey's pains were gone. Mabs asked her mother to stick the pin for her. 'I'm not sticking no pins in any poor girl's stomach,' said

Mrs. Tree, crossly, 'just because you want to breed a football team. Why don't you look after the ones you've got? Something terrible will happen if you go on like this, and it won't happen to her, it will happen to one of yours, and serve you right.'

So the image lay in Mabs' drawer, without a pin, but with a hole through its middle all the same.

Next time Liffey went to see Dr. Southey and lay on her back on his couch while he felt, with firm chilly fingers, the outline of the baby, she noticed a flicker of surprise on his face. She always watched his expression carefully as she lay, thinking she might find out more from that than from his words.
'What's the matter?' she asked, sharply.
'Nothing,' he said, 'but I think we might send you up for a scan.'
'What's a scan?'
'A sonic picture.'
'Is it bad for the baby?'
'No.'
'Does it hurt?'
'No.'
'Why do you want me to have one?' she snapped the question out, first things first.
'The baby seems rather high, that's all.'
'Too high for what?'
'It might be nothing. It might be placenta praevia.'
'What's that?'
'The placenta is attached below the baby, not beside it or above it.'
'Is that dangerous?'
'If there weren't doctors and hospitals in the world, it might be. But as there are, it isn't. You can go in for the scan, by ambulance, tomorrow.'
'Ambulance? Am I delicate?'
'No. It's simpler and more comfortable and I'll be sure you've gone. Your husband might like to come too. It's nice to see a picture of the baby, after all.'

Liffey rang Richard from the surgery. Miss Martin answered the telephone.

'I'm afraid he's at a meeting, Mrs. Lee-Fox. Is it important?'

'No.'

'I can take a message if you like.'

'No thanks.'

Sad, thought Liffey, putting down the phone, that nasty things are thought important, but nice things aren't. News of death travels faster than news of triumph. Miss Martin did not tell Richard that Liffey had rung. He was not in fact at a meeting, but chatting with a colleague down the corridor. She did not think Richard would go home that weekend, and if any question of the phone-call arose, the passage of time would have clouded the issue, by the time he saw Liffey again.

Liffey went by ambulance to the hospital, and marvelled at how smooth the ride was, compared to what it was like when she drove with Mabs. She sat between two white-coated ambulance men, who were friendly, and wondered at her courage, living all alone miles from civilisation, nearing her time, and without a telephone. Liffey, hearing it put like that, felt, for the first time, almost sorry for herself.

'I have friends and neighbours,' she said. 'The Pierces.'

'Mabs Pierce? Old Mrs. Tree's daughter?' said one. 'Well, as long as she's a friend and not an enemy.'

'Why do you say that?' Liffey asked, but neither man would answer directly.

Liffey lay on a slab with her stomach oiled, and a technician moved a scanner back and forth, back and forth, over the mound of the baby, building up a picture on a screen, as a child makes the pattern of a coin on tissue paper, shading the circle with pencil. There was the curve of the baby's backbone, the little hunched head. Liffey felt both reassured and shocked, at what seemed an untimely manifestation of spirit into flesh. The technicians pointed and murmured. Beneath the baby's head, banning its exit to the world, was the shadowy boat-shape of the placenta.

Mabs felt her spirits rise. She dressed up and went into town and had coffee with Carol, and had her hair done, and looked at her face in the hairdresser's mirror, and saw again the face of a young girl, Tucker's bride, happy to have left her mother's cottage and become mistress of Cadbury Farm, pregnant and fruitful, in the days before she knew the depths of her own malice, and anger and greed. That's what I was, thought Mabs; that's what I still could be: happy and simple and good. What happens to all of us, with time? But when she got home, all the same, she stuck a pin into Liffey. Tucker's baby was not to live in Liffey: she had every right to stop it. Debbie complained of a pain, but Mabs took no notice. Liffey came to Mabs in tears.

'They think I'll have to have a Caesarian,' she said.

'That's bad,' said Mabs. 'Why?'

'Otherwise when labour starts I'll just bleed to death, and the baby will suffocate.'

'They always exaggerate,' said Mabs. 'Dr Southey loves to frighten women. He's famous for it. Have some tea? Or a glass of wine to cheer you up? I've got some of last year's plum.'

'I'll have some tea.'

Mabs made some rosemary tea and sweetened it with honey and put in a pinch of dried mushroom powder.

'Placenta praevia,' marvelled Mabs. 'Dr. Southey said I had one of those with Eddie. But it moved over by itself: they always do. I had a perfectly normal labour.'

'And I'm so far from the hospital; supposing I don't get there in time.'

'We'll look after you,' said Mabs. 'Come to that we could always deliver you ourselves. Think of all the cows Tucker and I have done.'

It was meant to be a joke and Liffey tried to smile.

Mabs rang Richard on Liffey's behalf since she seemed the only one able to get past Miss Martin, and told him that Liffey was upset and why, that the doctor was just being an alarmist, and that Liffey looked all right to her, and a

Caesarian, in any case, was perfectly routine. Liffey listened.
'I expect she's got it all wrong anyway,' said Richard. 'You know what Liffey's like.'

Liffey went off to be sick and attributed it to nerves, not Mabs' tea. After all, Mabs had drunk it too. But it was the sort of thing she noticed, these days. When she got back Mabs had put down the phone.

'He had to take a transatlantic call,' said Mabs. 'But he sent you his love. He said Tina and Tony had got German measles. I don't think he ought to come down until he's out of quarantine, do you? If you get it the baby can be born blind and dumb.'

'I thought that was only in the first three months.'

'That's what they say, but I had a friend had it at six months and her baby was a mongol.'

Richard did not come back at the weekend, at Liffey's request. Tina and Tony coughed and groaned and sweated, out of sight and out of their parents' mind.

Richard had become suddenly afraid that the baby would be born deformed, that out of the once beloved, wholesome Liffey, a monster would emerge.

'That's guilt speaking,' said Bella. 'You believe you're so bad you can't produce anything good.'

'I expect it's true,' he said, and wept.

'Christ,' said Bella, 'don't I have enough with Ray, without you starting as well?'

Bella curled her legs around the small of his back and they rocked and rocked, and Richard's tears passed.

'You'll feel better when the baby's born,' Bella assured him. 'When I was pregnant with Tony, Ray went on a gastronomic tour of New Zealand; and with Tina, it was Tierra del Fuego. At least you've kept within telephonic distance.'

'I don't like the thought of Liffey being cut open,' said Richard.

'Saves you having to do your paternal duty and watch,' said Bella. 'I'm sure it's unnecessary, anyway. Doctors just make more money out of the National Health doing operations, than leaving things to nature.'

Liffey was frightened. The baby was silent. She felt that the scan had been in some way an insult to him: she'd been checking up on him. Giving him physical shape before he was ready.

The weather grew colder. It rained and rained, and slugs got the poor, sodden strawberries. Four cows broke through from Tucker's side of the stream, breaking down the fence, splashing through the water, trampling and munching her patch of vegetables. She asked Tucker to move them and he didn't, and she had been afraid to persist, for his kind and friendly eyes, as she asked, had taken on a speculative look and he had lain his hand on her stomach in the half-pleased, half-envious way people did sometimes, but which was somehow something different in Tucker, reminding her of what she would rather not remember. So there the cows stayed, staring and munching and splattering round her back door, and Richard not coming back for seventeen days, which was the incubation period for German measles, and a pain in her stomach every now and then, as if someone had pierced her through the middle with a laser beam, but which Dr. Southey told her was nothing.

As if a placenta praevia was not enough.

In-Laws

Richard's parents came down to stay as soon as Richard was out of quarantine. Liffey made the house as pleasant and pretty as a shortage of money and energy would allow. She dusted out cobwebs, and turned sheets side to middle, and noticed how quick the processes of dilapidation and depression were – when cracked cups were kept because there was no money to replace them, and burned saucepans scraped, not thrown away: and stained carpets merely scrubbed, and damp wallpaper patched. The houses of the poor take longer to clean than the houses of the rich: rooms must be tidied and polished before guests appear; a wealthy disorder is tolerable; the jumble of desolation is not.

Mr. and Mrs. Lee-Fox were shocked by the change in Liffey's appearance, but felt she was wholly to blame. She was letting herself go: she would depress Richard – she was young and healthy and had nothing else to do all day but look after herself – why was she not doing it properly? Mrs. Lee-Fox told Liffey how well she was looking, and remarked on how pregnancy evidently suited her, and looked forward to at least another six grandchildren.

Mr. Lee-Fox went further into the matter of Mory and Helen's occupancy of the London apartment.
'Of course it was a gift to you and Richard freely given,' he said, 'but we hardly expected it to be given away so soon!' He appeared to be joking; he smiled and smiled as he spoke. 'All the same,' he added, 'Collins is a fine solicitor; he'll get them out of there in no time. Of course the law of the land, these days, is on the side of thieves and vagrants.'

Mr. and Mrs. Lee-Fox liked their cups to rest on saucers, and their saucers on tablecloths and their tablecloths on polished tables, and Liffey did what she could to oblige. Her own daintiness seemed a thing of the past, her swelling belly on too large a scale to allow for a retreat into little, pretty, feminine ways.

When Richard arrived, having been delayed, or so he said, by queues of traffic leaving London, his car was laden with the exotic foods which once had been their staple diet. His parents marvelled.
'How well he looks after you, Liffey!'
'Worth waiting for, after all, Liffey.'
'All the goodies of the world on your doorstep, Liffey!'

'Why live near to the shops with a delivery service like this!'
'Isn't Richard a wonder! Where does he find the energy. Not to speak of the time. Makes the money, does the shopping, drives a hundred miles for a kiss, and comes up smiling!'
'Whose friends were they, Liffey, this Helen and Mory? Yours or Richard's?'

'Mine,' said Liffey.

Richard was kind, charming and hard-working all week-end. He was up early to make the breakfast, bring tea in bed for Liffey; then he fetched the papers, weeded the garden, mended the banister, peeled the potatoes, and washed up.

'Good heavens, Liffey, it isn't a husband you've got here, it's a servant.'

That night Liffey placed Richard's hand on her stomach, but he withdrew it as soon as he tactfully could. Being in his parents presence had focused the matter for him, forcibly. He did not want to be a father. He did not want to join the grown-ups. He wanted to be a boy-husband and have a girl-bride. Liffey was making him old beyond his years.

On Sunday afternoon, while Richard was out walking with his father, Mrs. Lee-Fox enquired further into Liffey's side of the family.
'Of course I met your mother at the wedding. What a brave and independent lady! I only wish I could have been like her, and flouted convention. But I never had the courage. What was your father like, Liffey?'
'Slippery, from the sound of him,' said Liffey. 'Apart from that I don't know.'
'But your mother *is* a widow.'
'No,' said Liffey. 'Unmarried and deserted.'

Mrs. Lee-Fox's hand trembled as she sipped Mabs' home-made plum wine. The wine contained a distillation of the seed of a flower known locally as 'Tell-the-Truth' and had been given to Liffey and Richard by Mabs on the grounds that, one way or another, it was bound to cause trouble.

'I'm glad you told me the truth, Liffey,' said Mrs. Lee-Fox. She wore many rings on her once pretty fingers and a thick gold charm bracelet on a still slender wrist. Her hair was grey and curled, and sad eyes battled for predominance over a mouth composed into an enduring smile.

'Thank you for telling me your secret, Liffey,' said Mrs. Lee-Fox, sipping plum wine.

'I shall now tell you my secret,' added Mrs. Lee-Fox. 'It's bigger than yours and I've kept it longer.'

'I've never really loved Richard,' said Mrs. Lee-Fox, her head spinning from Tell-the-Truth, 'because you see Richard isn't his father's child.'

'He has his father's nose and his father's neck,' confided Mrs. Lee-Fox, 'and his father is Mr. Collins the solicitor who treated me very badly. Talk about being seduced and abandoned!'

'No use looking shocked, Liffey,' reproved Mrs. Lee-Fox, 'because all women are sisters under the skin, and if this child of yours is Richard's I'll eat my hat. If it was his, he'd be here all the time. He's acting completely out of character, all this sweet talk and washing up; you're both of you putting on an act and I know what it is. You've cheated on him, Liffey, and he's agreed to stand by you.'

'No,' cried Liffey, on her feet. 'No!'

'Another secret,' said Mrs. Lee-Fox, calmly, 'is that Mr. Collins is an extremely bad solicitor, but I can hardly tell my husband that, in the circumstances, let alone my son.'

'I did my best to raise Richard properly,' wept Mrs. Lee-Fox into her glass, 'but he always reminded me of what I'd rather forget. And Liffey, Mr. Collins had a grandmother who was an Asiatic. I remember him telling me so. If the baby has slanting eyes, Liffey, for my sake, say it comes from your father's side. I have lived in fear of this for so long. It has clouded my whole life.'

Liffey put her mother-in-law to bed with a hot-water bottle.

When the older woman woke she seemed perfectly normal and the smile was back, and she and her husband departed with little conventional cries of pleasure and admiration and apparent ordinariness.

Inside and Outside

Thirty-four weeks.

'Still a placenta praevia,' said the doctor to Liffey. 'But never mind. We'll take care of you. And the baby will be saved the struggle of getting out, won't he?'

Ah, but what about me, doctor? What about my tight and stretching tummy? Where are you going to take your knife and slit it? From top to bottom or side to side?

'You'll have to ask the specialist,' said the doctor. 'I'll send you to see him this week.'

The hospital was large and new, hot and carpeted. Pregnant ladies walked bright corridors up and down, up and down, dressing gowns stretched to cover swollen tummies. Young men waited at telephones: faces elated or anxious or bored.

'We'll give you a bikini scar,' said the specialist. 'Just below the line of your pubic hair. Almost unnoticeable. That's if all goes well, of course. If we're in a hurry we do the best we can, for you and baby, and without a doubt the old-fashioned navel to pubis cut is quicker and safer; but there you are: you girls think of your figure more than your baby.'

Liffey didn't like the specialist. Nor did he particularly like women.

'We'll keep the baby inside you as long as we possibly can. If you start to bleed, which you probably will, soon, because the placenta's likely to tear when it's down there, you'll go on bleeding until the baby's out. So when I say come in quickly if you see so much as a spot of blood, that's what I mean. A placenta praevia is rare in a first pregnancy. You're sure you haven't been pregnant before?'

'Quite sure.'

'You're not hiding anything?'

She began to think perhaps she was, such was the force of his suspicion, his determination that all women were fools, and knaves, and the enemies of their babies. She tried to think, but could not: to give her past a reality acceptable to him. Yes, I have had measles, and mumps – but a baby? Did I? Her silence irritated him.

'Well, let's say you're just unlucky.'

Liffey thought, all of a sudden, Mabs did this to me. If she was unlucky it was because Mabs had done it to her. She had never been unlucky before. The baby danced and laughed, to confirm her conclusion. Mabs was not a friend, she was an enemy.

'Active little beggar,' said the specialist. His hands, she acknowledged, however much she disliked them were experienced and competent. 'You're lucky to have kept him inside this long. You're sure there's been no bleeding?'

'No.'

'No, you're not sure, or no, there's been no bleeding?'

Ah, he was a bully.

Never mind, sang the baby, never mind. I'll be all right. So will you. Liffey felt she had to protect such charming naïvety.

'No bleeding.' There will be no bleeding, either, until my baby is forty weeks old, give or take a day or two. My baby's no fool. Nor am I. I'll keep him in and he'll cooperate.

'He isn't the most tactful of men,' said the doctor, tentatively, of the specialist. 'But on the other hand, he won't let you die.'

Liffey was elated. She felt that things were better now between herself and Richard. She felt sure the baby would nudge the placenta praevia over when it felt like it. She did not believe her mother-in-law's account of her husband's birth. She would keep out of Mabs' way, and things would go better.

Thirty-four weeks. Oh, she was heavy, breathless, and languid, but she was still happy. Richard, had, for some reason, turned vegetarian so she worried in case she was not eating enough meat for the baby's welfare. Richard assured her that animal flesh did more harm to the human body than good. He wore a lovely pair of thonged sandals. They had a good weekend. He took her to the pub, which she liked but knew he hated. He had enough of people during the week. So he said.

Richard had lately met up with a girl called Vanessa. She had auditioned for a part in a television commercial, for oxtail soup, and failed to get it, but had given Richard her telephone number. She was an actress, had a degree from Oxford, a flat and slender crutch across which jeans strained, a mother who was a Countess and her own apartment. Richard thought she was just about right for him. She was a vegetarian and thought that sex was yucky and pushed off roving hands but Richard thought she would soon be cured of that. She was twenty-one.

He was particularly animated and cheerful that weekend. He told Liffey about Ray's love for Karen, and how it upset Bella.
'So long as she doesn't expect you to comfort her,' said Liffey.
Richard shuddered at the thought.

'Bella,' he said, 'is a withered hag who talks too much. I'm sorry for her, and she's good to me, but I could no more – oh, really, Liffey!'

'What about Helga?' Sometimes Liffey wondered about Helga.

'Helga is a Hausfrau and I don't go for Hausfraus. You'll be laying the finger on poor Miss Martin next.'

'You did go off with your secretary last Christmas.'

'Go off with? You mean she fell on top of me at a drunken party and if you hadn't been spying you'd never even have known.'

'I wasn't spying.'

But he was angry, and made her drink up and took her home. He relented as they passed Cadbury Farm and kissed her proffered cheek. Her skin, these days, was hot to the touch, as if fires burned inside her.

'I think Mabs *is* a witch,' said Liffey, as they passed the farm. 'That's a very unkind thing to say about a neighbour,' said Richard.

'If you nailed her footprint to the ground,' said Liffey, 'I bet she'd limp. That's how you can tell a witch.'

The next day, giggling and absurd, as in the old days, they crept down the lane when Mabs and Tucker were out, and found a footprint made by Mabs in the marshy ground where she went to feed her ducks, and hammer, hammer, Richard drove a nail right into it.

Then they watched and waited for Mabs to come back, and sure enough, when she did she was limping. They laughed and laughed, and went up later to the farm and asked what was the matter with Mabs' foot, and Mabs replied she'd stubbed her big toe and all but broken it, hadn't she, Tucker, and Tucker said yes, she'd walked straight into a tree stump, what's the matter with you two, for they were stifling giggles, but of course they couldn't say – ah, like the old times back again. Happy days. That night they lay curled like spoons together, and Richard stayed until Monday morning and

kissed Liffey goodbye as if he meant it and didn't want ⬛
And he didn't.

Honeycomb Cottage, as he looked back at it from the ca⬛
nestled amidst hollyhocks and roses like a childhood drean
of the future. This was surely what he wanted and enough
for any man.

And Liffey, waving goodbye, sensed it, and hoped yet to
achieve what her mother had not – an ordinary marriage, an
ordinary family, and ordinary happiness.

But the next day she had a nasty pain in her sacroiliac joint, at
the top of her buttocks, three inches to the right of mid-
point, and could hardly walk.

Mabs came over by chance with some honey, and sent
Tucker over to drive her at once to the doctor's surgery.
Liffey was in such pain she almost forgot her dislike of the
Pierce's car.

'Was that Tucker Pierce?' asked the doctor, manipulating
the joint.
'Yes.'
'He's changed,' said the doctor. 'It's not in his nature to do
good turns. Not in anyone's round here, come to that.'
He'd just sent the ambulance for the body of a recluse, found
badly decayed in the caravan he'd inhabited for fifteen years.
'His wife makes him,' said Liffey. She'd forgotten all the
nonsense about Mabs being a witch; all, all had been washed
away again in loving laughter, annd trust of Richard.

Liffey's back creaked and cracked as the doctor pressed and
dug, and the pain went, although the joint remained a little
tender.

'Well,' said Tucker, 'here we are, just you and me. Time we
had a little talk.'
'What about, Tucker.'

.'t get all la-di-dah with me. That's my baby you've got
here and don't you forget it.'
ucker!' she was horrified. 'You can't think that. It
ouldn't possibly be yours.'
'Mabs thinks it is. According to her sister's friend who works
up at the doctor's, it's as like as not my baby.'
'You mean Mabs *knows*?'
'Of course she knows. She's my wife. We have no secrets.'
'You *told* her?'
'Of course.'

Liffey was quite cold with shock. Gentlemen did not kiss and
tell, but Tucker, after all, was no gentleman. And secrecy
rose out of guilt, but Tucker felt no guilt: and if Mabs knew
what was there to stop her telling Richard?

Tucker's hand was unbuttoning her Mothercare blouse.
'No please, Tucker.'
'Why not?'
'I'm pregnant.'
'Anyone can see that. It's not comfortable in here. Come out
on the grass.'
'No.'
'Why not? What you do once you can do twice.'
'Tucker I can't, I mustn't. Please. My back still hurts.'
'I expect it does, at that,' he said, kindly. 'I'll be over in a day
or two. No hurry.'

He started the engine and they bumped back to the cottage.
I can deny it, thought Liffey, wildly. I can deny everything.
That's all I have to do. Tell Richard that Tucker tried to rape
me – tell Richard I'm coming up to London, I can't stay
here, he has to think of something, some way we can live
together.

Liffey packed a hessian bag with some meagre belongings,
hitch-hiked with a startled salesman to the station, and used
the last of the week's housekeeping for a ticket to London.
She had to change trains at Westbury, wait two hours for a

connection. The journey took five hours. She wondered how she had ever thought Richard could do it daily. She arrived at Ray and Bella's at half-past nine in the evening.

Events

Helga was cleaning up the kitchen. Liffey had met Helga once, in the old days, and not bothered to speak to her, since she was an au-pair, and au-pairs, like servants, were uninteresting. Helga did not much like Liffey, but was shocked by her appearance. What had seemed gamine now seemed undernourished, ill and almost ugly. Helga told Liffey that Bella, Ray and Richard were at the pictures. In fact Ray was at a discotheque with Karen but she thought that fact could perhaps emerge more kindly in the course of time.

'I only stay for the children,' said Helga. 'Every night I get to bed at midnight. It is a very messy family.'

'Doesn't Richard do a lot of baby-sitting?' asked Liffey. For that was how Richard described his evening occupation: sitting in the kitchen, working on papers from his briefcase, while the rest of the household had a good time.

'Oh yes,' said Helga. 'Of course.'

At midnight Richard and Bella came home. Ray wasn't expected until after two. Helga intercepted them in the hall.

'Liffey's here,' she hissed.

'Oh, Christ,' said Richard, furious. He had pushed Bella into her house with his buttocks and was looking forward to thus edging her up the stairs.

'Ask her up,' said Bella. 'She might as well know. Everyone might as well know.'

She had been drinking. So had Richard.

'I couldn't be so cruel,' said Richard. 'She only has me in the world.'

But he stood undecided until Helga pushed him into the kitchen, and Liffey ran into his arms.

Liffey did not mention Tucker. She merely said she missed him so much she'd decided to come to London, on the spur of the moment.

'But where are you going to stay?'
'I can share your bed, Richard.'
'My bed is the sofa. But you can have that tonight and I'll sleep on the floor. I've got meetings all tomorrow, too. I was hoping, just for once, to get some sleep.'

The temptations of power are indeed terrible. Richard succumbed to them. To hurt, subtly, yet appear not to hurt, made up for a little of his sense of loss in regard to Bella.

Liffey slept badly on the sofa. The noise of the London traffic kept her awake. Yet it appeared friendly, and companionable. She wondered how she had ever found it oppressive. To look out of the window and see not grass and cows, but people and buildings, and the safety of civilisation - was this not good fortune? Not for nothing had men yearned, over the generations, to escape the solitude of the countryside and make for the pleasure of the town.
Too late.

Breakfast with Ray and Bella was humiliating.
'Well,' said Ray, 'pregnancy has certainly made you look more like a woman and less like a boy. Everything going all right?'
'Well,' said Liffey, 'it's not really. They say I have to have a Caesarian.'
'They give everyone Caesarians these days,' said Bella, 'at the drop of a hat. The hospitals have to justify their monstrous expenditure on capital equipment. So the knife's back in fashion.'
'But I have a placenta praevia,' replied Liffey. 'It's nothing to do with fashion.' But Richard was reading *The Times*, and

Ray and Bella fell into an argument as to who was to talk to the Selfridges' Fish Buyer.

'I suppose you'll be meeting Karen out of school,' said Bella. 'That's why you can't do it.'

'She has her A-level Art today. I said I would, Bella. She's only a kid. She depends on me. Her own father neglects her terribly: she has to have someone.'

'Oh yes. Incest's so fashionable.'

'You are disgusting,' said Ray. 'You see sex in everything.'

'Please,' said Helga, 'not in front of the children.'

Liffey, out of the city for six months, started to cry. Mabs and Tucker back home; plotting: Richard reading his newspaper here; indifferent. Liffey fainted.

Helga took Liffey round to Bella's doctor, since Richard had an important meeting at half-past nine. The doctor said her blood pressure was up, what was she doing gadding about London, she should be safely at home in the country, and with a placenta praevia anyway she should try not to be too far from the hospital where they had her records.

'I'm not trying to frighten you,' said her doctor. 'I just don't want you to be silly. You have to think of the baby.'

Liffey rang Richard's office and got Miss Martin and left a message. Miss Martin gave Richard the first part, that Liffey was on her way home, but left out the part about the blood pressure and staying near a hospital, as he had another important meeting and she didn't want to worry him.

Liffey remembered, on the way back in the train, that she had no means of getting from the station to Honeycomb Cottage, and cried.

But Tucker was waiting for her at the station. It seemed inevitable. She did not even ask him how he came to be there. In fact, Richard had rung through and asked him to meet Liffey. Miss Martin had dialled the call, with reluctant fingers.

'I can't stand helpless women,' said Miss Martin. 'It isn't fair. If you're silly and helpless like your wife, you get looked after. No one ever looks after me.' And she cried into her typewriter – the big, ugly sobs of despised womanhood.

Later that morning Miss Martin said that she wanted to confess to Jeff, and Richard knew that once she did, once her guilt had been evaporated, puffed away in a careless word or so, she would begin to see herself as a proper person with feelings to be considered. She would stop being a humble typist, grateful for her boss' caress, and see herself as a mistress, with claims and aspirations to all kinds of impossible things.

Richard regarded his situation as dangerous. 'You'd be unwise to tell Jeff,' he said, as casually as he could manage, knowing that those who want too badly never get, and that to care too much is to lose power. 'He'd only get upset. It's not as if you and he ever slept together. You're doing him no harm: I'm only warming his bed for him a little.'

It was a phrase Bella used. Bella's phrases swam through all their lives. Even Karen had to put up with it. Bella was feeling thwarted and unsatisfied. She too seemed to be becoming a danger.
She said there ought to be more, somewhere, somehow, the other side of sexual acrobatics. She bought Richard a flat Victorian carpet-beater and asked him to thwack her bottom with it, but either her flesh was not young and smooth enough to be excited by chastisement, or he did it wrong, for all that happened was Helga threatened to give in her notice, since the noise they made upset the children.

'You must not,' said Helga. 'I will have to speak out. Mr. Ray will find out and we will all be murdered.'

Bella laughed at the idea of Ray as murderer. Part of her wanted to be murdered, another part of her wanted Ray to know, another part wanted the nights with Richard simply to continue.

So did Richard.

'Helga loves the drama,' said Bella, to Richard. 'She hasn't the guts to do it herself, so she lives through us.'
'Perhaps you ought to be quieter,' suggested Richard. 'It might upset the children.'
'Christ,' said Bella. 'It's how they were born, weren't they?'

Bella could justify anything in the world she wished to justify, thought Richard. Perhaps everyone could.

Ray bought Karen a pound of the first cherries of the season. She bit into them with her little white teeth. Red cherry juice ran down her chin. In the car he held her hand and bit into it with his own rather yellowed teeth.
'Your chin's all stubbly,' she said. Peter's hair grew fine and soft on his chin. Peter was young. Ray was old. She had not told Ray about her boyfriend Peter, a gardener drop-out, with whom she was sleeping. She thought he might be hurt.

Richard rang Vanessa but she was off to a summer school for the New Atlanteans, where communication was through the spirit not the body.

Richard thought about giving up Vanessa. Vanessa didn't think about it at all.

As for Liffey, little Liffey: Liffey lay naked on the bed, on her side, while Tucker entered her from behind. To submit gracefully, calmly, had seemed the best way of protecting herself and her baby and her blood pressure. Tucker had met her on the station: she owed him something for that.
'You shouldn't go rushing up to London like that,' he said. 'Bad for the baby. Bad for you. I wasn't going to harm you. Do anything you didn't want.' He spoke kindly, and what he said was true. He was concerned for her. She was grateful. Liffey grateful to Tucker!

He took her home, made her put her feet up, and made her

tea. 'I don't know what you're so frightened of,' he said. 'All you've got to do is what you want.'

'I know what pregnant women are like,' he said. 'I've had Mabs pregnant more times than I can remember. I like the feel of my child inside.'
'It's not yours,' she whispered. But she did not persist. She had to stay calm and bring her blood pressure down. Liffey felt the baby warning her. Careful now. Lie down. Do as he wants. It doesn't matter.

Tucker put his hand on her bare tummy: he lay down his head to listen to the baby's heart beat. That answered some kind of craving in her, too.

It was almost pleasurable; then it actually was: she forgot herself, she cried out. Liffey had an orgasm. Afterwards she cried: floods; all kinds of things, it seemed, got washed away with her tears.

Liffey, rightly or wrongly, felt she had changed. She would never easily look like a little boy, feel like a little girl, ever again. It was a loss: she knew it: she was at her best when very young. All charm, no sense. The days of charm were gone. Now she was real, and alive.

Liffey looked to no kind of future beyond the day of delivery. Everything worked towards that end.

Tucker seemed to like her tears. He made no comment on them. 'Don't tell Mabs,' he said, as he went, and Liffey was safe again, knowing he was cheating too. Their interests once again coincided.

She sang as she worked in the garden. She had to sit on the ground to weed; she found it hard to bend.

Waiting

The weather was hot. Liffey spoke to the birds, and the butterflies. Tucker came up from time to time to see how she was. She quite looked forward to his visits: she ran to make him tea – ordinary tea bags now, not Earl Grey – discussed the cows, Dick Hubbard's perfidy, the knack of making silage. Tucker made no more sexual assaults upon her. He seemed satisfied, having made his mark, having made her remember.

The baby kicked and heaved, and made her laugh and pant: it seemed to have a foot wedged under her ribs. She hoped he was all right: that a leg wouldn't grow crooked for being so long in one place.

The doctor said that was highly unlikely.
'No bleeding?' he asked.
'No bleeding,' said Liffey. Liffey still believed she would have her baby naturally. She felt that fate had dealt her quite enough blows. It could not be so cruel as to make her submit to the surgeon's knife.
Slice into the smoothness, the roundness, the taut health of her tummy? Ah, no. That was a bad dream. Liffey loved her tummy now. She lay on her back and sang to it. The earth was warm and so was she.

Liffey looked better. She was almost pretty again. The doctor said she would be delivered on October 10th. It was now the beginning of September.

Thirty-six weeks.

The first puffball of the season appeared. A blind white head pushed its way out of damp warm ground, down in the dip by the stream where once, a year ago, Richard and Liffey had made their ordinary everyday love and thought themselves much like other people. Then, when the world was innocent, and Liffey was not pregnant, nor Mabs so desperate to be so; and Richard was faithful and Bella nothing worse than bored; and Karen was a virgin and Ray was not a laughing stock: when Miss Martin still looked up to her fiancé, and Tucker contented himself with looking, through field glasses, at Liffey in the act of love – then indeed, the world was young.

Mabs was the first to see the puffball. She was out early, bringing the cows in. This was normally Tucker's job, but the night before she and he had drunk a bottle of whisky between them, almost inadvertently, one on either side of the fire, while the children, barred the kitchen, snivelled and snored upstairs.

Mabs was having trouble with Debbie. Debbie was dirty. Debbie wet the bed. In the mornings she'd stand at the sink crying and washing out her sheets, cheeks red from a slapping, and doing her best – even Mabs had to admit it – but she was a cack-handed child, and never seemed to get through before it was time for the school bus, so she'd have to leave it, and then Mabs would have to load the dripping mass into the washing machine and finish it off. And now it was school holiday time, it was even worse, for Debbie would spend the entire morning washing and getting in Mabs' way.

Debbie was eleven. She was a delicate-looking child: the prettiest of the girls and a throw back to some obscure ancestry. Mabs had the heavy jowly features and prominent eyes of the Norman invaders of these parts: Tucker the smaller, darker, cautious looks of the Celts. Once, in any case, the general belief was, in the very old days, there had been two races about, the giants and the little people, but time and civilisation had diluted the strain, and now everyone was much of a muchness – only Mabs would look

out, as it were, from the surface of her head, and Tucker
from within it. But Debbie seemed a new, neater breed,
incompetent with her hands, full of whims and fancies,
uncertain of necessities, a decoration placed on the face of
the earth instead of something part of it – and reminding
Mabs for all the world of Liffey.

Slap, slap. You dirty little thing!

Mabs sent the whole lot of them to bed early and then drank
more whisky than she meant, to calm her nerves. Soon she
was talking about Richard and Liffey.

'Of course he won't put up with her for long,' said Mabs.
'Dumping her down here is just the first stage. He's on his
way up in the world and she's a millstone round his neck.'
'You can't tell what goes on between man and wife,' said
Tucker.
'I can,' said Mabs. There was still a light left in the sky. The
Tor seemed very near tonight, as it did when rain was about.
'Judging by the things he lets slip,' added Mabs.
'I think he's interested in a whole lot of things,' said Tucker,
'not just his office.'
'It's going to rain,' said Mabs, as if willing it, and the Tor
stepped nearer, listening. Tucker told himself it was only a
sudden shift in the pattern of clouds above Glastonbury.
'I wonder who it will take after when it's born?'
'Not me,' said Tucker, rather too quickly.
'It had better not,' said Mabs.
'Well,' said Tucker, 'I don't know what you're complaining
about. We got the cows in Honeycomb field, didn't we?'
'Not for long,' said Mabs, and the rain started and drove
against the window pane in sudden gusts. 'She's a slut and a
thief and she came out of nowhere and stole my baby.'
'That's nonsense,' said Tucker.
'Then why haven't I got one?'

Mabs went to the cupboard under the sink, where the
candles were kept in case of powercuts, and lit one, and

waited until the wax began to melt, and then took the drips and began to mould them. First came the head, white and blind, with a pinch for the neck, and then a half-pinch, not at the waist, but where the trunk joined the legs, so that the belly curved out round and full.

'Don't do that,' said Tucker, 'it gives me the creeps. Who is it?'

'Who do you think?' said Mabs. 'Liffey. I've done one for the baby; that one's in a drawer keeping its strength, but this one's the mother. I'll get them both. Why not?'

She took a hairpin from her head and was about to pierce the belly, but Tucker thrust her hand aside and slapped her, and then bore her down on the floor, pushing up her old skirt and down her pretty, slippery knickers, and had her, while she laughed and panted and struggled.

'Why do you do it?' Tucker asked, later. 'It's a wicked thing to do.'

'She stole my baby,' Mabs persisted.

'If she did, it's not her fault,' said Tucker, doubtfully. Perhaps such things did happen: who was to say? Certainly Liffey was pregnant, and Mabs was not. And Liffey had never been pregnant before, and Mabs usually was.

'That's neither here nor there,' said Mabs. She slept peacefully afterwards but Tucker did not, and he groaned and moaned, so in the morning Mabs kindly rose and brought in the cows on his behalf from Honeycomb field. And there, down in the long grass, as a kind of omen and reward, was the puffball.

Mabs stared long and hard at it and after breakfast went up and knocked on Liffey's door. Liffey was hemming cot-sheets. Liffey quite enjoyed the task: to sit patiently, sewing, each stitch an act of faith in the future of both her child and herself, stemmed up anxiety and sorrow and made her feel at peace. But Mabs wouldn't have it.

'It's unlucky to sew for babies before they're born,' said Mabs, peering over Liffey's shoulders.

'I hadn't heard that,' said Liffey.

'Well, now you have. It's tempting providence.'

'I suppose it is, in a way.'

'Come over and use my machine. And stay for lunch,' said Mabs.

So Liffey took the pile of old flannelette sheets which Mrs. Lee-Fox senior had sent her by parcel post, and walked over to Cadbury Farm and sat in the kitchen where Mabs' children yammered and cowered and snivelled and were slapped and shouted at, and used the sewing machine and wondered if she really wanted a child.

The baby kicked Liffey. It had changed its position. Its head lay somewhere over her left groin: its legs tucked under her right ribs. Sometimes it waved its elbows and made her gasp. It's not what *you* want, it seemed to say, it's what *I* want.

Tucker was out with the cows. A cat sat by the fire. Eddie crouched beside it, poking at its eyes with a stick. Jab, jab. 'You leave the cat alone,' shrieked Mabs, 'or I'll have you put away.'

Jab, jab, jab, went Eddie, until his mother seized him and flung him half across the room.

Mabs served cabbage and bacon for lunch. She would let the cabbage cook for a couple of hours, then squeeze and press some of the water out of it, and cut it into wedges.

Mabs walked with Liffey back to the cottage, after lunch. She said she wanted the exercise. Liffey wished she didn't. Moreover, she ran her large hands over Liffey's tummy before they set out, and Liffey wished she wouldn't do that either.

'It's a girl,' said Mabs, 'you can tell. What do you want? A boy?'

'I don't mind,' said Liffey. 'So long as it's human.'

It was a little joke she made, but Mabs seemed to think she was serious.

Mabs saw the puffball.
'Look,' she said. 'Isn't it horrible!' And she pulled back the long grasses, and ran her hands over its surface rather as she had run them over Liffey's tummy.
Then she straightened up and kicked the puffball, and it spattered into pieces.
'I can't abide those things,' Mabs said. 'Coming up from nowhere like that.'

Liffey felt quite sick, and trembled, but Mabs smiled pleasantly and they walked on.
'They're only big mushrooms,' said Liffey presently. 'They don't do any harm.'
'Can't abide them,' said Mabs. 'Nor does Tucker. No one round here does.'

Liffey sat for a while after Mabs had gone. It was a lovely, warm afternoon. Bees droned, sun glazed, flowers glowed.

Preparations

Changes had recently been occurring in the lower part of Liffey's uterus. It was gradually softening and shortening, in preparation for labour, and it was to this lower part, of course, that the baby's placenta was attached. Now the placenta separated itself fractionally from the uterus, and Liffey lost a few drops of blood, but failed to notice. For there was a thunderstorm over the Tor that evening and lightning struck a cable, so that there was a powercut. Mabs had to take out her candles again, but Liffey had none and had to undress in the dark and did not notice the staining.

'Make the lights come on again,' said Tucker to Mabs, half-joking, and no sooner had he spoken than they came on. 'You're a witch,' said Tucker, 'that's your trouble,' and then had to spend half the night pacifying her. She did not like to be called a witch by anyone, let alone her husband.

The doctor sent Sister Davis the midwife up to see Liffey. Sister Davis was a slender, doe-eyed girl, who had no intention of ever having a baby herself.
'No bleeding?' she asked.
'No,' said Liffey.
'The minute there is,' said Sister Davis, 'you'll come along in to hospital, won't you.'
'Of course,' said Liffey.
'I don't know why they haven't taken you in already,' said Sister Davis. 'Of course, they're short of staff up there, and it's a question of priorities.'
'I feel fine,' said Liffey. 'I really do.'
'Up here, on your own,' said Sister Davis, running expert hands over Liffey's tummy. 'No telephone, no husband. It isn't right.'
'It's very peaceful,' said Liffey.
'And you have good neighbours,' said Sister Davis, 'that's the main thing. Mabs Pierce is an old hand at motherhood. I wonder when her next will be? She's leaving it longer than usual.'
'I don't think she wants any more,' said Liffey, surprised.
'No? What a pity. She's such a lovely mother. The babies slip out like loaves from a greased tin!'

Sister Davis reported to the doctor that Mrs. Lee-Fox seemed in good health and spirits, and she was sure that Mabs Pierce would keep an eye on her. The doctor replied that somebody ought to be keeping an eye on Mabs Pierce and sent the health visitor up.

The health visitor called in to see Mabs.
'You'll keep an eye on Mrs. Lee-Fox, won't you,' said the health visitor, an eye on Eddie's facial bruises.

'Of course,' said Mabs.
'What's the matter with Eddie's face?' asked the health visitor.
'Fell into the grate,' said Mabs, 'didn't you, Eddie?'
'That's right,' said Eddie. Mabs clasped Eddie to her, with a spurt of genuine affection. She was feeling better. She felt that in some way or other she'd off-loaded a bit of bad.

Eddie looked up at his mother with such evident pleasure and gratitude that the health visitor decided she'd better let well alone. Even if you feared a child was being battered, the problem of alternatives remained. Mrs. Wild was of the opinion that short of death, a natural home was better than an unnatural one, with changing foster parents or in institutions. The child's spirit died, in any case, if the mother failed to love it, no matter who intervened; just the same way as its body would die if she failed to nurture it. And once the spirit died you could do what you liked with the body, and make yourself feel better, but scarcely ever the child.

Eddie's spirit hovered on the brink of life and death.

Liffey's baby floated free and wild. In normal first pregnancies the baby's head descends into the cavity of the pelvis at the thirty--eighth week: a process known as lightening, inasmuch as the pressure on lungs and heart and digestive organs lessens and the mother thereafter feels more comfortable. Liffey's baby's head did no such thing: it could not. The placenta barred its way. Liffey's baby did not care. Liffey's baby, headstrong, trusted to a providence which had already acted against it, whether twisted by Mabs' malevolent will, or merely by the laws of chance. One pregnancy in a hundred is a placenta praevia: does every one of those foetuses have a Mabs in the background? Surely not; such foetuses are merely accident prone, or event prone, as some individuals are; at one time or other in their life. Ladders fall on them or pigs out of windows, or bombs go off as they approach; or, in country terms, their crops fail and their cattle sicken and a witch has overlooked them.

Liffey's baby, overlooked or accident prone, take it how you will, leapt in Liffey's womb, and its umbilical cord – now twenty inches long – exerted gentle pressure on the upper side of the placenta, so that it slid further over to cover Liffey's cervix fully. And then it leapt again and contrived an actual knot in the cord, but fortunately – or whatever we mean by that word – the knot did not tighten, and the cord continued to supply the foetus with blood, through its two ingoing arteries, and remove it, through its single outgoing vein. But there the knot was, annd should it tighten, that would be the end of that.

The baby sang to Liffey: Liffey drowsed: the knot did not tighten. Nor did Liffey's blood pressure rise: it stayed at around 20/77 of mercury – the upper figure being the pressure reached within the blood vessel at the height of a heart beat, and the lower figure being the minimum level to which the pressure falls between heart beats. The upper figure could vary, safely enough, with exercise, fatigue, excitement and emotion – and indeed had risen dramatically when Mabs kicked the puffball to pieces – but the lower figure could only vary as a result of some fundamental change in the circulation, which might tend to reduce the blood supply to the uterus, placenta and baby, and result in, what must at all costs be avoided, premature delivery.

Catharsis

In London the sun shone day after day. It was hot. Karen's boyfriend Pete was found asleep in the potting shed and lost his job. He turned up at Karen's house and introduced himself to Karen's mother. Karen's mother was a psychotherapist, and asked him in.
'How dare you have him in the house without asking me first,' shouted Karen, all red hair and spoilt pout, already on her way to Ray's.

Helga let her in. Ray and Bella and Richard were all out. Karen watched Helga wash dishes and peel potatoes and despised her.

Ray came home and was both disconcerted and delighted to find Karen in his kitchen.
'I've left home,' said Karen.
'You can stay here,' said Ray. 'Bella won't mind. You can help Helga with the children.'

They went upstairs. Helga clattered and crashed. Karen revealed to Ray that Bella was having an affair with Richard, an item of news she knew from an unkept confidence in her mother. Ray hit Karen, so shocked was he; Karen fell into Bella's arms, as she returned home with Richard. Ray knocked Richard down the stairs and Karen ran shrieking from the house.

Ray's nose bled heartily from Bella's blow, and she had to mop him up in the bathroom, her own eyes blurred with tears of remorse and indignation mixed. Richard rose, dazed and alone, from the floor, and gathered his belongings and prepared to leave, out into the night, wondering where he would go.

But Bella and Ray barred his way.

'Don't go,' said Ray. 'We must talk everything out,' and they led him by the hand to the kitchen, and there they sat all night, eating French bread and Brie, and drinking coffee, and more coffee, and whisky and more whisky, while tears ran and voices grew husky, and childhoods were remembered and rankling incidents recalled, and marital failures and erotic disappointments mulled over.

Richard realised that he was a bit-part player in Ray and Bella's drama: and he feared he had much the same rôle in Miss Martin's life. He was her route to self-esteem, not the gratification of her desires; and in all fairness, she was his.

He understood at last that Liffey, his marriage partner, was his true love, his true security, his true faithful companion and his happiness. Richard said as much. He wept. They all wept.

Ah, what a night it was, the Night of the Confessional, of remorse and whisky and embraces and the signing of pacts and the announcement of good intentions, and as the day broke and the noise of traffic grew, and the grass of the park emerged out of dawn grey into brilliant morning green, all felt purged and re-born.

It was only when *The Times* was stuffed through the letterbox, and Tony and Tina were still asleep, and the replacement kitten yowling with hunger, that it was realised that Helga had gone.

Packed her bags and gone.

Richard left for the office. Tina and Tony emerged startled from their bedrooms and organised their own breakfast and departure for school, and wrote their own notes apologising for their lateness, which they presented to Bella for signing. Ray took offence at this. Both children were weeping over Helga's leaving, but neither parent showed much concern. 'For God's sake,' snapped Bella. 'Stop whining. She was only the maid. It's not as if she was your mother.'

Richard knew he must break off his relationship with Miss Martin. She made it easy for him.
'You're never going to marry me, are you, Richard?' she blurted, out of her typewriter.

Richard was startled. He could not remember her ever using his first name. She had so far avoided it, as he avoided hers. He was not even sure, come to think of it, what her first name was.
'No,' he said.

'I'll tell your wife about us,' said Miss Martin: her eyes were hollow and her cheeks sunk. Her figure, no longer solid and shapeless, seemed scraggy and shapeless. Her eyes were malevolent.

Richard rang through to the Personnel Department and arranged to take its head out to lunch.

Miss Martin was sent for by Personnel during the course of the afternoon and transferred to the Computer Room.
Her replacement was a young woman with downcast eyes, a demure look and practised ways, lately transferred from the Manchester branch. Richard read invitation in the eyes, eventually raised to his over lunch – it was customary for bosses to take secretaries out to lunch on the first day of their appointment, so they could get to know each other – but steadfastly refused the invitation.

Now he was free of Bella, Helga and Miss Martin, he would concentrate on loving Liffey. It was clear to him that the world and the people in it were not perfectable; that one person's happiness could only be gained by the unhappiness of another; that if Liffey were to be happy, Miss Martin must be unhappy, and Bella, and Ray, and even himself. For deprived so suddenly of the sexual activity of which he had been accustomed, Richard was restless and wretched and irritable, and dissatisfied, and jealous, and very very hungry. But he bore all for the love of Liffey and in a mood of self-congratulation and sorrow mixed, and with a feeling of achievement and some kind of personal storm weathered, did he return, on that the thirty-eighth week of Liffey's pregnancy.

Bella, Ray, Tina and Tony went too. Bella thought Tina and Tony would benefit from a weekend in the country. Ray wondered if Liffey would be up to it, but Bella said of course she would: anyway, she, Bella would look after Liffey: she felt she had behaved badly towards her and wanted to make amends.

It was the children's half-term the following week and Bella thought perhaps she should leave them behind, to look after Liffey. They were really very good. Tony could help carry shopping and Tina could make beds and bread or whatever.

Didn't Richard think so?

Inside Liffey (10)

Thirty-eight weeks.

Liffey's baby was eighteen inches long: its weight was six pounds one ounce; it was layered nicely with subcutaneous fat. The vernix creased richly in the folds of its body. It lay head down, knees meeting wrists, ankles turning little feet towards each other, buttocks jutting out at a point just above Liffey's umbilical cord. The baby was now almost fully mature, and had it been born into the world that day would have had a ninety per cent chance of survival. Only the lungs were not quite ready, and would have had some trouble in performing their required task, the converting of oxygen.

Liffey herself was languorous and uncomfortable, and the normal relief expected at such a time, when the baby's head drops into the pelvis, and the maternal organs are relieved of this untoward pressure and that, did not occur. It could not. The placenta, positioned as it was, prevented it. The baby swayed and moved, and stayed free. What yet might prove its undoing remained for the time being a blessing.

Liffey moved slowly about the house. From time to time she breathed heavily and deeply. Every now and then her uterus contracted, painlessly, but growing taut and hard. It was a reassuring sensation, as if the body at least knew what it was doing. The contraction would last some twenty seconds and then fade away.

Liffey dreamt. How she dreamt! Were they the baby's dreams, or hers? She dreamed of strange landscapes, and of the dark, warm, busy world that was inside her. She dreamed that the baby was born: that it jumped out of her side and ran off laughing. Its hair was curly and it was aged about two. She dreamed she gave birth to a grown man and when he turned his face to look at her, it was Richard. She dreamed she gave birth to herself: that she split into cloned multitudes. She dreamed that Madge tied her feet together and forbade her to give birth at all. She dreamed that Mrs. Lee-Fox shut her in the seaside cottage and the waves rose and broke against the window; and rockets flew overhead: and she escaped in a junk. But there was a kind of blank panel in the mural of all her dreams, where the face of Mabs should have appeared but never did.

In the mornings she woke slowly, and dressed slowly, and the evenings came before the day had scarcely passed. She had very little sense of the passage of time; she functioned, yet her senses closed down around her: she saw and heard and touched the world through a dark film, as if preferring to see and hear and touch as the baby must – rocked and lulled in the dark.

Guests

And here they were, on Friday evening, pouring out of Richard's car, and yes, they were real: Richard and Ray and Bella and Tony and Tina: and yes, they were chattering and laughing and looking for sleeping bags and oh, they were hungry and tired, and no, Liffey mustn't move, not an inch, they were going to do everything, everything, only where was the tea and were there any more towels and no, Liffey, don't move the beds, get Ray to do it – where's Ray? Looking for flying saucers: everyone is, these days, and this is UFO country, isn't it – and Liffey, is there any brown paper we can use for the loo; newspaper is so crude, isn't it? And Liffey, no Liffey, sit down – just tell us where the onions are so we can make a sauce for the spaghetti – oh, in the garden – where in the garden? – ah, there – where are the plates, Liffey? Liffey is there any hot water, and Liffey, Tina's fallen and hurt her knee on the torn mat; yes, thank you for the plasters, and I do think the mat ought to be moved – where's Richard? Ah, taken Ray to try Tucker Pierce's cider, how like a man, to leave everything to the womanfolk. How long, Liffey? Two weeks! Now if we can just get the table laid and the candles – where are the candles? – lit, everything will be ready by the time the men get home. Can Tony just have some cocoa and go to bed?

That's one dinner saved! And Tina had better have some too. They simply love the country. You're so lucky, Liffey, right out of the rat-race, and I'm sure one gets on better with a husband for not seeing him all the time and of course Richard, as everyone knows, adores you, Liffey, and is fundamentally absolutely, totally faithful to a vision of you, Liffey. Liffey, is there any ice? I can't seem to get it out of the tray. Most people have plastic, Liffey, not tin. Now you're not to overtire yourself.

Liffey, exhausted, faded back into a kind of gentle stupor. Richard came back from Cadbury Farm in a luxurious and loving mood. His arms were full of puffballs. He laid them in rows of ascending size upon the kitchen table.

Who needs shops, when the fields are so abundant?

Liffey waited until the guests were in bed, and Richard had made gentle, affectionate remorseful love to her and fallen asleep, and got up and cleaned the kitchen and laid breakfast, feeling that this was the way she could best allocate her strength, and then went back to bed and propped pillows beneath her back, and slept as upright as she could manage. A light, uneasy sleep. She thought the baby did not want the visitors. But they kept Mabs away.

In the morning Richard sliced a sharp knife into the biggest puffball, and where the cut was the flesh gaped wide, as human flesh gapes under the surgeon's knife, and Liffey stared, aghast.

'What's the matter?'

'Nothing.'

He dipped the slices of puffball into first flour, then egg, then breadcrumbs and fried them in butter. Bella and Ray and Richard ate with enthusiasm; Tina and Tony politely declined and made do with Weetabix, and Liffey fainted dead away.

'Perhaps we'd better call the doctor,' said Ray, when Liffey had been patted and coaxed awake, which took only half a minute or so.

'Honestly, I'm all right,' said Liffey.

'I'd better leave Tony and Tina,' said Bella. 'She shouldn't be on her own, should she.'

'I don't know why puffballs should have such an effect,' said Richard.

'It's because of the operation,' said Tina, softly. No one, usually, listened to Tina.

Liffey wondered about whether or not to go to the doctor about her fainting fit, but the assembled company, now sitting in the garden in the early sun, drinking coffee, clearly did not want to get into cars and drive her anywhere so boring. Liffey, the general feeling was, was showing her hypochondria again. Pregnant women fainted; everyone knew that.

Liffey went inside and swept floors and made beds. Tina helped, and told her about Helga, and how Helga was now working for her girlfriend's boyfriend, making Indian sweetmeats. She had no work permit for anything other than domestic work so was earning only fifteen pounds a week but don't tell Mummy because her visa has expired and if Mummy tells the Home Office Helga will be deported and we'll never see her again.

'Why should Bella do a thing like that?' asked Liffey, surprised.

Tina shrugged. She was a sad, sallow little girl with a round face and button eyes. She kept her eyes fixed on Liffey's tummy.
'I don't think I want a baby,' she said.

Her brother Tony wandered around the garden, kicking at tufts of grass and slashing the heads off what he claimed to be weeds but were usually budding flowers. He stared at Liffey's stomach too, but in a more prurient, less sympathetic way.

'It's because Helga's left, I'm afraid,' said Bella. 'She really was an irresponsible little bitch.'

Tony watched Liffey and Richard together, and giggled, and sniggered, as if imagining them in the act of love.

'I don't know why it is,' complained Bella. 'I thought if you brought children up to be open about sex, they didn't get like that. I expect it was Helga. What a little prude she always was.'

Ray lay in the sun and Bella rubbed his back with oil.

'Do we really have to stay here two whole days?' asked Bella. 'I'm missing a perfectly good publishers' party on Sunday.'
'We can't just dump the children and go,' said Ray.
'It's not dumping,' said Bella.
'Anyway, I like it here,' said Ray.
'I don't,' said Bella. 'It's tiny, and scruffy and fancy having to eat pork and beans at our time of life, and the beds are uncomfortable and Liffey lumbers round making everyone feel bad – she used to be such fun, do you remember? – and Richard can only talk about freeze-dried peas.'
'You don't like seeing Richard and Liffey together. You're jealous.'

'I could have Richard any time I wanted him but I don't want him any more.'

She didn't either. She felt quite happy with Ray. She had forgiven him for not being her rightful husband. Anger and guilt had been purged by the confessional. She could even accept the episode of Karen as her rightful punishment for past sins. Like candyfloss in the mouth – so much abundant glory gone, melted, nothing. All she was now was bored.

'Can't we go tomorrow morning?'

But no, Richard had accepted an invitation to Sunday lunch at Cadbury Farm.
'Oh Christ,' said Bella to Ray. 'Now we'll all get food poisoning. What does Richard see in those boring peasants anyway.'
'They're *real* people,' said Ray, turning his mottled chest to the sun. 'Bred out of the soil.'

He still yearned for Karen. Karen told her friends how she had seduced Ray, and about the sorry state of his legs, and the funny mottled colour of his member, and was believed; and wherever they saw his picture at the head of his column in the *Evening Gazette* she and her friends laughed, and felt less powerless in the world.

Miss Martin's mother had a bad night with her daughter, who presently demanded to be admitted to a mental hospital. They spent a long morning waiting in the out patients department of a psychiatric hospital, only to be told that the case did not require in-patient treatment, and that pills would do. Jeff was most supportive, but believed on balance that Miss Martin was fantasising, and feared his own liking for pornographic magazines was somehow to blame.

While Bella oiled Ray and complained, and Liffey toiled, and Tony and Tina mourned, Richard talked to Tucker about the benefits of planting in phase with the moon.

'Never heard of anything like that,' said Tucker.

'It's part of the old knowledge,' said Richard. 'It's died out here where it originated. Now the city folk have to bring it back to the countryside. Root crops are planted at the waxing of the moon: leaf crops at the wane.'

'His brain's weakened,' Tucker complained to Mabs. 'I hope you haven't been giving him anything.'

'I've no quarrel with him,' said Mabs. 'Only with her, and that's your fault.'

'I don't really want to go to the farm tomorrow,' said Liffey to Richard, at tea. He was cutting open another puffball. Its rich, sweet, sickly scent stood between her and the fresh clean air her lungs demanded. She opened the window. 'You are full of whims and fancies,' he complained. 'Why not now?'

'Mabs frightens me,' said Liffey.

'Mabs!' he laughed.

'She kicked one of those puffballs to pieces,' Liffey said.

'Country people are superstitious about them. I don't know why.'

'She wants to harm me, Richard.'

'Why, Liffey?' Richard sounded quite cross.

'I don't know.'

'Perhaps you've been messing with Tucker?' He was joking.

He sliced into the next puffball and Liffey thought of her own pale, stretched flesh.

'Supposing the baby starts early?' she asked. 'Supposing I start to bleed.'

'Liffey, you are making ever such heavy weather over this pregnancy.'

'Sorry. I suppose London's full of girls just dropping their babies in a corner of the office, and going straight back to the typewriter?'

'Well, yes. More or less. That sounds like the old Liffey.'

The old Liffey. Little lithe silly Liffey. Liffey remembered her old self with nostalgia, but knew it was gone for good.

Tucker had driven it out of her. Mabs flew shrieking through her mind, perched on a broomstick; heavy, smooth, nyloned legs ready to push and shove and get her in the stomach. All Richard did was slice puffballs, and smile, and pretend that nothing had changed. But it had. Richard had changed, too. He had grown from a boy into a man and she was not sure that she liked the man.

But she had to. He paid the rent. He bought the food. She and the baby had to have a home. And he was the baby's father. Richard, I like you. I love you.

Please, dear God, let me like you, love you, trust you.

'Don't you love the smell of puffballs?' Richard asked. 'Wonderful!' said Liffey. 'Of the earth, earthy.'

Tucker, with earth beneath his nails. That was not love, nor lust, nor folly, nor spite: that was nothing to do with the will, with the desire for good or bad, that was simply what had happened. An open door, and someone coming through it, further and further until he was not just inside the room but inside her as well.

'I don't know what you had to go and ask them over for,' grumbled Mabs. She was preparing a distillation of mother-wort for herself, and syrup of buckthorn for Debbie, who complained of stomach pains, presumably due to constipation. Debbie was locked in her room for not having properly cleaned the kitchen and was using the pains as an excuse.

Mabs was in good spirits. Tucker had taken her to a dance at Taunton. She'd had her hair done at the hairdresser and bought a new flowered skirt.

The milk yield accepted and paid for by the Milk Marketing Board was higher than it had ever been; the cattle sheds could be retiled: it had been a good spring for silage, and a fine summer for hay. Apart from Liffey's baby, and her own inability to conceive, it might almost be called a lucky year.

The bad times were nearly over. Mabs felt that once Liffey's baby was delivered she would start her own. That was the way things went. And she confidently expected Liffey to die under the surgeon's knife.

Mabs gave Tucker a twist of thornapple in his elderberry wine, which made him mellow and complaisant, and took the edge out of his complaints, and she felt it was rather an improvement. His lovemaking lasted longer, too.

Early on Sunday morning Ray took Tony out for a walk. They went up the hill and stopped at the point where there was an excellent view of the Tor. As they paused, and puffed, for neither were in good condition, they saw a round red spinning disc of considerable size but unclear distance from them, move towards them, move away again, vanish, re-appear, shift colour from red to orange, and depart again, not to reappear.

Ray and Tony were silent.
'That was a flying saucer,' said Ray, eventually.
'Don't be stupid, Dad,' said Tony, embarrassed. 'Anyway don't call them flying saucers. They're UFOs.'
'But you do agree we saw one?'
'No, I don't,' said Tony, wretchedly.

Ray ran back to report his sighting, and had to wake a sleeping house to do so. Bella was angry.
'Your brain's gone to jelly,' she shouted. 'You're so afraid of your own mortality you've taken to seeing things.'
'It was real, Bella.'
'Tony, did you see the same thing as your father?'
'There was something, Mum, but it could have been a fireball or a shooting star or something.'

Ray took hold of Tony and shook him.

'If you ask me,' said Bella, 'that's the first physical contact you've had with your son since the day he was born.'
Ray stopped shaking.

'Everything wonderful in my life,' he said to Bella, sadly, 'you destroy. I can't even see a flying saucer but you entirely spoil and diminish the event.'
'UFO,' said Tony.

The quarrel continued until it was impossible for Bella and Ray to stay under the same roof. Tony and Tina wandered in the garden. Bella demanded that Richard take her to the station at once, and Ray got in the car at the last moment and Liffey did what she could to comfort Tony and Tina. Their parents did not have the spiritual energy left to say goodbye.

Bella got to her publisher's party.

Richard was laughing when he got home.
'Oh Liffey, darling,' he said, 'how lucky we are. We've had our hard times but things are going to be better from now on.'

He touched no wood as he spoke.

The Unexpected

Sun glazed, flowers glowed, bees droned. Richard and Liffey walked down the lane from Honeycomb Cottage to Cadbury Farm, on the way to Sunday lunch. They held hands. Tony and Tina, taken aback by their parents' sudden departure, walked behind, subdued.

Now, in late summer, after a season of Liffey's tending, the cottage might have graced the top of a chocolate box. Hollyhocks, roses and wallflowers tumbled together against the whitewashed walls; swallows dived and soared above the thatch; Tucker's black and white cows grazed serenely in the field behind; down on the stream moorhens paddled against the current, in the dappled shadow of weeping willows. Peas and beans and carrots flourished in the small vegetable patch: and there would have been potatoes in the field had it not been for the cows.

'You do make the best of everything, Liffey,' said Richard, contentedly, as they walked.

He carried a puffball with him. It was tucked under his arm. It seemed to stare ahead, as he walked; there were, by chance blemishes spaced like eyes and mouth on its smooth surface. He was taking it as a gift for Mabs.

'I'm not sure she'll appreciate it,' Liffey said.
'But they're so nourishing,' Richard replied, 'and so delicious. I'll convert her.'

They came to the end of the wood. The long grey building of Cadbury Farm lay before them, with its crumbling dry stone walls, and the neglected outhouses, with their collapsing red tiled roofs. Away to the right of them, the ground swept down and across the levels of the valley, past small villages and hedgerowed meadows, threaded by ribbons of road, where toy cars and lorries trundled, to where the Tor rose, suddenly and dramatically, at odds with the gentle landscape which surrounded it.

'They say there's a magnetic force line straight from the Tor to Jerusalem,' said Richard.
'Who says?'
'Can't remember,' said Richard. It had been Vanessa. She had told him to find a pine tree on a ley line and lean against it, when ever his system needed revitalising. She had told him about twisted apple trees and yews which marked the radiating force lines from the Tor; about the old roads between Stonehenge and Glastonbury; about how it was no coincidence that he lived in London in the shadow of

Primrose Hill – also a seat of power – and in the country, in the shadow of the Tor. Deciding, by virtue of his dwelling place, that Richard must be a rather special person after all, she had allowed him to sleep with her, and declared herself revitalised by the encounter and not – as she had feared – enervated. But she would not repeat the experience, no matter how his by now practised hand strayed over her long, young, cool body. Once was enough – she said. They knew all there was about one another now – she'd as soon recharge herself against a pine tree or a ley line. But could he get her another modelling job?

Richard thought he probably couldn't, but since then had regarded the Tor with more respect, as something with spiritual meaning, which could bring good things about, rather than a tourist trap for ruined abbey and UFO freaks. Things had gone wrong, since then. He'd talked to Vanessa about Liffey.
'I didn't know you were married,' she'd said, surprised. 'I don't want to get into all that scene. You should have told me.'
'I didn't think marriage mattered to you lot, one way or another.'
But it had seemed to; she had said she'd ring him when she'd worked things out, but hadn't rung: and Richard was vaguely sorry, since Vanessa was restful, and her expectations from sex so few that he was bound to please, and his attempts at seduction for that reason unclouded but relieved as well. All that was behind him now.

'You're not tired?' he asked, now, solicitously.
'No,' said Liffey. But she was. From time to time she had a dragging pain in her abdomen.

Labour

Thirty-eight weeks. The average duration of pregnancy is forty weeks, but can vary from woman to woman, and from

236

one pregnancy to another, and from one marriage to another. Each pregnancy differs: each woman differs. Liffey's baby was ready. All through life the muscles of a woman's uterus, like the muscles in the rest of her body, contract and relax from time to time, lest they waste away. All through pregnancy uterine contractions occur, every half hour or less, for about half a minute at a time. In late pregnancy, they become noticeable, though not painful: they are known as Branston Hicks contractions. When labour begins, these contractions become regular, stronger, and more forceful. They last for forty seconds or more: they mount to a crescendo more slowly, fade away more gradually. As labour progresses, uterine contractions come at shorter and shorter intervals; they are designed to eliminate the canal of the cervix without damaging its muscle, incorporating it into the lower uterine segment, so that the baby can be expelled. The upper uterine segment, where the contraction begins, and which consists almost entirely of muscle, behaves during labour in a unique way, known as retraction. It shortens itself slightly after every contraction, thus increasing its pulling power on the lower segment, which is already much stretched and weakened by the baby it contains. The pressures produced inside are considerable. The cervix, as the canal above it is, little by little, inexorably, drawn up, widens, or dilates, eventually making an opening some nine-and-a-half centimetres in diameter, enough for the baby's head to pass through – all going well with the baby, that is. This first stage of labour, as it is called, takes a different length of time in different women, varying from two hours to twenty-four but with some exceptions either side. It is not possible to anticipate the duration of a labour, nor whether the contractions will be experienced as discomfort or pain: but as a rough working estimate it requires some one hundred and fifty contractions to produce a first child, about seventy-five for a second or third child, and about fifty for a fourth.

Liffey, walking down the lane with Richard, had a mild backache, and a slight dragging pain in her tummy: but so she'd had from time to time over the past few weeks. Earlier in the morning she'd had an uprush of energy: had swept and cleaned and even scrubbed, under and around her warring guests, but this had now passed, leaving her soft and languid.

'What a pity,' said Mabs, when they got to the Farm, 'I was expecting your smart London friends. So was Tucker. Weren't you, Tucker!'

'They had to get back in a hurry,' said Richard.

'London folk are always in a hurry,' said Mabs, shooing Tina and Tony out into the yard. 'I suppose my invitation wasn't good enough for the likes of them.'

She was annoyed. Richard offered her the puffball by way of pacification. It made her laugh.

'God-awful things,' she said. 'You're quite mad, Richard.' But she consented to slice it, a little later, and place it under the roast to catch the drippings, and serve it like Yorkshire pudding.

'Just because I never have,' said Mabs, nobly, 'is no reason why I never should.' Her annoyance seemed to have evaporated. She smiled at Liffey, and pulled back a chair for her, saying, 'Don't go into the parlour, since it's only you. Stay and talk while I work.'

Tucker served elderberry wine, clearing a space on the crowded table for bottle and glasses.

'How are you keeping, Liffey?' he asked. 'No pains?'

'No more than usual,' said Liffey.

'She's not allowed to produce for another two weeks,' said Richard. 'I can't take time off until then.'

'You're not going to be *there*,' said Mabs, in horror.

'Fathers are supposed to be,' said Richard, helplessly.

'Liffey, you wouldn't want him to see you in that state?' demanded Mabs.

Both Mabs and Tucker wore their Sunday best. Tucker was wearing a collar and tie, which somehow diminished him. It made him seem uneasy and ordinary, and grimy rather than weathered, as if the ingraining accomplished by sun and wind was the mark of poverty. Mabs wore an oyster coloured silk blouse, already splashed by juices from the rib of beef she was roasting and the sprouts she was stewing, but her hair was pulled firmly and neatly back, showing her broad face to advantage. She has lost weight recently, Liffey decided, and that made her high cheek bones more prominent and her dark eyes larger and more glittery than usual. Moreover, Mabs, who seldom so much as looked in a mirror, but saw herself, as it were, defined by sky and hills, had today outlined them with black.

A witch, thought Liffey. A witch preparing for witchery. The ceremonial has begun.

Nonsense, thought Liffey. My neighbour, about whom I sometimes get strange fancies, connected, no doubt with my pregnancy. My neighbour, the salt of the earth.

'I don't think it's going to apply,' said Liffey. 'I'm going to have a Caesarian, anyway. Or so they say.'
'They only say you might, Liffey,' said Richard. 'Don't exaggerate.'
'It's natural for her to get nervous,' said Tucker, 'at this stage.'
'The way I look at it,' said Mabs, 'a man's place during childbirth is down at the pub.'

Everyone laughed, Even Liffey.

Tony and Tina had been given a bag of crisps each and sent out to play with the others. The others were nowhere to be seen, so they sat on a wall and swung their legs and waited, with some alarm, for further events to transpire. They were hungry, but relieved not to have to sit down with the grown-ups for dinner. They were accustomed to the stripped pine furniture, uncluttered lines and primary colours of home, and found the rich dark mahogany and oak, the dust, and litter and the crumbling walls of the Pierce's kitchen oppressive. They were accustomed, moreover, to adults who talked to them, and who did not offer them crisps in lieu of conversation. They were accustomed to Richard, but did not trust him; liked Liffey but judged that she was hardly in a condition to look after them; were angry with their parents for abandoning them; and missed Helga. They munched and crunched their crisps, and were silent, faces impassive.

Mabs had got their names wrong: had taken Tina for a boy, Tony for a girl.

'You can't tell which is which,' she complained, in their hearing. 'I'd be ashamed to let my children out, looking like that.'

Debbie was locked in her room again. Today the reason given was that she failed to clean her father's Sunday shoes. She lay with her legs drawn up to her chest, occasionally vomiting and groaning. She had had another dose of buckthorn to cure her constipation.

Buckthorn was a tall shrub which grew in the woods around. It had little creamy white flowers in spring and inviting black berries in autumn; and grew, in these parts, without thorns. The thorny kind, or Spinachristi, provided Christ's crown of thorns; Mabs' kind, though without thorns, provided a powerful cascara-like purgative, which she prepared, with sugar and ginger, from the dried berries, and with which, as her mother, grandmother and great-grandmother before her, she dosed her children, doing them one damage or another. It was a local custom so to do. Dr. Southey would suggest to mothers that they keep it for cows, but they politely agreed and kept on dosing. Sometimes he thought he would emigrate, and take a post in Central Africa, where superstition and witchcraft would be something clear and definite to be grappled with, not a running, secret thread through the fabric of life.

Eddie played silently in the corridor outside Debbie's room.

He crouched on the floor, listening to her groans, zooming his hand over the rug like a dive-bombing plane. There were blue bruises on his upper arms. Eddie was waiting for Audrey to come back from church. Audrey had a nice voice and a natural ear and had joined the church choir, partly because she could make 35p a wedding and more for funerals and partly because she fancied the curate, Mr. Simon Eaves. She looked at him with large, glittery, inviting eyes and he struggled to believe there was no invitation in them; she was a child.

Today Audrey asked if she could stay behind after church and speak to him, and Mr. Eaves felt he could not very well refuse, and also that it would be prudent not to see her alone.

'Well,' said Mabs, preparing the puffball for the oven, 'I don't know about you lot, but I'm certainly looking forward to the baby. You've really made me feel quite broody, Liffey.'

She sliced into the puffball with too blunt a knife, so that the edge crumbled as if it were a ripe Stilton she was parting, and not an edible fungi.

As she cut through the flesh, not cleanly, but bruising and chipping on the way, she stared at Liffey's stomach.

'I'm imagining it,' thought Liffey. If she were doing it on purpose, surely Richard would have noticed? But Richard smiled amiably on, his mind on good red meat juices and the creamy texture of roasted puffball. And Tucker stared into space and drank.

'But why does Mabs hate me,' wondered Liffey. 'I am not a hateful person. I am a nice person. Everyone likes me. They may forget me, but if I'm around, they like me.'

'I have slept with Mabs' husband but Mabs doesn't know that. Mabs can't know. Tucker was lying.'

When the knife had pierced to the very centre of the puffball Mabs gave it another twist.

'She hates my baby, too. She wants to kill it.'

Liffey looked at Richard for help. Richard was speaking. 'Puffballs are truly amazing. Nature's richest bounty. And you can hang them up and dry them, and then they make wonderful firelighters. Did you know that, Tucker?'
'Can't say I did,' said Tucker. 'We use a gas poker to light our fires, in any case.'

He smiled at Richard as he spoke, as a grown-up might smile at a rather slow child; and then he looked at Liffey with a sympathetic expression on his face, which would have been pleasant enough except that Mabs was watching Tucker watching her, and Mabs' eyes seemed not just brown, dark brown, but deepest black.

Things fell into place.

'Mabs knows Tucker comes up to see me. Tucker wasn't lying. Mabs knows. Knows he came up again, and I let him.'

Make it a dream.

Dinner is served, in the cold dining room, on the French polished table. It is a room that is hardly ever used.

'So, Liffey,' said Mabs brightly. Tucker carved. Mabs served. A face appeared briefly and hungrily at the window, and disappeared again. Tina's. 'Only two weeks more to go. I expect you'll be glad when it's over.'
'I like being pregnant,' said Liffey, brightly. Liffey knew that she must now assert her will against Mabs: must oppose bad with good: must send out against her such spiritual forces as she could muster. Mabs had a strong, evil battalion already assembled: as she doled out mixed thawed peas and carrots, and roast and mashed potatoes both, she doled out

spite, anger, enmity and mystery. They were hers to distribute.

Wonderful dinner! Liffey said so.

Liffey must be cheerful, honest, ordinary, positive and kind. Then all might still be well. She must set up a bulwark of good will. Her defence must be an armoury of opposites. She had no attacking weapons. She could not love Mabs, who had stuck a knife through Liffey, into Liffey's baby, and twisted.

Mabs, who limped when you drove a nail through her footprint.

Ha-ha.

Yes, Richard. Mabs, witch. Do you know? Are you part of it, too?

O madness! Paranoia! Pregnancy!

Liffey looked down at her plate. On Richard's plate, and Tucker's, were good thick lean and shapely slices of roast rib of beef. On her, Liffey's plate, was a little mound of fat and gristle.

Mabs watched Liffey watching her plate. Liffey raised her eyes and stared at Mabs.

Mabs smiled. Mabs knew. Mabs knew that Liffey knew that Mabs knew.

Richard noticed nothing, or pretended to notice nothing. He was fishing for more puffball slices with Tucker's carving fork.

'Give Liffey a decent piece of meat,' said Tucker, mildly. 'She doesn't want too much at this stage,' said Mabs, 'do you Liffey?'
'I'm fine,' said Liffey, 'really fine with what I've got.'

Well done, Liffey.

Of course what it's all about, thought Liffey, with the calmness born of certainty, is that Mabs thinks it's Tucker's baby.

'Have some puffball, Liffey,' said Mabs, 'now Richard's found it. I was hoping he'd forget but no such luck.'
'No, thank you,' said Liffey. Ah, that was wrong. She should have accepted, devoured her own flesh and blood. Or at any rate her own white, bloodless flesh. The life blood drained away. Too late.

'Liffey,' said Richard, 'you must at least taste. I insist. After all the trouble everyone's been to.'

Eat, said the baby. You must choose now not between good and bad, but between the lesser of evils. Eat, smile, hope.

'Really, Liffey,' chided Richard, 'you're supposed to be eating for two.'
'Don't upset her,' said Tucker. 'Not in her condition.'
'It's an entirely natural process,' said Richard. 'Nothing to worry about. African mothers go into the bush, have their babies, pick them up and go straight back to work in the fields.'
They all looked at Liffey, to see how she would take this.
'And then they die,' said Liffey, before she could stop herself.
Open a chink to let doubt out, and a tide of ill will would surge back in.
Bright, brave, bold! That's the way, Liffey. If ever you fought, fight now.

Liffey laughed, to show she didn't mean it.

'Exactly when is the baby due?' asked Mabs.
'October 10th,' said Richard for Liffey.

Mabs got up and rummaged in a drawer amongst old batteries, dried-out pens, bills, string, ancient powder puffs and tubes of this and that with stubborn tops, and rusted skewers, and brought out a leaflet the cat had walked upon with muddy paws. 'The doctor gave me this,' she said. 'After the fifth baby, in just about as many years. He said I might work it out for myself.'

'Work what out?' Tucker was nervous.

'When it was, you know, conceived. It's wonderful the way they can tell, these days. They know everything there is to know in hospitals.'

'It was back in December or January, some time,' said Liffey, swiftly, vaguely.

'According to this,' said Mabs, 'it was over Christmas.'

'We moved in on January 7th,' said Liffey, thankfully.

'So you did,' said Mabs. 'Do you remember, Richard? What a terrible time you both had? You had to rush straight off back to London, Richard, didn't you, and then that weekend poor Liffey had an upset stomach. I remember clearly thinking, you poor things; if you expected a second honeymoon, you certainly weren't getting one then. Such lovebirds you seemed. Of course if Liffey was pregnant that explains her upset stomach.'

'Yes I expect it did,' said Liffey.

'Nothing to do with my cooking after all,' laughed Mabs. Then she seemed to look at the leaflet more carefully. 'No, wait a minute. Christmas was your last period. The baby must have been conceived just around the time you moved in. I must say, Richard, you don't lose much time! In between all that running around and train catching. Remember?'

Richard remembered very well. The days were seared into his memory.

'Of course Tucker was over a lot, helping Liffey out,' said Mabs, into the silence. 'That's so, isn't it Tucker?'

Mabs laughed. Tucker grunted.

'Of course you London people are different,' said Mabs, 'but I don't see anyone round here so easy about rearing another man's child.'

Nobody laughed or grunted or spoke.

Richard blinked, as if by shutting his eyes he would then wake up into a more real and more believable world.

Upstairs Debbie screamed, but the sound went unnoticed.

'Do shut up, Mabs,' said Tucker, 'or I'll break your bloody jaw.'

'I think you'd better take me home, Richard,' said Liffey. 'I don't feel very well.'

The dull pain was gone but the piercing pain now seemed established as a permanent reality and was increasing in intensity. A sizeable segment of placenta had torn away from the uterine wall. Liffey, although ignorant of this fact – indeed, having known remarkably little of what had been going on inside her for the last nine months – nevertheless felt something was going wrong somewhere. Mabs' allegations and revelations seemed to Liffey, now, of no particular relevance.

But for Richard, of course, they were.

'Home,' he said. 'What do you mean by home, Liffey? I don't think what we have is a home.'

Mabs, Liffey realised, was on her feet, arm outstretched, pointing at Liffey: black eyes staring.
'Thief,' she cried. 'You stole what was mine. I hope you die.'

'Richard,' observed Liffey, 'I do have a pain. I think we ought to go.'
'You can't pull the wool over my eyes,' said Richard. 'What do you think I am? A fool? I could see the way things were

246

going.' But of course he hadn't. All the same, the claim to knowledge lessened the humiliation, just a little.

Tucker spoke.

'No reason to think it's my baby,' said Tucker to Richard, man to man. 'Might be yours: might be mine.'

Richard turned his blue eyes, no longer merry, but still crinkling, of executive habit, to Liffey's, and found them abstracted. He slapped her. Her head shook, and her body, but her look of indifference remained.

'Don't you see what you've done!' shouted Richard. He had trusted Liffey with the better part of his nature, and she had betrayed his trust. There was, he felt, nothing good left in the world. And she had stolen so much of his past as well. She had invalidated so much – the love and concern she had elicited from him; his worry about the growing child; the guilt and inconvenience he had endured; the conscience, and indeed the money, he had expended – all had been for nothing, had meant nothing: had been as little to Liffey as it had been, once, to his mother. And Liffey seemed not even to notice his distress.

The placenta tore a little further. Liffey's uterus began to bleed. No doubt Mabs' curse – for curse it was, a malevolent force directed along a quivering outstretched hand, and not a mere overlooking or ill-wishing – had something to do with it, if only by virtue of the sudden alteration in Liffey's hormonal levels, as shock and anxiety assailed her, and the rise in her blood pressure occasioned by sudden emotion.

Liffey was not aware, so far, that she was bleeding. But the pain intensified.
'Take me home, Richard,' said Liffey.

Richard was staring at Tucker. Little grimy Tucker in his collar and tie. Richard did not really believe that Tucker, by virtue of his way of life, was his superior. Richard had been playing games, as the rich and confident will do with the humble and struggling. Richard despised Tucker.

A wife may be unfaithful with a prince, and not be considered defiled. Glory can be transmitted via the genitals. But Tucker!

'Richard,' Liffey was saying, 'I have to be looked after.'

'Let him look after you,' said Richard, and left Mabs and Tucker's house, head hunched into his shoulders, walking briskly, stonily through the yard, mangy dogs yapping at his crisp blue denim, Tony and Tina falling in behind, up the lane, looking neither to left nor right, to where his car was parked outside Honeycomb Cottage, and piled Tony and Tina in the back, while they protested about hunger and clothes and homework left behind, and drove to London. Quickly, for fear of further pollution, as if evil followed him from the Somerset sky, as if Glastonbury was beaming out some kind of searchlight of dismay, meant especially for him.

Richard, too, got to Bella's publishing party in time, but he was feeling sick with misery, resentment and disillusion, and possibly also from Mabs' dinner, and did not enjoy the party at all. Afterwards he went to see Vanessa, who was pleased to see him, in the way a rather busy person is pleased to see a stray cat, and told him she'd been stoned out of her mind for the last few weeks but had now reformed, and encouraged him to cry gently into the night for his lost Liffey, while she, Vanessa, rang girlfriend after girlfriend to discuss the ethics of whether or not she should own a car, positing the good of comfort against the evil of lead pollution of the sky. He heard himself referred to as a strung-out executive hung-up on a wife who was having it off with a cow-hand, and fell asleep, reassured by the ease with which words could modify experience.

Tucker left shortly after Richard did. He just took the car and went.

'You'd better walk on back up to Honeycomb, girl,' he said

as he left. 'There'll be no sense out of Mabs for an hour or two.'

Mabs strode the room, up and down, up and down. She seemed to have forgotten Liffey, who drooped over her belly, willing the pain away. The floor seemed to shake beneath Mabs' footfall, although surely it was made of solid stone. Mabs seemed larger then life, like a giantess.

Liffey's baby was quiet. Liffey knew it was apprehensive: she had not known it like that before. All right, said Liffey to her baby, reassuring where no reassurance was, all right. She made a conscious effort to modify her own mood: to lessen shock and fright, to accept pain and not to fight it, as Madge had once tried to teach her, while Liffey had refused to learn. Little Liffey, long ago, refusing Madge's knowledge, that the world is hard and you'd better learn to manage it.

All right, mother, you win.

Liffey stood up. Blood streamed down her legs. It was bright, almost cheerful.

'Mabs,' said Liffey, 'can I use the phone?'
Thus the habit of politeness spoke, foolishly. Madge would just have grabbed, before worse befell.

Worse befell – Mabs, barely pausing in her pacing, answered by ripping the telephone wire out of the hall and throwing the receiver across the room and breaking it.
'Mabs,' said Liffey, 'I'm bleeding.'
'Good,' said Mabs.

Liffey went to the door.
'Tucker,' she yelled. 'Tucker!' There was no reply. There were tyremarks in the dust of the yard. Tony and Tina were gone. A swallow swooped down, and up again, and was gone. It was quiet. The dogs did not yap and prance, as they usually did. They sniffed around, the rich red smell of Liffey's blood, perhaps too strong and strange for them.

Liffey had another pain now, of a different kind: a more patient, slow, insistent pain, travelling round from back to front, as the uterus, damaged as it was, began the business of taking up the cervical canal.

'Mabs,' said Liffey, 'get me to hospital.'
'Can't,' said Mabs. 'The car's gone.'

There was a trail of blood wherever Liffey moved.
'Mabs,' said Liffey, 'I'll die.'
'Good,' said Mabs.

Missions of Mercy

Audrey put her hand trustingly into that of the curate. Hers was warm and small. His was cold and bony. They were alone in the vestry, and he wished they were not.
'What's bothering you, Audrey?'

Audrey sang loud and lustily in the choir, but gave the impression, in church, of being some kind of emissary from a foreign power, and not a particularly friendly one at that. It might, he thought, have had something to do with the way her eyes roamed, with prurient speculation, over the males in the congregation. Most of them were elderly.
'It's my sister Debbie. She's ill. She needs the doctor.'
'Then surely your mother will fetch one?'
'My mum's not like that.'
'But why come to me? Why not go straight to the doctor?'

He knew the answer even as he asked. Audrey did not even bother to reply. Audrey fancied him. She did not fancy the doctor. He wished he were back in theological college. He did not know why he felt so helpless. Audrey's hand, which he had thought to be so childish, moved like an adult's in his, suggestively.

'My mum says Debbie's just constipated, but I know she's not, because she keeps messing her pants, and I'm the one who washes them so I should know. And my mum keeps on giving her buckthorn.'

'What's that.'

'It's all right for the cows, I suppose. It's just berries she boils up. Makes your mouth green.'

The curate took back his hand. Audrey looked disappointed and concluded the interview.

'Anyway,' she said, going, 'I really am worried about Debbie.'

Liffey stood bleeding in the yard of Cadbury Farm.

Mabs had slammed the door behind her. The piercing pain was worse: her brow was clammy, her clogs were full of blood. She took them off.

Well, thought Liffey, no good standing here. No good screaming, or crying, or fainting. No use lying down, either. If I do nothing, I will simply bleed to death. If it was only me, I wouldn't mind. I really wouldn't. I am not sure, on my own account, that I wish to stay in the world, considering its nature. What about you, baby? She felt the touch of its spirit, almost for the last time, still clear, still light and bright, almost elegant. The baby didn't have to want to live: it *was* life. She felt the touch on her hand, and there was little Eddie, standing in front of her, looking up at her, mumbling something incoherent, talking about Debbie. He pulled her forward, down the lane towards the road.

Liffey started walking.

'Only blood,' said Liffey aloud. 'Not even the baby's blood. My blood. Lots more where that came from, Eddie.'

But she wasn't so sure. She walked as fast as she could, but she was also aware that that was very slow, because Eddie kept standing in front of her, facing her, waiting for her to catch up. And as soon as she did, he was off again. Pain counted now as sensation. It had to. She had no idea what the time was, or how long she walked, and bled. The sun glazed in the sky behind the Tor; it was surprisingly high. She walked into it. She did not suffer, particularly. She travelled because she had to, as a bird might travel to a warmer climate, or a salmon cross the sea to the river it had to find.

The curate, though delayed by Audrey, presently arrived at a drinks-before-Sunday-dinner party at the new solicitor's house, and here he encountered the doctor, who was telling the solicitor's wife, not without pride, of the extent to which the old herbalism was still practised in the neighbourhood, and the fact that the village even boasted a wise woman, old Mrs. Tree, who claimed to have cured one of his terminal cancer patients with stewed root of Condor Vine – and admittedly the patient was still in remission. The curate, casually enough, mentioned buckthorn berries and his conversation with Audrey, at which the doctor groaned, said all Sundays were much the same, left his drink unfinished and his wife without transport, and took off for Cadbury Farm. 'His partner once had a child die from buckthorn,' said the doctor's wife, sadly. She finished her husband's sherry. The new solicitor was not going to be lavish with the drink.

The doctor found Liffey just where the lane joined the main road. He took Eddie into the car as well, since he could not leave a small, half-daft child standing by himself on a main road. He drove to the hospital, stopping briefly to talk to a policeman on the way.
'Aren't you going rather fast?' Liffey asked.
'Not particularly,' he said. 'Why didn't you use the phone?' He went through a red light as if it wasn't there at all.
'It was out of order,' said Liffey.
'Where's your husband? Isn't he home? It's Sunday, isn't it?'
'He had to get back to London,' said Liffey, easily. She rather enjoyed the ride; the piercing pain had dulled and she could now allow the other ones to come and go at will. She was sitting on a pile of curtains the doctor happened to have

in the car, on the way to the cleaners for his wife. He had prudently put them under Liffey to save his car upholstery. What funny bright red damp curtains, thought Liffey. I'm sure I have better taste than his wife.

Three nurses and a doctor and a wheeled stretcher, with two drips already set up, one clear, one red, waited at the top of the hospital steps.

'I say!' said Liffey.
'She might be drunk, or something,' said the doctor. 'She's euphoric. Tell the anaesthetist,' and hoped they heard him as they ran down the corridor away from him.

There had been valerian and coltsfoot in the elderflower wine; Mabs thought now that perhaps she had overdone the coltsfoot, and made everyone quarrelsome, including herself. Well, it was too late now. What was done was done. She wiped up the blood on the doorstep and worked out a story to tell when Liffey's body, with any luck, was found, and went upstairs to tell Debbie to stop that racket.

The doctor had forgotten all about Eddie but of course there he was, still sitting in the back of the car, crying.
'Christ,' said the doctor. 'This is supposed to be my day of rest.'

He sped and jerked Eddie all the way back to the village, and then bumped and banged him all the way down the lane, and parked amongst the yowling dogs because there was nowhere else, just as Mabs came out of the front door with Debbie's unconscious, or dead, body in her arms. The doctor got out of the car and ran, kicking at the dogs. He'd forgotten about the buckthorn berries.

'The phone's out of order,' offered Mabs by way of explanation, 'Eddie broke it, and Tucker's gone off God knows where, and I came back in from the cows and found blood all over the step and Debbie fell out of bed and must have banged her head because I went up and found her like this.'

'The blood is Mrs. Lee-Fox's,' said the doctor, laying Debbie flat, running his hands over her stomach. She groaned. Good. 'Fine neighbour you make: never in when you're wanted. She's in hospital now.'
'My, that was quick,' said Mabs. 'She was right as rain at lunch. Had a bit of a row with her husband, though. Well, she imagines things.'
'Why was the child in bed?'
'She's dirty. Wets the bed. She's got to learn. Is it bad?'
'Ruptured appendix,' said the doctor. 'Stands to reason. Help me get her in the car, quick.'
'I'll come to the hospital too,' said Mabs. 'Might as well. Will Mrs. Lee-Fox be all right?'
'I'd worry about the child, if I were you,' said the doctor, but he'd known mothers like this many a time, the object of their concern shifted to something more tolerable than danger to their own child. At least he hoped it was that.
'Mrs. Lee-Fox is in good hands.'
'It's a punishment on me,' said Mabs, and began to cry, though what was the punishment she did not make clear. Eddie had stopped crying. He stayed in the car while the doctor drove back to the hospital. This time they did not pass a policeman and when they reached the hospital the doctor had to stamp and roar to get attention, by which time he feared all hope for Debbie was probably lost.

'Two emergencies in one afternoon,' grumbled the theatre sister. 'You can tell it's Sunday.'

Birth

Bells rang, red lights glowed, people ran.

Liffey had been in the operating theatre for twenty minutes.

254

She had gone in fully conscious, been given one injection to reduce the secretions from her throat and mouth, another one which part-paralysed her and prevented her struggling, and an anaesthetic which was of necessity light, in case the baby was anaesthetised too. Liffey sensed the passage of time, and of terrible, painful, momentous events. Of struggle, and endeavour, and of the twists and turns of fate, and of life taking form out of rock.

'Was there breakthrough?' enquired the anaesthetist later. 'Sorry. Sometimes it's hard to judge, not too much, not too little and there wasn't much time.'

The foetal heart had showed no signs of distress. The baby's supply of oxygen remained adequate, in spite of the knot in the umbilical cord, in spite of the haemorrhage behind the placenta, in spite of the frequency of the uterine contractions – each one obstructing the blood and oxygen supply to the placenta for, at their height, one minute in every three: in spite, in fact, of anything, everything Mabs could do. The umbilical knot remained loose; the area of haemorrhage was limited; the placenta remained able to provide enough oxygen in two minutes to carry the baby through the next. The heart remained at a steady 140 beats, falling to 120 at the height of a contraction.
'Lots of time for baby,' said someone, surprised. 'What a lucky baby. Not much for mother, though.'

The uterus had to be emptied before it could fully contract. Until it was fully contracted, it would continue to bleed. Difficult to drip as much into Liffey as she dripped out. The surgeon made an inverse incision from side to side across the abdomen, just above Liffey's pubic mound. He then separated the muscles of the lower abdominal wall and opened the abdominal cavity. The bladder was then dissected free from the lower part of the anterior of the uterus. A transverse incision was then made in the lower uterine segment, exposing the membranes within. The baby's head slipped out of the surgeon's hand: membranes closed.

Mabs seated herself, coincidentally, in the waiting room of the theatre block, and took up a magazine and flicked through it.

Poor woman, thought the voluntary worker who organised the tea bar there.

The baby, conscious of distress, moved violently, tumbled and turned and pulled the umbilical knot tighter and the surgeon re-exposed the membranes and found the baby's buttocks, and Liffey, conscious of struggle within, tried to cry out and could not.

The surgeon found the head: used forceps. He sweated. 'Little beggar,' he said. 'You seem to like it in there. If only you knew how unsafe it was.'

The surgeon lifted out the baby.

'A boy,' someone said. Someone always names the sex. Everyone wants to know. It defines the event. Liffey heard.

'I'm really sorry,' said the anaesthetist later. 'Still, we do our best.'
'At least,' said Liffey, 'I am left with a sense of occasion, not just in one minute and out the next.'

The baby was held upside down. The baby did nothing. Then the baby breathed, spluttered, coughed and cried, and tried to turn itself the right way up, slithering in restraining hands. His colour was pinkish blue, changing rapidly to pink, first the lips, then the skin around the mouth, then the face. He was covered, beneath the slippery vernix, with fine hair. His muscles were tense.
'Doesn't seem premature. Got her dates wrong, I expect.'
The umbilical cord was clamped in two places, and divided between the clamps.
'A knot, too. See that? Only eight lives left.'
'About five, I'd say. How far did she walk?'
'A mile, someone said.'

'Christ!'

More anaesthesia. The placenta was removed. Ergometrine, to contract the uterus.

'How much has she lost?'
'Two, three pints since she's been in. Can't say, before.'

The bleeding stopped. A morsel of puffball, undigested – for during labour the digestive processes stop – rose up in Liffey's gullet, propelled by retching muscles as the anaesthetic deepened, and such was its light yet bulky texture, might well have been inhaled had the nurse stopped bothering to exert pressure on Liffey's neck. But she was young and frightened and doing as she was told. So much so that Liffey's neck retained the bruises for some weeks. But she lived.

Mabs, sitting outside in the waiting room, was conscious of defeat, and sighed and was brought a cup of tea by the voluntary worker.

Repair

The incision in Liffey's now firmly contracted uterus was repaired with catgut. The bruised bladder was stitched back over the lower uterine segment. Liffey's fallopian tubes and ovaries were inspected. They looked young, healthy, and capable of function in the future. The anterior abdominal wall was sutured. The incision in the skin was then closed with individual stitches.

'I wouldn't want to do that again,' said the surgeon. 'Next?'

The baby lay in an incubator in the special care unit. His

temperature was ninety-eight degrees. His heartbeat, 120 at the moment of delivery, had fallen to 115, and would slow gradually over the next three days to between eighty and a hundred, where it would stay for the rest of his life. He breathed at forty-five breaths a minute, with an occasional deep, sighing breath. The breathing came mostly from the abdomen – the chest itself moved very little. He grunted a little but that would soon stop. He was immune, for the time being, to measles, mumps, and chicken pox, thanks to antibodies present in Liffey's system which had crossed the placenta.

With his first breath he had inhaled some 50cc of air, opening up the respiratory passages in his lungs, forcing blood through the pulmonary arteries, establishing an adult type of circulation. He weighed six pounds and six ounces, he was nineteen-and-a-half inches long. Grasp, sucking, swallowing, rooting and walking reflexes were present. That is, his palm would clench when pressure was applied to it, any pressure on his palate would start him sucking, a handclap would make him throw out his legs and arms, he would swallow what was in his mouth, he would root for food, following touch on his jaw: when he was held under the arms and his feet touched a firm surface, he would seem to walk.

His nails reached the end of his fingers; his eyes were blue, but already, unusually, changing to brown. He could not see, in adult terms, but could differentiate light from dark. His tear ducts worked so well he could not cry. He sneezed from time to time. He could hear. He had already passed a quantity of meconium, the sticky dark green substance present in his intestine at birth. Liver and spleen were slightly enlarged at birth, which was normal. His testicles had descended, and his urinary passage was normal.

Everything was well with the baby. Very well.

In the operating theatre next door Debbie hovered between life and death, and finally came down on the living side. The nurse who went to tell the mother so, found her eventually in a phone booth, where she was having a long, wrangling conversation with her sister Carol. as to whose fault it was.

Mabs seemed annoyed at having to bring the call to an end, rather than gratified with the message brought. 'What a fuss!' she said, 'about nothing.'
Mabs did not enquire too closely into the nature of Debbie's illness, its cause, or its prognosis.
'I expect you'll want to stay with your little girl, till she's out of the anaesthetic,' said the nurse.
'Well, I can't get back till Tucker comes with the car,' said Mabs. 'How's Mrs. Lee-Fox doing?'
Liffey had been wheeled past her on the trolley, ashen white, head lolling.
'She'll be all right,' said the nurse. 'We only lose one mother a year and we've already lost her!' It was their little joke.

Murder

Mabs heard Liffey's baby cry. A pain struck through to Mabs' heart, not just at this final, overwhelming evidence of her impotence to prevent this birth, but at the injustice it presented. Tucker's baby emerging from the wrong body, so that she, Mabs, was left ignored in a waiting room while the gentle, powerful concern of authority, and the dramatic indications of its existence – masks and lights and drugs and ministering hands – focused down on the wrong person. Mabs sat beside Debbie's bed and waited for her to wake up, and scarcely saw her.

Liffey woke up to ask how the baby was and was told it was fine, which she didn't believe, and sank back into sedated sleep. When she woke next she cried with pain, exhaustion and lack of a baby to put in her arms.

'Baby's perfectly all right,' said the nurse. 'Don't fuss. All Caesar babies go into special care for a couple of days, that's all.'

The staff treated Liffey with automatic kindness; moving her up in the bed when she slipped down, changing pillows, sponging her face. The desire to empty her bruised bladder was enormous; the ability to do so lacking: the pain and humiliation of being lifted to use a bedpan overwhelming. She had more drugs.

She remembered the baby.

'Don't let Mabs get the baby,' she said. Of course this was hospital and Mabs was at the farm, but Liffey kept saying the same thing. 'Bring the baby here. Please bring the baby here,' and they promised her they would, to keep her quiet, knowing her sense of time was confused.

The Almoner's Department tried to trace her husband but he could not be found at his office, and had a new secretary who was not helpful. They did rather better with the Personnel Department, who proffered the information that Mr. Lee-Fox might well be having a minor breakdown: that this sometimes happened to executives under stress at the time of a major life event; of which having a first baby was certainly one. They were concerned but not anxious, and thanked the hospital for their help.

Liffey lapsed back into slumber and pain and woke to find Mabs in the room. Liffey tried to sit up but could not. She had no strength in her abdomen, thighs, arms or shoulders.

'Well, well.' said Mabs. 'Feeling better, are we? Congratulations!'
Liffey said nothing.
'I never had to have a Caesar,' said Mabs. 'Perhaps you have narrow hips? You should have taken some of my rosemary tea. I always drink it when I'm pregnant and never have any trouble. Is Richard pleased?'

Liffey said nothing.

'I do think a girl's easier for a man to accept,' said Mabs, 'but there's not much we can do about that. Do you mind me just chatting on? Don't talk if it tires you. I know what it's like by now. The doctor told me you lost a lot of blood, too. Why didn't you come down to me instead of setting off like that, all by yourself. Mind you, the phone was out of order. Eddie broke it, the naughty boy; I didn't half wallop him. Debbie was taken ill with appendix, and of course the one time I really needed the phone, it wasn't working.'

'Is it visiting hours?' asked Liffey. Perhaps she was dreaming Mabs?

'No,' said Mabs, 'it isn't. I'm living in, with Debbie. She's been quite poorly. Isn't it a coincidence, the two of us here together? So I can pop in any time I please. Where's baby?'

Dreamed or not, Liffey wasn't replying to that.

'In the special care unit, I suppose?' went on Mabs. 'I'll just nip down and see him. Poor little mite, all wired up. No baby of mine ever went into special care.'

Mabs saw the bruises on Liffey's neck.

'Who ever tried to strangle you?' she asked, as she left. 'Now who would want to do a thing like that?'

And Mabs was gone.

I dreamed it, thought Liffey. There was a great hollow under her ribs where the baby used to live, and a hole in that part of her mind which the baby had used. She had endured some kind of fearful loss. Liffey sat up and cried for help.

No one came.

No. She had not dreamed Mabs. Mabs had been real.

Liffey remembered Richard's going, the pain, the broken telephone, the slammed door, the blood, Eddie, the walk. Mabs. Witch, Murderess.

Liffey got out of bed. She took her legs with her hands and dropped them over the side of the bed, and let the rest of her fall after them. Once she was out of bed and on the floor, progress was possible. Surprisingly, movement begat movement. Liffey began to crawl. She still wore a white surgical gown, tied with tapes across her back.

Mabs was already at the special care unit, at the far end of a wedge of post-natal wards. The walls of a corridor turned to glass, and there, behind the glass, under the bright yet muted lights, were ranks of plastic incubators, and in them babies, wired up to monitors by nostril and umbilicus, or linked to drips or life support machinery: tiny mewling scraggy things.

Baby Lee-Fox, there only for observation, unwired, un-linked, lay in a far corner, breathing, sighing, snuffling, doing well. Masked nurses sat and watched, or moved about the rows on quiet urgent missions. An orderly at the door handed out masks and gowns for parents and close relatives. 'Baby Lee--Fox?' asked Mabs. She looked like many women in these parts, large and strong, yet soft.

The name Lee-Fox with its pallid hyphenated ring, its overtones of refined home counties, sat strangely on her tongue, but not strangely enough for the orderly to doubt Mabs' right to be where she was so clearly at home; amongst these small babies, hovering between dark and light, at that moment of existence where the ability, the desire, to go forward peaks again towards reluctance.

At Honeycomb Cottage doors and windows stood wide. Rain had fallen in the night and splashed unheeded on to papers and books. A column of ants now filed through the sunny front door and into the sugar bowl on the kitchen table. The rain had washed out most, but not all, of the marks where Richard, in his anxiety to be away, had scored the lane with his tyres.

Up at Cadbury Farm Tucker was in charge. He liked being

alone with the children. They sat round the kitchen table eating large plates of cornflakes, liberally sprinkled with sugar and swimming in milk. Audrey made a cake. Eddie sat on his father's knee and poked his fingers up Tucker's nostrils. They missed Debbie. The radio was on. All remembered a time when Mabs had been kind, and Tucker felt at fault for not having earned them, of late, a remission. Each remission, of course, meant another mouth to feed for the next fifteen years. Now, it seemed, he had earned one by proxy.

Mabs leaned over Baby Lee-Fox. Mabs laughed. The tone of the laugh disturbed a nurse, who came over and looked as well.

Baby Lee-Fox clenched and unclenched fists; struggled to open eyes.
'Lovely little baby,' said the nurse. 'Of course Caesar babies usually are. They don't get so squashed.'

Mabs laughed again: it was a strange deflating sound, as if all the air and spirit was draining swiftly out of a balloon, so that it tore and raced annd hurled itself about a room, before lying damp and still.
'Is it that funny?' asked the nurse, puzzled.
'He's the image of his father,' said Mabs.

'Just like Richard,' said Mabs to Liffey, laughing again. Liffey had been picked up from the floor outside the special care unit and put back to bed, and the drips set up again, and Baby Lee--Fox brought into her room, since she was apparently earnest in her desire to see her baby.
'Why shouldn't he be?' asked Liffey, wearily.

Mabs smiled, a really happy, generous smile.
'All's well that ends well,' said Mabs, 'and Debbie's fever has broken. If they'd let me give her feverfew in the first place we'd have had none of this trouble. What a fuss they make in here about every little thing.'

Mabs leant over and picked Liffey's baby out of its crib. She

did it tenderly, and reverently. Liffey was not afraid. Mabs had dwindled to her proper scale. The world no longer shook at her footfall. Mabs handed Liffey the baby.
'But where's Richard?' asked Mabs, all innocence. 'Where's the father?'

Liffey's memory of the Sunday lunch was vague, overshadowed by the events that had followed it. She remembered as one remembers on waking from sleep, the feeling tone of the preceeding day rather than its actual events – that Richard had left angry and that this had been a practical inconvenience rather than an emotional blow. As to the details of the rest, it seemed irrelevant.

The baby lay in Liffey's arms, snuffling and rooting for food. She sensed its triumph. None of that was important, the baby reproved her: they were peripheral events, leading towards the main end of your life, which was to produce me. You were always the bit-part player: that you played the lead was your delusion, your folly. Only by giving away your life, do you save it.

'The little darling,' said Mabs. 'How could anyone hurt a baby?'
The baby smiled.
'Only wind,' said Mabs, startled.
'It was a smile,' said Liffey.
'Babies don't smile for six weeks,' said Mabs, uneasily.
The baby smiled again.

Resignation

Liffey slept. The baby slept. Mabs went home.
'It wasn't your baby after all,' she said to Tucker, and they went upstairs to try for another one. This time sufficient of Tucker's sperm survived the hazardous journey up to Mabs' fallopian tubes to rupture the walls of a recently dropped ovum – fallen rather ahead of time, by virtue of the emotions

264

of tenderness and remorse, mixed, which had flooded Mabs when she marvelled over Baby Lee-Fox, and laughed at his looks. Richard's bemused air of competence combined with innocence, Liffey's gentle generosity: as if the baby, wonderfully, had captured both their good qualities as they flew, and let the others pass.

Mabs, being pregnant, became quiet and kind as if, in her, body alone dictated mood. She had no rational knowledge that she had conceived: only her body, setting off on its forty-week journey, conveyed a general impression of contentment, which the mind accepted.

Mabs came downstairs, smiled at the children, and brought them all fish and chips, and even lemonade to go with it.

The doctor came up to Cadbury Farm presently to say that Debbie was to be sent off to a convalescent home, and to take a general look around.
'Rather them than me,' said Mabs. 'She's a dirty girl. She wets the bed. Still,' she added, magnanimously, 'the others miss her.'
'You nearly lost her altogether,' said the doctor.
'No,' said Mabs, 'I knew I wouldn't.'

There had been no signs, after all – no owls hooting out of nowhere, no lightning out of a clear sky, no yew brought into the house – no signs or portents. Only Mabs twisting a pin in a wax image when she should have left it to others: enough to damage and frighten, but surely not to kill. Debbie had always been safe enough; but how could she tell the doctor a thing like that?

'I'd like to hear a little less about home remedies,' said the doctor, 'and a little more about visiting the surgery when anyone's ill.'
'All right,' Mabs acquiesced. It was a genuine capitulation. She yawned. She was tired. It occurred to her that Tucker and she were not as young as once they had been.

She allowed the doctor to put Eddie on a course of antidepressants, and Audrey on the pill, and she herself on valium to cure the rages she now admitted to, and Tucker on Vitamin B because he drank so much home-made wine. With every act of consent, every acknowledgment of his power, her own waned. She felt it. She didn't much mind.

Mabs told the doctor that she and Tucker would fetch Liffey and the baby home from hospital. They'd look after Liffey. Well, the husband had finally gone off.

Liffey's drips were removed. Her stitches came out. Snip, snip – eight times. The skin that had stretched and smarted around the catgut resumed its natural place. She could sit up now, of her own accord. She could lie on her back and lift her legs. She could do without the physiotherapist, who thumped her hard from time to time to make her cough and clear her lungs. She could take a bath, albeit on her hands and knees. She rang her mother, hardly knowing what to say. Madge was cool but friendly, and busy with a Royal visitor to the school.

Mrs. Harris from the shop came to visit; and Audrey brought the curate, who saw God's hand in the deliverance of both Liffey and Debbie. The incident had even reached the local paper. Audrey wished to be confirmed; he was undertaking it. Mabs and Tucker came, with flowers. Tucker wore collar and tie, and sat on the edge of his chair and seemed embarrassed by his surroundings, but he was robust and solid, and dignified: powerful, dark and male in a pale female world.

And certainly as Mabs lost power, Tucker gained it. He knew it: he was rough with Mabs now; he told her what to do: he shouted at her if she behaved badly to the children. He recognised that she was deflated, that although she still stared at the Tor, the clouds around its summit neither reflected her will nor shadowed her intent. Her sly looks requested rather than commanded, and he performed at his own pleasure, and not hers. He thought she was a better mother, and high time too. As one set of energies drained out of her, others took their place.

Richard did not visit Liffey.

Ripples

Richard, after a whole week's absence, unaccounted for and so far unexplained, went back to the office.

'Welcome back!' said Personnel. 'We'll ask no questions and be told no lies. You have a fine son and mother's doing well. Can we be of any help?'
'No, thank you,' said Richard.

He knew he had a son. His attention had been drawn to an advertisement in *The Times* which said, 'Lee-Fox. To Liffey and Tucker, a son'. Miss Martin, Richard rightly guessed, had inserted it. Miss Martin, as did everyone in the company, via Vanessa's connection with the director of the Canadian ox-tail soup television commercial, knew all about the fathering of Liffey's baby. Malice does not evaporate: it bounces round like a rubber ball, striking here and there, sometimes in the most unexpected places, gradually losing energy. It almost stops. Then up it starts again – the cosmic ball of ill will.

Richard wangled Vanessa another modelling job, so that she could buy a car for herself, but after that left her alone. She had heard him weep: she would never respect him. The battle, he could see, was to find a woman who would.

He had spent the whole week with Vanessa: she had made him, for a while, believe that his work was unimportant, that he was only money-grubbing in a rat race: fortunately, common sense reasserted itself. He wished to behave well towards Liffey: to shame her with kindness; to continue to support her. For that he would have to earn more. He owed it to his parents to get promotion, do well, carry on along the road on which they had first set his stumbling footsteps. He could not fail Liffey, or disappoint them.

When he hated Liffey, it was because of the distress her behaviour would have given his parents. He put off telling them. How was he to put it? Yes, mother, Liffey has her baby but it is another man's child. Not your grandchild. Not, after all that, after all those years, your flesh and blood.

Ah yes, I am sure. So sure. It explains so much. Why I betrayed her. It was all her doing. Once the sacred tie is loosed, chaos ensues; the forces of love, of trust, and faith are in disarray: lust sweeps in. Liffey loosed them, quite deliberately. Untied the snowy white robe of her purity and let Tucker in.

Mrs. Lee-Fox senior telephoned.

'Darling, what *is* happening? How's lovely Liffey?'

Lovely Liffey had Tucker's child, mother.

Mrs. Lee-Fox senior wept. See, Liffey, what you have done? My mother weeps. All my life I have dreaded this minute, this moment. I knew it lurked somewhere, waiting.

Liffey, I hate you. I would kill you if I could.

Richard went to stay with Bella and Ray. Bella still couldn't get over the way Liffey had behaved towards Tony and Tina.
'Not even bothering to pack their homework!' said Bella. 'Not even making them a sandwich. They were dreadfully upset. I can't help thinking you're well out of it, Richard.'

'Next time choose someone who can cook,' said Ray. 'Does that sound crude? But it's no good being romantic. You're past the age of falling in love.' Ray had felt infatuation for

Karen, not love. Bella had explained it all. Ray was glad it was over.

No one has a baby alone. Every pregnant woman carries with her the aspirations, the ambitions and the fears of others – friends, relatives, and passers-by – and good and ill wishes of such intensity as might put the sun right out.

Good Fortune

As Mabs' ill-wish evaporated so Liffey's good fortune returned. Or perhaps it was merely that now she carried the baby in her arms, the ordinary up-and-downness of life returned.

Tucker and Mabs brought Liffey home from hospital. Their car no longer reeked of menace. It was an ordinary, shabby, littered family car. The baby seemed to enjoy the motion. Home was cosy and familiar. Mabs had put flowers in vases: Tucker had dug over the garden.

The telephone had been installed.

There was a pile of letters. One was from the bank to say that a final payment from the trust fund had been paid in on her last birthday but had inadvertently not been entered to her credit. Twelve thousand pounds. Another was from Mory and Helen. 'Wonderful about the baby!' they wrote. 'Just to say the flat's yours if you want it, even without the £1000 Richard couldn't raise. Mory's been offered a wonderful job in Trinidad, and Helen can't stand the British climate any more. She's pregnant.'

Cruel Richard, thought Liffey. Cruel, cruel Richard. But she did not want the flat back. She wanted very few now of the things she had wanted before.

It was a wonderful month for late sun and over-ripe roses. Liffey could take off the baby's clothes, and let the sun get to his little chicken limbs.

The telephone rang. Friends, who had seen the announcement in *The Times*, and wanted to know what was going on. Liffey told them. Liffey, they thought, was quite fun again.

Fortunately no one who knew Tucker and Mabs read *The Times*, so news of the announcement did not reach them. Personnel fired Miss Martin, however. Enough was enough.

On Friday nights Liffey would find herself nervous, wondering if Richard would come back: half wanting him to, half not. She needed the full width of the double bed for herself and the baby, rolling over in the night as he woke, to pick him from his crib and feed him. Richard would have been in the way.

'What's his name?' people asked.
'Baby Lee-Fox,' she said. She was waiting.

Madge wrote out of the blue saying that the name of Liffey's father had been Martin, and in retrospect had behaved well according to his lights. They just weren't Madge's lights. Why didn't Liffey call the baby Martin?

She called the baby Martin.

'After his grandfather,' she told milkman, dustman, postman, proudly. They all came up the drive now.

The baby's legs looked more human: he lay in his cot working rather than resting, making sense of the world, recognising kindness, censorious of carelessness.

There was a brief rain-sodden autumn. The last of the rose petals fell. A few last blackberries stayed on the brambles. The days became cold and short.

Eddie would come up with firewood; he liked to hang close by Liffey's side. Audrey came to talk about sex, and religion, and whether she preferred the vicar to the curate, the former being older, wiser and richer, but married. Debbie, though still pale and fragile, would trudge over the fields unasked, to get Liffey's shopping. Liffey thought perhaps she was quite content with the company of children.

Local events became important in her life. Carol's husband broke Dick Hubbard's jaw in a brawl and was sent to the local prison for two weeks to teach him what the magistrates called a lesson. Carol did not visit him on visiting day, but was seen in the car park in Dick Hubbard's car. Public opinion finally turned against Dick Hubbard.

Mabs laughed. She and Tucker drank a bottle of sherry between them. They let Audrey have a sip. Mabs was pregnant; the price of beef was high, of foodstuffs not so high as usual; one of the dogs had a puppy, unexpectedly: they were happy. Liffey lived in Honeycomb, properly subdued. It had taken them a year to achieve it. Christmas was coming.

Conclusion

Liffey's baby lay in its cot by the fire and smiled. It seemed, to the outside eye, a perfectly ordinary baby. It spoke to Liffey, silently, but less and less, as its body grew into better proportion to its being. It gave up all apppearance of being in charge, of knowing best. It left all that to Liffey, now.

Liffey looked at herself in the mirror and laughed. She thought she seemed a very average person: no longer pretty, or elfin, or silly, or anything particularly definite, any more. She was much like anyone else. She thought that she too had become what Richard wanted. He had triumphed in his absence.

She put on another jersey. The baby wore two pairs of leggings. The wind turned to the north. Black clouds heaved around the Tor: sometimes it was obscured altogether by mist and rain. In the very cold weather the fire smoked to such an extent it would put itself out, like a scorpion which stings itself with its own tail. On Christmas Eve Liffey ran out of kindling wood to relight the fire. It was raining, and the branches and twigs outside were wet and useless. She went into the outhouse and there found the withered remnants of Richard's puffballs. They were tough, withered and leathery, and she remembered what Richard had said about their use as firelighters, laid them in the grate, and lit them. They burned slowly, patiently and brightly, and she thought there was some good in them after all.

She wanted the baby to speak, to mark so momentous a thought, but his spirit was finally cut off from hers. He smiled at her and that was all.

The fire lit by the puffballs stayed in over the Christmas holiday, to Liffey's satisfaction. The baby smiled at the flames. On Boxing Day a car drew up outside. It was Richard, and his arms were full of soft fluffy toys – white bears and pink fish and orange lions. Liffey thought that vitamin drops and disposable nappies would have been more sensible.
'Christ, Liffey,' he said. 'I am sorry. I don't care whose baby it is.'

Liffey opened the door, not without reluctance. But she knew the baby liked to see people. He enjoyed company more than she did. He would smile at everyone, Liffey told herself, at Mabs and Tucker and the postman and the milkman. But now he smiled at Richard too, claiming him for a father, shuffler of the genes, and she knew that that was that. He claimed them all, everyone, as bit-part players in his drama, dancers in his dance, singers to his tune.

Come in Richard. Here is Liffey.